"Hey," she said, shaking his shoulder. "Wake up."

His eyes cracked open. If she'd thought about it at all, she might've expected them to be blue, given his fair coloring and blond hair, but they were a warm brown, just like her papa's had been.

"You're all right," she said, and if her voice was breathless with relief, he was the only one around to hear.

"Can you sit up?"

She put her hands beneath his shoulders and nudged, hoping that he would take the hint and sit up. She'd rescued him, and now he needed to move on, before Pop caught wind that he'd been trespassing on their property.

But as she pushed on his shoulders, he gave a horrible groan. One hand went to his chest, and then he promptly passed out.

She unbuttoned the top of his shirt and found ugly purpling bruises covering his upper chest. And he was breathing funny. Even passed out, his mouth was a grimace of pain.

He wasn't going away anytime soon.

What was she going to do now?

NOV 0 5 2015

Lacy Williams is a wife and mom from Oklahoma. She has loved romance from childhood and promises readers happy endings in all her stories. Her books have been finalists for an RT Reviewers' Choice Award (three years running), a Golden Quill Award and the Booksellers' Best Award. Lacy loves to hear from readers at lacyjwilliams@gmail.com. She can be found at lacywilliams.net, facebook.com/lacywilliamsbooks or twitter.com/lacy_williams.

Books by Lacy Williams

Love Inspired Historical

Wyoming Legacy

Visit the Author Profile page at Harlequin.com for more titles

LACY WILLIAMS

Her Cowboy Deputy

HARLEQUIN® LOVE INSPIRED® HISTORICAL

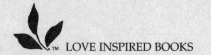 LOVE INSPIRED BOOKS

Recycling programs for this product may not exist in your area.

ISBN-13: 978-0-373-28332-3

Her Cowboy Deputy

www.Harlequin.com

Printed in U.S.A.

Two are better than one,
because they have a good return for their labor:
If either of them falls down, one can help the other up.
But pity anyone who falls
and has no one to help them up.
Though one may be overpowered,
two can defend themselves.
A cord of three strands is not quickly broken.
—*Ecclesiastes* 4:9–10, 12

With thanks to my cousin T.,
who provided insight on having a broken collarbone.
Any inaccuracies are mine.

Chapter One

May 1902

Sheriff's deputy Matty White stumbled out of the bunkhouse, still pulling on his left boot.

In the corral just outside, his brother Seb swung a lasso above his head, aiming for one of the green broke geldings trotting anxiously back and forth and tossing their heads.

Except for Seb, the barnyard was eerily empty. Matty's big family worked the family ranch together, and nearly everyone showed up for family breakfasts and suppers, so the absence of his older brothers was unsettling.

And it was easy to see why.

Matty clapped his hat to his head as a burst of wind threatened to send it flying. He didn't like the looks of the swirling clouds, low and heavy in the sky.

"Get those horses in the barn and get inside," Matty called over his shoulder to Seb.

Seb waved him off. Probably Pa had already told him the same. And…while it was hard to remember sometimes thanks to his antics, his youngest adopted brother was twenty now and man enough to know when it was time to take cover from a storm.

This particular storm looked to be a nasty one, judging by the sky's sickly green hue.

Hailstones thumped against his shoulders and hat, stinging slightly, as Matty's boots hit the porch steps.

He burst in through the door, calling for his ma. Penny White was in the parlor with Walt, Ida and Andrew, her and Jonas's biological children, lined up on the sofa. She was disheveled, a state he rarely saw her in. Her auburn hair was coming out of the simple braid she must have rushed to put it in.

Andrew and Ida, ages five and eight, sat with wide, bright eyes, obviously alerted to the potential danger of the situation.

"Good, you've got the little ones," Matty said. He had to speak loudly in order to be heard above the hail pounding on the roof.

"We're not little," eleven-year-old Walt growled. "I'm plenty big enough to ride out with Pa. He shoulda let me go with him."

"Pa went out?" Matty directed his question to Penny, worry skittering through him. The hail would be uncomfortable or could possibly cause injury. And what if Jonas's horse spooked?

"Breanna was worried about her mare that's close to foaling," Penny explained breathlessly. It seemed she shared his concern. "She ran out of here before either of us could stop her, and Jonas followed. He'll keep her safe. They can take cover at Oscar's cabin or Davy's, depending on where they find the horse."

If they found her. The animal was half wild—a little like his stubborn seventeen-year-old sister—and would likely hole up wherever she could find shelter. The family ranch had expanded as each adopted brother gained his majority, and there was plenty of land to cover. Seb, Matty and Breanna were the only unmarried siblings left at home.

But Penny was right. Now that his older brothers had married and built their homes around the ranch, Jonas and Breanna could take cover with one of them. Even Maxwell and his wife, Hattie, both doctors, had a place out here. They split their time between home and the nearby town of Bear Creek, where their clinic served those in town and the neighboring areas.

Seb burst through the door, snapping it closed against the wind that threatened to tug it out of his hands. "It's getting bad out there." He wiped the brim of his hat, and his hand came away wet. Several hailstones clattered to the floor at his feet.

"You got any quilts handy?" Matty asked Penny. "Get the children huddled up beneath them. Just in case."

He didn't go after the blankets himself. He'd grown up in this house, but as the White family had grown with Jonas and Penny's biological children and as the older boys had begun wanting more independence, they'd moved out to the bunkhouse. And he knew how particular his ma was with how she preferred her house to be kept.

Penny disappeared into the hallway toward the bedrooms and reappeared moments later with an armful of quilts.

"I ain't no baby," Walt protested, attempting to shove away the thick quilt that Penny extended to him.

"Listen to Ma," Matty said sharply. He didn't like to take that tone with his younger brother, but this wasn't a moment to assert his independence—things could get dangerous, fast.

"Matty—" Seb's murmur drew his gaze to where the younger man stood in the kitchen, looking out the window over the washtub. Matty's feet took him there almost of their own accord.

"Get the children down behind the sofa," he said over his shoulder to Penny.

And then he was standing outside on the porch, his brother beside him, without really meaning to.

A soft curse escaped his brother's lips. Matty would've chastised him, except the word conveyed all the terror he felt this very moment.

At the edge of their property and rapidly moving closer was a funnel dropped from the clouds.

"Tornado," Matty whispered. The silent prayer that had been rolling around the back of his brain since he'd run out of the bunkhouse this morning suddenly shouted loud in the forefront of his mind. *Keep my family safe. Please, Lord.*

Noise, like a rolling freight train, pressed in on his ears. The ground at the base of the tornado was obscured in a cloud of dust and debris. On its current trajectory, it would come close to their barn. Or demolish it.

"Turn, *turn*," Seb murmured. Matty could barely hear him over the tornado's roar.

For long moments, they both simply stared at the oncoming horror. A full-grown tree pulled free of its home as if it weighed nothing. Earth crumbled from its roots as it was engulfed in the tornado's debris.

Please, God.

And as if God had heard their frantic prayers, the tornado *did* turn. Although it remained on the ground, it swerved to the west, taking out a copse of cedars.

He and Seb stood on the porch watching as the tornado ripped its way across the family property, knocking down two fences as it passed.

"I need to get to town," Matty told his brother. "Sheriff Dunlop will want his deputies—" of which Matty was one "—scouting the area."

Seb nodded.

"Check on Ma and the kids," Matty said. "Then Edgar and Fran, and Daniel and Emma. I'll stop at Oscar's and Davy's places on my way to town. Maxwell and Hattie are probably already on their way to town." Daniel and Emma were Fran's grown siblings and lived in a cabin nearby.

He could only pray they weren't needed, but knew that if the tornado had caught folks in Bear Creek unawares, there could be injuries. Or worse.

The only brother who didn't live nearby was Ricky, who planned to buy out his father-in-law's ranch up north. Ricky and his wife, Daisy, raised sheep, in contrast to the Bear Creek contingent, who raised cattle and horses.

Matty was torn as he ran out to the barn and saddled up his buckskin gelding. Part of him wanted to stay and help his family. They'd need to move any cattle or horses out of the pastures where fence had been knocked down.

He didn't even want to think about leaving them to deal with any animals that might've been caught in the tornado's path.

But he'd made a commitment to the town when he'd taken on the badge only three months ago. When Sheriff Dunlop had pinned the tin star to Matty's chest, he'd felt the weight of expectations—both from the man and from the town he'd sworn to protect.

For now, his family would have to clean up without him.

* * *

Hours later, Matty was exhausted, covered in mud and hungry. His bedroll would be nice, right about now.

He was also several miles out of town, in the opposite direction of home.

He guided his horse around an uprooted tree, barely seeing the devastation surrounding him. The protruding roots and scattered earth showed the destructive path the tornado had taken. He'd ridden through the storm that followed. The driving rains had flooded local waterways, and hail had demolished crops and buildings. In town, strong winds had damaged several buildings. But the worst part had been discovering that the tornado had resulted in two deaths.

Sheriff Dunlop had sent his four deputies in each direction, north, east, south, west, scouting for folks who needed help and telling them that the Bear Creek school building was being used to house anyone who'd lost their homes.

Heading north had forced Matty to check on the McKeever family, including Luella McKeever, who'd just last week told him not to come courting anymore.

She hadn't given him a clear reason why she didn't want to see him anymore, and the rejection still stung. But a bigger part of him was relieved to find her family unharmed, even if they had lost a couple of head of cattle to the hail.

She hadn't made any move off the porch, and he'd stayed in the saddle, but their eyes had held for a long moment before he'd tipped his hat and taken his leave.

Maybe it was a coping mechanism to keep his mind off the horrors he'd witnessed today, but he couldn't stop thinking that maybe things weren't finished between them.

After everything he'd seen today, he realized that life was too short not to try to grab a second chance. His family had been blessed that the tornado had only flattened two fences, but many others had suffered.

He wanted to live each day to the fullest, starting now.

Or after he'd had a chance to wash up and get some rest. He'd ranged so far out of town that the last homestead he'd passed had been almost an hour ago. He didn't know many of the folks out here, but everyone he'd come across had been thankful to see him.

But there were no houses in sight and Dunlop had told him once he got to the creek that cut through the Samuelses' property, to turn back.

"You ready to head home?" he asked his mount, patting the animal's neck. Clouds had gathered on the far horizon, possibly threatening another storm or letting him know that one was hitting miles away. He breathed in deep, the scents of horse and moist ground and wet earth filling his senses.

But as he let his eyes take one last scan of the horizon, movement just beyond the next rise caught his eye. Was that…?

He urged his gelding forward and caught the flash of movement again. It was a person. A teenaged boy, looked like. With his hat pulled down over his brow, the lad was leading a mule several yards back from a creek bursting its banks.

Matty whistled to catch the boy's attention. The young man's head whipped up. But instead of halting, waiting for Matty to cross the creek and come to him, the boy took off, shouting something at the mule.

That wasn't the reaction of a law-abiding citizen.

Matty bit back an uncomplimentary exclamation as

he urged his horse into a gallop. Whoever this was just made a long day even longer.

He leaned into the horse's neck as the animal cleared the slight rise, approaching the rolling creek on the down side.

The boy and his mule were disappearing into a copse of bushes across the stream.

The waters blocked his path; the stream had overrun its banks.

"Hey!" he shouted. "Stop! I just wanna talk to you!"

But the boy faded into the underbrush, becoming a shadow.

Matty couldn't see the bottom of the creek, only eddying, murky brown waters. He had no sense of how deep it was, and that meant danger.

He risked his horse—and himself—if they got caught in the raging water and swept away. He could turn back.

But why would the boy run away from him? Had he broken some law? Would he have even been able to see Matty's tin star from that distance?

He needed answers.

He urged his horse along the creek's edge, looking for a place that looked wide enough to cross safely. Finally, he saw what appeared to be a flat stretch and turned his gelding to cross.

He was halfway across when a low roaring sound met his ears. He jerked his head up to see a wall of water advancing on him, with debris caught in the floodwaters. He spurred his mount with a "hiyah!" but it was too late. The water swept against his horse. The animal lost its footing, and Matty managed to get his feet out of the stirrups just before he was thrown from its back.

Immediately, he got dunked and inhaled a mouthful of muddy, foul-tasting water. He coughed and spluttered when he was able to kick his head above the water. He couldn't get his bearings, and then the creek turned a curve and he saw a tree growing right smack in the center of the creek—or maybe the waters had just risen that much that it had surrounded the tree.

He scissored his legs, but then a huge branch with lots of small, twiggy offshoots rolled over him in the water. He went under, and then the branch and the water combined and it was too late—he was shoved into the standing tree with bone-shattering force.

From her position downstream, Catherine Poole saw the stranger, dressed as a cowboy, get swept up in the flooded creek and then crash into the tree. He didn't resurface.

Her grandfather "Pop" Poole had cautioned her time and again to stay away from strangers.

And she well knew the danger of those who called themselves friends.

Men meant danger, and that's why she'd run when she'd seen the rider. At first glance, she'd thought he was her neighbor Ralph Chesterton.

But what if the man died? Even though he'd been chasing her, she couldn't leave the man to drown, could she? There was no harm in checking on him.

She wouldn't have even been out here—there was plenty enough to do around the homestead with the damage the storm had inflicted—but the mule had broken out of its stall in fright from the thunder and she'd had to track it down.

She left her mule behind and moved away from the creek's edge, where she'd used some wild plum bushes to camouflage their presence. As she ran alongside the swirling, dangerous waters, she was careful not to slip on the muddy banks. If she tumbled in, who would rescue her?

This was when her habit of wearing men's clothing—trousers, shirt and boots—was beneficial. In a long-skirted dress, she would have been hampered, but her trousers made it easier to run.

Even as she watched for the man, she kept her wits about her. He could've pretended injury when he'd fallen into the water and be waiting even now for a chance to grab her.

She caught sight of him floating facedown, yards ahead of her, still being swept away. Worry spiked through her like one of the bolts of lightning that had split the sky this morning. Was he dead?

Her boots slipped on the muddy banks.

How was she going to fish him out of the water? If she had rope, she could form a lasso, but there wasn't time to run home and get some.

She knew this land. She'd been raised here and survived off the farmland and what nature provided. She knew that the creek made another twist up ahead and she put on a burst of speed. If she could get to the dog-leg, she could possibly snag the cowboy when he passed.

She was panting, her chest clutching, but she didn't slow down. The sudden fear for him overshadowed her own concerns. She couldn't let this man die.

Her sleeve caught on a blackberry bramble; it scratched her cheek. But she dismissed the stinging pain.

She slid down the slight incline, scrambling for purchase, and nearly fell headlong into the rushing waters, but caught herself before she would have pitched into the water.

There he was! Still yards away but coming in her direction and quick.

She stretched out her arms as far as they would reach, arching out over the water, but she could see that it wasn't going to be enough. She wasn't tall enough to reach him.

He was going to float right by her.

She scrambled frantically, but there was nothing to help her, no branch, no rope…

The cowboy was upon her and there was nothing for it. She let her legs slide into the cold, murky water, up to her calves. Its chill made her gasp. Behind the small hill of land that made up the dogleg, water eddied. It pulled at her, but the slight protection of the shape of the land kept her from being swept away herself.

She caught the man around the waist, locking her hands together, bracing her feet against the muddy creek bottom. The water made him buoyant, but the weight of his wet clothes and boots dragged him down. She wobbled, almost losing her balance, which would have been a disaster for both of them, and threw herself backward. Her momentum was enough to land her backside on the bank, the rest of her following. The cowboy landed on top of her, stealing her breath with a *whomp* of his weight atop her.

He wasn't breathing.

She shoved at his shoulders—he was much bigger than her—and finally rolled him up the bank and off her.

She pushed herself up to kneel at his side. His face was ashen, his blond hair matted to his head. A large bump and gash near his temple worried her, blood trickling from it down into his ear.

"Hey," she said, shaking his shoulder. "Wake up."

Nothing. He made no response.

Fear twisted through her, giving her hands force. She beat her fists against his torso. And he coughed. A burst of air and water expelled from his mouth. She turned his head to the side so he wouldn't choke as he gurgled and spit liquid.

She was leaning over him as he finally gasped an inhale. His eyes cracked open. If she'd thought about it at all, she might've expected them to be blue given his fair coloring and blond hair, but they were a warm brown, just like her mama's had been.

"You're all right," she said, and her voice was breathless with relief. He was the only one around to hear.

"Can you sit up?"

He didn't answer, his eyes remained open but narrowly, as if he was perhaps holding on to the edge of consciousness by a thread.

She put her hands beneath his shoulders and nudged, hoping that he would take the hint and sit up. She'd rescued him, and now he needed to move on, before Pop caught wind that he'd been trespassing on their property.

But as she pulled on his shoulders, he gave a horrible groan. One hand went to his chest, and then he promptly passed out.

Face flushing at the intimacy, she unbuttoned the top of his shirt and found ugly purpling bruises covering his upper chest. And he was breathing funny. Even passed out, his mouth was a grimace of pain.

He wasn't going away anytime soon.

What was she going to do now? Pop was *not* going to be happy about this.

Chapter Two

Matty regained consciousness in a haze of pain, lying flat on his back in a dimly lit room that smelled of damp earth and woodsmoke. Where was he?

Every breath hurt, like fire streaking across his chest. He moaned. "Pa?"

Where was Jonas? If his pa would come, he'd help Matty. He knew it.

"Easy." A cool, dry hand rested on his forehead.

"Ma?" He tried to turn his head and see who'd spoken, but throbbing pain pierced his skull and he cried out.

"Be still," the voice said, but it wasn't Ma.

There was movement at his shoulder, and he again tried to turn his head.

Blinding pain changed his mind.

"I told you not to move," the voice came again. "You've got a gash on your head, and I've just about got it to stop bleeding."

The voice was calm. A midrange contralto.

"Wanna see you," he mumbled, the effort costing him in the pounding of his head.

A shadow fell across his face and he opened his eyes. An adorable pixie face, capped with dark curls and bright blue eyes fringed with inky lashes. It was too hard to focus on the darkened room beyond her.

"Who're you?" his voice emerged more of a growl than he had intended, but he didn't apologize. Where was he? Who was this?

"A friend," came the implacable answer. "And things will go better for you if you're as quiet and still as possible."

The part of him that had taken lessons in suspicion from the local sheriff sent prickles of awareness down the back of his neck. What did that warning mean? Had he been set upon by a gang of bandits? How had he gotten here? What had happened?

Why couldn't he remember?

His breathing quickened as those panicked thoughts swirled in his mind, and that was painful, too. He forced himself to slow both the thoughts and his breathing until his pain eased slightly.

"I'm an officer of the law—" he started.

"Ssh!" Something soft touched his mouth at the same time as she shushed him.

Her fingers, he realized, when his eyes flew open. When had his eyes closed? He needed his wits about him. The blinding pain continued, but he forced his eyes to stay open.

She took away her hand, which was really a shame, because her fingers were soft as a dandelion puff, and leaned close. He got a whiff of sweet woman and sunshine and then coffee as she spoke again, this time from much closer. Close enough for him to see the light sprinkling of freckles across the bridge of her nose.

"I've taken your gun belt," she whispered. "And hidden it somewhere safe."

That didn't sound innocent.

He tried to reach for his shoulder, where he kept a silver star pinned, but trying to move his arm wrenched awful pain across his chest and he gasped.

"Be still," she said, censure in her tone. "You'll injure yourself worse. You may have a broken collarbone."

"What...what happened to me?"

"Do you remember trying to cross the creek? Getting swept up? Nearly drowning?"

At her words, memories flooded him. Chasing the young man who'd run. His horse caught by the rushing waters and a floating tree. And then blackness.

Where was the young man?

How had this young woman come to rescue him? And why had she taken away his gun belt? His intuition shouted that danger was still present.

"My ride?" he demanded, his voice hoarse.

"I didn't see," she said, her voice soft with what might be empathy. "Maybe your horse climbed out downstream."

The water had been rushing with such force that Matty didn't know if the animal would have been able to recover, not with the floating debris that made it so dangerous. The buckskin had been a good mount, a trusted friend. It was a difficult loss.

"What's your name?" the voice asked.

"Matty. Matty White."

There was a soft intake of breath.

"Do we know each other?" he asked, watching the play of emotions as she ducked her head.

She shook her head minutely. "I'm Catherine." Her eyes flicked to the side, as if she wasn't being entirely truthful that they weren't acquainted, but he would recognize her if she'd been at any church socials or town functions in the past couple of years. There was no flicker of recognition within him at all.

"Thanks for fishing me out of the creek."

It had been a guess, but he saw the quick flare of pride in her eyes before she stood up. "You should rest."

Catherine stood up and turned to stoke the fire in the short stove across the room. The dugout she shared with her grandfather was small, this distance not far enough for her to catch her breath.

She was deeply unsettled by the cowboy's nearness. The deputy.

A deputy shouldn't be an immediate danger, but that discounted *this* particular deputy.

Matty White.

She hadn't recognized him until he'd said his name.

Back in their school days, she'd known him as Matty Standish.

Why did it have to be him?

They'd known each other for all of a week when she'd been eight years old. That had been nearly fifteen years ago now.

Her hands were busy with supper preparations, but she couldn't keep her mind from whirling back to the past.

He'd been one of her tormentors. He and Luella Mc-Keever. That first day in the schoolhouse, they had poked fun at her homespun dress and her bare feet and lack of a bonnet, though it had been late fall and she really should have been wearing shoes by that time of year. She'd been unbearably shy, coming to school for the first time at age eight. She'd been behind the other children in lessons, and they'd made fun of that, too.

It had only grown worse from there.

But now it looked like he'd grown up. He'd been skinny to the point of being scrawny back then. Now his shoulders had broadened, and he'd filled out a tall frame. His jaw was firm and forehead strong. God had certainly blessed him with handsome features.

She'd had a hard time hauling him back to the soddy. She'd constructed a litter out of two long poles and a few branches she'd found, and gone back for the mule. Luckily the contraption had held until they'd reached the dugout, several hundred yards from where the cowboy had fallen into the creek.

She'd pretended that the exertion had made her face flush, but she feared it was a reaction to the man. She wasn't used to being near someone so comely.

Or maybe she'd been isolated on the homestead for too long. Hopefully that was the true explanation.

She had no use for men—other than Pop—and didn't trust a one of them. She needed to figure a way to get the cowboy off her property, but he could barely move from his injury.

He was silent. She'd seen the stark emotion cross his face when he'd learned his horse had been lost, and something inside her had responded with a corresponding surge of grief. She knew loss, didn't she?

But she didn't know the cowboy. A previous acquaintance over a decade ago did not a friendship make. And even though he cared for his animal, it didn't mean he was a kind man, did it? She needed to tread carefully, for if he was still as cruel as he had been in the past, she wanted none of it.

And then there was Pop to consider. She'd sent him to the garden they kept out back of the soddy to see what damage the storm had wrought. She needed to prepare him before he came in and saw the bedridden cowboy.

And then she needed to check the barn, the second, open-sided soddy they used to house the mule, milk cow and few chickens and their winter supplies. It was closer to the creek, and she thought it might have suffered damage in the storm but had been too busy with the cowboy to check.

The work never ended, out here on the prairie.

"Miss?" The word and then a gasp had her whipping toward her bed in the corner.

Matty had rolled his head on the pillow and was looking at her, though his eyes were narrowed and lips pinched with pain.

"Where'd she go?" he asked.

"Who?"

"Catherine. She was just here."

She froze; words died on her lips. He was looking right at her, and she knew what he must see. A teenage boy.

The clothes were a protection. As she'd blossomed to adulthood, Pop had convinced her of the need to dress like this, but she'd never considered that up close, someone would mistake her for a male.

Her cheeks flamed.

"I guess it don't matter," he mumbled. "I need someone to get word to my family. They'll come for me."

She was shaking her head before he'd finished speaking. "I can't."

Her grandfather couldn't handle having folks around, not with his delusions. And though he still roamed their property, he couldn't be left on his own due to his failing memory. She checked on him often during the day, couldn't work long distances from the house. A few weeks ago she'd come in from milking the cow to find he'd let water boil over on the stove and flooded part of the floor in that corner of the dugout. Before that, it had been him running out in the field wearing his long johns with a bedsheet tied around his neck, flying like a cape behind him.

And she also couldn't take Pop with her to town. Not only did he refuse to go, but his aversion to people could take a violent turn sometimes. He still thought strangers were Rebel soldiers, ready to kill him.

It wasn't possible.

"I'm real sorry, but you're stuck here for now."

The cowboy laid out on the bed tried to sit up, groaning with the effort. He got one elbow under him before he collapsed, groaning in pain.

"That ain't acceptable," he growled—*growled!*—to the ceiling. "I've got folks that'll be worrying for me. And they'll take me off your hands—doctor me up at home."

"I'm sorry," she said softly. "I can't leave the homestead."

She left it at that for now, knowing he was still in deep pain, knowing he was likely exhausted and addled from his ordeal and nearly drowning.

She did feel bad for him, but she was virtually on her own out here. If it was just her, she would do what he asked, but she had Pop to think about. She would nurse Matty here until he could leave on his own. It was the best she could do.

It wasn't as if she wanted him here, either. Once he got his wits about him, he'd see that she *was* Catherine, dressed in men's clothes. No telling what censure he would show then. Would he make fun of her as he had when she was a child?

The thought made her breath catch, even now.

"I've got to go check on my grandfather," she told the cowboy. "Stay in that bed and don't hurt yourself. Further."

She found Pop standing near the edge of the garden plot. Their plot took up more than an acre, the brown earth that she and the mule had tilled earlier this spring. Around a bend in the woods was the wheat field they'd cultivated for years.

Standing at the edge of the plowed dirt field, it was easy to see the damage that the storm had done.

Hail had ripped through the delicate leaves of her tomato plants, had decimated the cornstalks. Her okra was ruined. A few of the hardier plants had survived with only minimal damage.

Pop stared at the horizon, lost in thoughts she would never be able to guess.

"We've still got time to replant, Pop," she said, winding one arm through his elbow. He felt more frail than he had even six months ago, felt as if his bones themselves were lighter. And the knowledge pierced her heart, made her breath catch.

He took a deep breath and came out of his mind and looked at the devastation around them, then at her. "The Rebs ruined our crops."

"The storm ruined them, Pop. Do you remember the nasty thunder and lightning that passed through in the night?"

His cloudy eyes cleared slightly, but he shook his head.

"We're on the family homestead in Wyoming," she reminded him, something she had to do at least once a day.

"We can replant the tomatoes," she said. "If the summer hangs on long enough, we'll still get a decent crop."

She didn't mention the wheat. Hail had decimated their crop of partly grown plants. It would take days to see whether the crop could be salvaged.

He didn't respond. Before his eyes could get that far-off look again, she squeezed his arm.

"I have something to tell you."

His rheumy blue eyes flicked to hers.

"There was a man riding out on our property today."

"You shoot him?"

"No, Pop. He fell off his horse and got hurt—broke his collarbone. He's laid up at the dugout."

Pop tensed, bristling immediately, as she'd known he would.

"He's hurt. He's not your enemy," she said quietly. "In fact, he's a sheriff's deputy for Bear Creek."

He spit in the dirt at their feet. "That don't mean nothin'. I've seen plenty a man wear a badge and use it for their own purposes. Even kill folks just 'cause they could."

The irony was not lost on her that she was being forced to defend a man she didn't like in the least.

"He's not wearing a gun." Because she'd taken and hidden it. She'd put away the rifle and shotgun when Pop had gotten bad, only taking them out when she needed to hunt to supplement their food supply.

"Don't mean nothin'."

This side of Pop scared her. When he became silent and violent and angry and nothing she said to him could get through.

"I won't let you hurt him." She said the words firmly, showing him with a steady gaze that she was serious. "We're going to nurse him until he's better and then send him home. That's all."

Pop grumbled but didn't argue as he followed her

back to the soddy. She didn't trust his acquiescence. He could be wily at times. Which meant she would have to watch over the cowboy.

The one thing she *didn't* want to do.

Chapter Three

The next time Matty woke up, his head was clearer and didn't ache quite so badly. He rolled his head in both directions and didn't experience the same intense pain he had before.

His first thought was escaping—he couldn't stay trapped here—but when he tried to push up, the same breath-stealing pain streaked across his chest. What had Catherine said before? Broken collarbone? He'd never broken a bone before, but this intense pain didn't feel like a simple bruise.

His mind flew to his parents. They would be worried about him. Sheriff Dunlop might even send a search party out. And what would Luella think? She was another reason to get home as fast as he could.

There was no one around, and he took advantage of the fact to discover more about wherever it was he'd been kept.

It was a soddy, he realized. Dug into the earth, with exposed wooden beams. He could see earth and some roots hanging down from the ceiling through woven wooden slats. Also peeking out was straw that they'd probably used to insulate holes when it grew cold outside. A small black stove and another narrow bed took up two other corners of the small room, and small triangular shelves had been built into the corner behind the door.

A small glass-paned window revealed bright, yellow morning sunlight streaming inside. His stomach grumbled at the latent smells of ham and fried eggs, as if someone had already eaten breakfast and he'd missed it.

The one-room home was simply furnished. The two beds—cots, really—were covered with faded, well-worn quilts. A simply constructed table and lone chair took up the rest of the floor space. Atop it was a folded blanket and thin pillow.

Baskets of foodstuffs, a frying pan and a deeper pot dangled from hooks set into the rafters. It was neat and tidy.

But most folks he knew chose to build a wooden home or use the rocks pulled from nearby creeks to build their homes. He knew folks who'd come west on wagon trains or begun homesteads in the distant past had used soddies, but who would choose to live in a home like this now? It was the early days of the twentieth century! He'd even read newspaper accounts of a horseless carriage that folks could ride around in.

And if they were close to the place where he'd seen that wisp of smoke, they were on the far edge of the rural areas surrounding Bear Creek. Far enough outside of town to keep a low profile and escape most folks' notice. Sheriff Dunlop hadn't told him of any folks who lived out here. Did the sheriff even know about Catherine and the young man and... Had she mentioned a grandfather?

The door opened, and the young man backed in, dark hair curling over his collar, the blue of his shirt long faded to near white, a pair of moccasins beneath his brown trousers.

His hands were full, and as he turned, Matty saw he carried a large woven basket.

And that *he* wasn't a he at all. It was Catherine. Without his head pounding quite so painfully, Matty saw what he'd missed last night in his delirium.

It had been Catherine all along. She wore her hair short, as a man would. It curled around her face and at the back of her collar, and her pixie features were in sharp relief in the morning sunshine. Dark lashes surrounded her bright blue eyes.

And there was no denying that it was a woman's body beneath her shirt and trousers. He didn't know how he'd mistaken her for a young man last night, other than the pain.

She was the boy he'd been chasing. The reason he'd taken that spill and was now laid up.

"Good morning," she said quietly, with only a glance in his direction.

"Why'd you run away from me yesterday?" It had been yesterday, hadn't it? With the bump on his head, he couldn't be sure.

She was close in the small space, but he only had a view of the side of her face. It was enough to see the twist of her lips.

"Why'd you chase me?" she countered.

"Usually when someone runs from a lawman, it's because they're a criminal. Or they've got something to hide."

She still didn't look at him, but her chin jutted out. "I'm no criminal," she muttered.

He noticed she didn't deny having something to hide.

"You took my weapon. That's suspicious."

She muttered something else that he couldn't make out. And then remained stubbornly silent. He started to grind his back teeth together, but the pain shooting through his skull made him think twice about it.

Right this moment, he didn't care if she was a bank robber or cattle rustler. He wanted to get home, where Ma would cater to him and his brothers would drive him crazy and he wouldn't be as good as alone out in the middle of nowhere.

"I'm...sorry." He gritted the words out, even knowing his ma would have his hide for the rudeness. "Sorry I scared you into running off and sorry for thinking you were a boy."

Her expression remained shuttered.

She juggled the basket against her waist and used her other hand to move the blanket and pillow from the chair to the foot of the second bed, then deposited the basket in the chair.

Maybe this wasn't the way to get home.

He sighed. "Look, I know you want me outta here, and there's folks at home worrying about me."

She shrugged. "I'll help you up if you want to go outside and...have a few private moments."

He did need to find an outhouse. And maybe once he was upright, he could find a way to get back to town. His thoughts flitted to the sheriff. The town that would be busy rebuilding by now. He needed to get back.

She must've seen his thoughts on his face, because she shook her head. "We're nearly fifteen miles from town. If you're thinking about walking, you should consider something else."

"You got a horse I could borrow?"

She shook her head, those dark curls bouncing around her face. "No horse, just the mule and she don't take to riders. Doubt you could ride anyway."

He frowned. Was she right?

She moved toward him, reaching for his shoulders. "I'm going to give you a pull, and we'll have you sitting up."

Her hands were small—she couldn't be any taller than his ma, who was fairly petite—but she had strength enough to assist him. By the time his feet were on the floor and he was sitting upright, sweat poured down his face.

It hurt like nothing he'd ever felt before. The ache was centered across his chest, but as he moved it spread like a creek overrunning its banks, making his limbs tremble with residual pain.

He got his feet under him and he managed to push up to standing. She steadied him when he would've fallen back to the bed.

He stiffly moved outside, squinting in the bright sunlight.

A creek meandered several yards away, the ground behind him sloping down to meet it, except where the soddy had been built into the bank. The creek was lined with woods on the opposite side, creating a sort of clearing. A hundred feet downstream was another structure, this one open across the front, shadowed inside. Probably where Catherine kept her livestock.

Other than the creek, there were no identifying landmarks. His last memories from yesterday before he'd been swept into the creek were how far out he'd come from town.

After a few moments taking care of his private business, he was sweating even worse, nauseous with the pain. He leaned his shoulder in the doorjamb to keep himself upright.

He was forced to admit the truth. He wasn't getting home under his own power.

He knew his brothers would come looking for him when he didn't arrive home. They might already be looking for him. But since he'd been traveling alone, the sheriff would only have the direction that he'd traveled to give them.

Would anyone even think to look for him this far out?

He needed to convince Catherine to send for help. If she didn't want to go to Bear Creek, she could at least fetch a neighbor to go on his behalf.

He perched on the edge of the bed, not wanting to lie back down just yet.

"You all right?" she asked, looking up from where she sat on the end of the second bed. She had small papers—on second look, perhaps they were small envelopes—laid out on the table's surface as she sorted them.

She handed him a plate with slices of ham and a fresh scrambled egg—she must've cooked it while he'd been outside—and two slices of toast topped with jam. The room was small enough that she could hand him the plate without getting up off the chair.

"Thanks."

She nodded and then went back to sorting, stacking several packets to one side and taking several more out of her basket.

"What's that?" he asked when she didn't offer any conversation. He was used to noise, being surrounded by his brothers and sisters and now their kids. The silence unnerved him.

"Seeds," she said, her head still down so he couldn't see her eyes, only her profile. "The hail destroyed part of our garden and we need to replant. The wheat crop, too, but that's a job for next week."

He licked his thumb, where a drop of grease from the ham had slid down. He was ravenous, and her food was good.

"Was it bad?" he asked when he'd gulped down another bite of eggs on toast and she hadn't said another word. Was she shy or upset about having him here in her place?

"Bad enough."

"How'd you get so many of those?" From up close he could see they *were* sheets of paper, folded into small envelopes with handwritten names on them. *Carrots. Peas.*

"Years of growing and saving some back."

Why was she so prickly?

Catherine kept her eyes on her task as she returned several seed packets back into the storage basket, their bumpy contents rattling as they settled.

She was surprised by the cowboy's friendly manner. Was he simply bored of being alone in the house? Obviously he didn't remember her, or he wouldn't be talking to her like this, would he?

He'd almost inhaled the entire plate of food she'd kept warm for him on the stove, and the eggs she'd quickly scrambled.

"You always so talkative?" he asked.

"Are you?" she returned.

"I've got a big family. Get lots of practice."

Before he could try to engage her in more conversation, Pop came shuffling into the doorway.

Matty looked up, his expression turning curious.

She saw Pop the way the cowboy would. White hair thinning on top and tousled from being outdoors bareheaded. Bushy eyebrows and silver stubble. His dear face. Suspenders holding up trousers that had seen better days and missing one button from his shirt.

She prayed the cowboy would be polite, or this could end badly.

"Howdy, sir," Matty greeted.

Pop skewered him with a glare.

She got up off the bed, hurrying to get the basket out of the way. "Here, Pop, come and sit." Her pants brushed the cowboy's knees in the close space.

"I'm Matty White, sir." Matty reached out his arm toward Pop, wincing as he did so. Pop stood woodenly, not reaching out to meet his handshake, and finally, the cowboy's arm dropped back to his side. Also with a wince.

"My grandfather Geoffrey Poole," she said, trying to ease the near-tangible tension in the room.

"Poole," the cowboy repeated, his eyes coming back to settle on Catherine. "Catherine Poole."

She saw the moment when recognition lit his eyes. His head tipped up and his eyes took her in from the top of her head to the tips of her moccasins. She could see his mind working quickly.

Nerves had her turning toward Pop. "Matty is a deputy from town," she reminded him, though she'd already told him the same outside.

"Don't like no town folks." It was the first thing Pop had said and the ire in his voice was easily heard.

Unaffected, Matty said, "Thanks for taking me in. I know my family will want to show their appreciation in a tangible way, once I get home."

Was that his attempt to escape their homestead? To try to inspire Pop to help him get home? To bribe him?

She should tell the cowboy it wouldn't work.

"What 'sactly were you doin' trespassing on our land?" Pop asked, his voice and stance unfriendly.

She eyed the kitchen knife, tucked in its spot behind the stove.

Would Pop really attack the cowboy, simply for being on their land?

"I wasn't trespassing," Matty said, still calm, still implacable. "The tornado damaged several buildings in town and some folks were hurt. Not to mention the flooding." He sent her a wry smile that made her stomach swoop low. What was that?

"The sheriff and town council sent me—and several other men—out to the surrounding areas to see if families or individuals needed some help."

Pop harrumphed. "We don't need no help."

Matty's eyes slid to Catherine again. She'd just told him the garden had suffered.

"We ain't got no use for strangers around here," said Pop.

Matty opened his mouth. She didn't know whether he would attempt to argue with Pop or what he would say, but she rushed to fill the short silence. "Matty will get out of our hair as soon as he is healed up, Pop. Right now he can't get there on his own steam."

The cowboy's upper lip was covered in a fine sheen of moisture. It was obvious he needed to lie back down. He'd braced himself on both fists pressed into the straw tick mattress.

"Can you help me check on the barn?" she asked Pop.

"What if he steals all our stuff?"

"He can barely sit up, Pop. I don't think he's going to carry off our things."

Pop harrumphed again but thankfully went out the front door.

The cowboy had gone white in the face.

"Why don't you lie back down?" She moved to assist him, and he groaned as he did so.

"Do you need anything?" she asked, the words popping out before she'd really thought about them. "More water?"

"I need you to ride to a neighbor's place and send someone home to come get me," he mumbled.

"I can't," she said.

He sighed heavily and closed his eyes. She guessed that meant their conversation was over. She ducked out the door to join her grandfather.

Approaching the barn, she and Pop found that part of the corner nearest the creek had washed away, revealing the bare bones of the framing that supported the front of the structure. The creek encroached, closer to the door than it had been for a good long time, flooding its banks.

A few feet closer and it would begin to wash away the structure itself.

"Does it seem the creek's edging closer this year?" She'd noticed the land eroding over the past decade, resulting in the flow of water widening its banks in places.

It could make things difficult for them if it continued flowing close to the barn.

He shrugged, mind elsewhere as he stood at her side. He'd always been difficult. She hadn't realized how much until her mama had passed when she'd been thirteen. But in these recent years he'd aged more—and his mind had taken him to the past more and more.

"Pop?"

"Hmm? What?"

Was he fading away? What would she do if she lost him, too? It didn't bear thinking about.

"Nothing. Let's go into the barn and see if there's damage inside."

* * *

Matty woke to a mumble. He was disoriented and overheated. Why was his bedroom so *close*? Why was it so smoky?

Where was he?

The storm. His injury. Catherine Poole and her grand-pop.

Starlight shone through the single window, illuminating the foot of his cot. He tried to kick off the quilt, but twisting his hips caused intense pain to flare across his collarbone and he gasped, the sound loud in the dark room.

"Who's there?"

That was Pop Poole's voice. And it sounded just as unfriendly now as it had earlier.

"It's no one, Pop." There was Catherine, her voice coming from slightly to the side and lower. "Were you dreaming? Go back to sleep."

Matty turned his head on the pillow and saw movement on the floor. A flash of white. Like the shoulder of a nightdress.

Was Catherine sleeping on the floor? He squinted, but in the darkness, he couldn't make out if it was her or the older man, but if he had to guess, he believed it was her.

She'd given up her bed for him. If that didn't give him a kick in the gut.

He could still remember her in the schoolroom. He'd been nine, and she must've been around the same age when she'd come shyly in the door, a few minutes after the teacher had called them to order.

All the other children were already seated. Luella was his seatmate that autumn, and her whispered, *Look at her dress!* was audible, even from across the room.

Pink climbed into Catherine's cheeks as her eyes darted their way, then quickly to the floor.

He wouldn't have noticed her dress if Luella hadn't pointed it out. But once he'd noticed, it was impossible to ignore that it was different from the other girls' store-bought dresses.

And after a quiet conversation with the teacher, Catherine took a seat next to one of the *little kids*.

Luella must be right. She was different.

And he was so confident in his place, he wanted to show off for his friends, so he stage-whispered, *You think she's slow or somethin'? That why she's sitting with the little kids?*

Luella and another friend who sat just in front of them tittered, and he earned a rap across his knuckles from the teacher. It was worth it. He was grinning as he returned to his seat.

Until he'd seen the tears sparkling in Catherine's eyes.

She looked down at her desk quickly, but he saw the swipe of her hand against her cheek.

That had been Monday. On Thursday, he'd come across her alone behind the corner of the school, where she'd been curled in a ball behind the wall of her knees and skirt, her face tearstained. When she'd seen him, she'd scrubbed at her eyes with her hands and left streaks of dirt across her cheeks.

And he'd turned and run away.

Friday, she hadn't returned to the schoolroom.

He'd been a stupid kid. More so because he'd forgotten about her after a few weeks. And at the end of that winter, his parents had died, and his entire life had been uprooted.

He'd forgotten about Catherine, forgotten to wonder what had happened to her.

Until now.

Now he couldn't seem to stifle his curiosity. Why did she live out here with no close neighbors and a crotchety grandpop?

His job as deputy had taught him to collect information. He wanted that to be what drove his curiosity, but if he was honest with himself, he knew it was the woman herself.

She was striking. Her pixie features and sharp eyes drew him in somehow.

Why did she cut her hair like that? And wear men's clothes?

There was a groan. Too deep to have come from Catherine, so it must've been her Pop.

"It's all right, Pop." Her voice came soft in the darkness.

"Catherine? What're you doing on the battlefield? It's too dangerous for you to be here, girl!"

Battlefield? Was the old man dreaming? Matty hadn't seen any signs of danger around the soddy. There was nothing around, no close neighbors.

"Pop, we're safe here at home in Wyoming."

He couldn't see well in the dark and with his head at the foot of Pop's bed, and he worked to get his elbow under him, biting back a groan at the lightning shot of pain across his chest.

"Who's there?"

"Pop—"

"Ssh! Girl, get down. There's someone out there. He's close. Where's my bayonet?"

Something cold slithered down Matt's spine. *Now* he sensed danger.

"Dirty Rebs," Pop growled. "Sneaking and spying at night."

Rebs. Rebels? As in, Confederate soldiers?

Suddenly it began to make sense to Matty. The old man must be caught in memories of the War Between the States.

Matty went still. He didn't know if Pop had a weapon.

"There are no soldiers here," Catherine said softly, calmly. "We're in the soddy. Home in Bear Creek."

"We are? Catherine?" Now the old man's voice had changed, turned weaker.

"Breathe in deep, Pop." Her voice was almost ethereal in the darkness. "Can you smell the Wyoming air? Smell the pine just outside."

Matty found himself following her directions. She was right. There was a bite of pine in the brisk air.

"Smell the earth. Did the earth in Georgia smell like this?"

"No." Pop sighed. "You're right. We're at home."

Matty carefully laid his head back on the pillow, not wanting to rustle around too much. Not wanting to draw Pop's notice, when she'd done such a good job settling him.

Matty had gotten a small glimpse of what kept her here on the homestead. Her Pop had seemed lucid today, but did he also have episodes during daytime hours?

Was she in danger from her own grandfather?

It didn't set right with him.

And, not knowing if the old man had a weapon in his possession, it was a long time before Matty got back to sleep.

Chapter Four

Catherine had spent the dark hours of morning tearing out the decimated garden plants so she could replant them later in the day. She'd also mucked out the barn, milked the cow and gathered eggs, all before breakfast.

She was dirty, smelly and tired. The storm had pushed laundry day back in favor of more urgent tasks.

And she still had to deal with the cowboy, who no doubt would make more demands about her returning him to his family.

Which is why she hesitated outside the soddy door, leaning her shoulder against it. She could just rest here for a bit in the silent, peaceful moment.

Was that movement across the creek, in the woods? She squinted against the shadows but couldn't be sure, even as a fearful tingle crawled up the back of her neck.

She'd caught Ralph Chesterton loitering in the woods two weeks ago and had been unsettled ever since. He'd asked her *again* to marry him, and she'd turned him down flat.

She couldn't understand why he continued to ask when she'd fairly run him off her property. Once with a pitchfork. Since that sighting, she'd had the feeling of seeing something out of the corner of her eye. But when she'd turn to look, nothing was there. Maybe she was going mad like her grandfather.

And Pop's middle-of-the-night spell hadn't helped her relax any. She was on edge, strung tight as a wire.

But there was no use dawdling anymore. Breakfast needed cooking.

When she kicked open the door, as she was holding three eggs in one hand and the milk pail in the other, she nearly dropped both when she caught sight of the cowboy sitting in the chair, stirring something in the skillet.

"What are you doing?" she asked, her voice sharp.

He glanced up at her, his brown eyes touching her and glancing off. "Cooking breakfast."

She sniffed, not smelling the charring there would be if he'd burned something. Instead, there was the familiar woodsmoke and the floury scent of biscuits.

Bacon popped and he calmly used the wooden spoon to shift something in the skillet.

Pop sat on his bed, whittling. His face was grim and he kept shooting glances at the cowboy wielding the spoon.

"Are you sure you should be up and about?" She set the pail of milk on the table.

"There's not much *up* about sitting here," he responded with a cheeky smile, but she didn't miss the white lines around his mouth. It was costing him to sit upright.

"Here." She put the three brown eggs into his hand, her fingers brushing against his palm. A tremble zinged up her arm at the touch of skin on skin. She felt his gaze rise to her face but edged away instead of looking at him.

A splash of water from the basin cooled her burning

cheeks. She took extra moments patting down her face and hands, drying off, trying to regain her composure.

Why did he affect her so intensely?

He was handsome. But surely it was more than that. It must be that so much time had passed since her last interaction with anyone other than Pop. She didn't count the marriage proposals from Ralph Chesterton. Mostly, she tried not to think of them.

When she got used to the cowboy's presence, it would be better. She wouldn't be so affected.

And then he would leave. And that would be even better.

She got three tin mugs down from the shelf, conscious of how her trousers brushed the cowboy's knees in the enclosed space.

She heard the series of cracks and the following sizzle as the cowboy must've broken the eggs into the skillet. She put the table between them, dipping milk for each cup out of the pail and then perching on a stool.

"I was just telling your Pop about my brothers and how their families have been growing."

She hadn't been aware that he had brothers. She remembered him being an only child. Hadn't he been? He'd been friends with Luella McKeever then; they'd been thick as thieves. Had she just forgotten those details?

She doubted it. Those horrific days were seared into her memory and had been for years. They had been enough to make her quit coming to school.

Looking up, she found him watching her. One corner of his mouth turned up, and all she could remember was him at nine years old, standing shoulder to shoulder with Luella and pointing at her, laughing, because her dress hadn't been like the other girls'.

Was he still laughing at her now?

She must be different from the other women he was used to. And that wasn't even counting her parentage. If he knew about that, no doubt he would look down on her even more.

Tearing her eyes away from the cowboy, she averted her gaze to the window, where bright morning sunlight streamed in.

"Do you want to hear about my family?"

She shrugged, figuring it was safer not to say anything, in case he was looking for a way to poke fun at her. Pop had taught her how to track and hunt, how to watch her surroundings for danger.

And family could be a dangerous topic for discussion.

"You probably didn't know I *had* brothers," he said easily, as if she'd answered him. "My parents died when I was ten. Man named Jonas White took me in—only, he already had five other kids. Four adopted sons and a daughter. And then about nine months after I'd come to be a part of the family, two other boys joined us—they were orphans, too."

She was sorry to hear that his parents had died. That wouldn't have been long after she'd left school. She could relate to how it felt to lose the person closest to you.

"You always been the only child?"

She startled, realizing he'd asked her a direct question. A quick glance showed he was stirring the pot, not watching her.

"Yes." Her voice sounded rusty. She realized she hadn't spoken all morning. She offered no details. Didn't want him guessing her shame.

"I was, too, up until that point. You can probably imagine it was a shock to me, going from being the only kid at home to having to share everything." What must that have been like? Growing up, she'd wanted a bigger family. A father at least.

Was he trying to befriend her? Make her feel companionable with him?

Suspicion filled her. What was his motive? Just to make her want to help him get home?

She tensed, still not answering him, still not knowing what the right thing to say was.

After all the years of isolation, she *couldn't* imagine having more of a family. She felt Matty's intrusion acutely, couldn't be inside the soddy without him being in her space.

And he talked. A lot.

To have seven others…she couldn't imagine the noise level, couldn't imagine having that many people close.

Her skin prickled just thinking about it.

Matty sensed Catherine's interest in his words. Why was she being so standoffish?

He gave the scrambled eggs and then the fried potatoes a last stir and grabbed a plate from the shelf above the stove and began filling it.

"Pop?"

The old man grunted what Matty thought must be assent, and Matty passed him the plate. It landed on the table with a thump.

The spoon clinked against the skillet as he worked at filling Catherine's plate. It didn't escape his notice that her pants were grubby at the knees and she'd had dirt rubbed into her knuckles before she'd washed up. She'd been in the garden and the pail of milk and eggs told that she'd been working at chores. If he hadn't cooked up breakfast, would she have come inside and done that, too?

It didn't seem fair for a young woman alone to be running an entire homestead.

"Catherine?"

She jerked when he said her name, then accepted the plate from him silently.

He worked at piling food on his own plate, and the silence began to grate on him. "Five of my older brothers are married now. Oscar, Edgar and Davy have built their places on the family land—we've got a big spread, plenty of room for everyone—Edgar and Davy run cattle with my pa, and Oscar raises cutting horses. Then Ricky lives with his wife on her family's ranch up north near Sheridan. And my brother Maxwell is married to Hattie. They're both doctors and split their time between town and the family homestead."

"Your sister-in-law is a doctor?"

There. There was the interest he'd been waiting for, in her soft-spoken question about Hattie.

"Yep. She trained as a nurse under her father—old Doc Powell—and then went to three years of medical school down in Denver."

He saw the light of interest in her eyes before her inky lashes came down and hid her gaze from him.

And he felt the stirring of curiosity, as well. "Did your family move away from Bear Creek for a while?"

He wanted to know why she'd disappeared from the classroom without coming right out and asking about it.

"Lived on this very land since 1871," Pop growled through a mouthful of eggs.

"Oh."

Then why had she stopped coming to the schoolroom?

"Will your brothers come looking for you?" she asked softly, her fork scraping against the edge of the plate.

"I expect so. I'm not sure they'll find me this far out.

I visited the Samuels family and the Chestertons two days ago, so maybe they'll follow my tracks."

Pop harrumphed. "No good Chestertons. They'd better stay out of our business."

Matty didn't know the two bachelors well. They'd been courteous enough when he'd checked on them. He could only hope the sheriff or his brothers would find him. He couldn't stay out here. The isolation, the quiet, was about to drive him crazy, and it had only been one day.

Catherine set her fork down, still silent. Was she upset that he was here, as her grandfather was?

He couldn't get a read on her, and that was unusual for him, and frustrating. He was an open and honest kind of guy, and most folks responded to that. Not her.

Was it old scars from their childhood that were still between them? He needed her on his side so she could help him get home. He had to find a way to make things right.

Catherine had left off clearing the field last night. Half of the ground had been rebroken, the rich brown soil turned up, while the rest bore the signs of the damaging storm, plants beaten into the ground and destroyed. She could finish this plot today, if the weather held and Pop behaved.

She approached the plow she'd left in the field, marking her place, with the mule slightly behind her, tugging its leading rope when it stubbornly slowed. And saw one person she could've done without seeing ever again. Ralph.

"What are you doing here?" she demanded.

He stood with arms crossed. He would've been handsome, tall and dark-haired, except for the hard light in his eyes and the unkempt state of his dress. And if she got close enough, the smell of his unwashed body.

His lips opened in what must've been supposed to be a grin, showing his crooked teeth, stained brown. "Came to see if you'd had the same damage we had. Looks like ya did."

"We're managing." She hated the way that he looked at her. She always did. From the way his eyes lingered when it would've been polite to glance away, to the slight narrowing of his eyes.

She started buckling the mule's harness, trying to pretend he wasn't there. He made no move to help her. Just stared.

"Was there something else?" she asked.

He gestured to the field. "It's a lot of work and just you to do it. Seems like you need a man in the worst way."

A shudder snaked through her. "I do just fine. And I've got a man. Pop."

"That old geezer ain't no help to you no more, and you and I both know it."

She kept her eyes on the buckle, on the movement of her hands at the mule's flank, though her attention did not waver from the man. From the sidelong glances she sent his way, she could see his posture was relaxed, but she wasn't fooled. He was a threat.

"You been thinking about the partnership I proposed?"

She knew the partnership he was talking about. Marriage. She wouldn't give him the satisfaction of mentioning it aloud.

He stepped closer. "Your big secret don't matter to me."

She inhaled sharply at his reminder. He knew about her shame. And wasn't above trying to use it as leverage, apparently. "I gave you my answer the last time we talked. It's still no."

He went on as if she hadn't spoken. "You lost your crop thanks to the hail. Ain't no way you're gonna catch up on all the work you need to do to make it through the winter. We could help each other."

"I said *no*." Now she let her eyes raise to him to make sure that he wasn't going to attack because of her answer.

His face had gone crimson; his eyes had a hard glint to them. "You'll change your mind."

"No, I won't."

He gave her one more leer that she did her best not to show any reaction to. As he walked away, he kept glancing over his shoulder until he made the tree line and disappeared into the shadows.

She had never been so glad to see someone leave her property.

She checked the last buckle on the mule's harness and slapped the old girl into motion. Now that Ralph was gone, she began to tremble. His words tumbled through her head like water over a rocky creek bed. Had he been threatening her? Maybe his words hadn't been an overt threat, but she felt it just the same. He and his teenage brother lived on a small homestead not far away. They had never caused trouble for her until about two years ago, when Ralph had started calling—if you could call his visits such. Lately it seemed that Ralph had been trespassing on their property more and more.

She had enough things going on with the cowboy hurt back in the dugout and trying to figure out a way to get rid of him. Didn't need something else to worry about. But with Ralph her closest neighbor, she never could relax.

For hours, Catherine trudged behind the mule, its leather reins laid over her shoulders as she guided the plow in the furrow next to the several she'd just created in the grassy plain, the brown soil sending its pungent smell into the air. Her boots sank into the soft, loose earth.

If it came down to replanting the wheat, she would need to increase the field so they could plant enough to put some back and start rebuilding the stockpile.

Every time she walked past the crushed stalks, a frisson of worry slithered through her. All that seed lost. The driving hail had left nothing untouched.

"You want a water break?"

Surprised at the unexpected voice, she wiped her forehead with the back of one hand and found the cowboy standing at the edge of the field.

She gave the mule the command to halt. The cowboy didn't wait for her to untangle herself from the harness, he just brought a pail and the dipper to her.

She saw the strain, saw what it cost him to carry the pail in the clenched set of his jaw.

"Thank you," she murmured as she sipped noisily from the dipper.

"You're welcome."

She saw his eyes trail over what she'd done, and unbidden, her spine straightened. The Matty she'd known in the schoolroom had found fault with nearly everything she did. Would he find fault with the work she'd done today?

She pushed her bangs out of her face, hating that he saw her like this, dressed like a man, grubby, thirsty.

Cathy, Cathy, homemade happy! Those awful voices from her childhood pattered through her memories like raindrops that sometimes infiltrated the roof of the dugout. It made her self-conscious as she drank from the tin cup.

"I figure I owe you an apology," he said.

She choked.

He gave her long enough to stop sputtering. "Guess you weren't expecting that?"

"I didn't know for sure you'd remembered me."

His gaze was steady on her, and the intensity of his eyes was hard to hold. "Yeah. And I remembered how awful I was to you. I'm sorry for the things I said back then."

It was the very last thing she expected him to say. And he seemed to be able to read that in her expression. His lips quirked up in an endearing half smile, one that made her stomach swoop. She dropped her eyes.

She had to remember that he wasn't her friend. He hadn't been back then and right now he wanted to get home. He was using her. Trying to get her to help him.

He might've been waiting for a response. Silence lagged between them, and she didn't fill it.

Finally, he sighed.

She gulped the rest of the water and offered him the cup. But instead of taking it and walking away, he caught her fingers against the cup. The contrast of his hot fingers against the cool metal unnerved her and her chin jerked up as she met his eyes.

"Does your Pop have nightmares like that a lot?"

That he saw the issues closest to her heart unnerved her even more than his touch, and she jerked her hand away. She couldn't afford him to discover the truth about her heritage.

His eyebrows ran up toward his hairline. She flushed, hating that he saw that he had an effect on her.

"Not every night," she said smartly. "Will you move?"

He didn't. "Is he a danger to you?"

"Of course not. He would never hurt me."

"Does he always know it's you?"

She went still. How had he guessed that sometimes Pop was so lost in his memories that he didn't recognize her?

"Pop is the only family I've got left. We take care of each other."

He took a slow look around them, prompting her to do the same. There was nothing out of place, only the familiar rolling plain, in the cup of the valley that kept them out of sight of the neighbors, unless they got too close.

"I only see *you*, taking care of everything," he said quietly. "Have you ever thought of moving closer to town, where you'd have more help?"

And there it was. Of course he'd brought it back to getting to town. Because he wanted to get home.

And while she wanted him gone, she also couldn't leave the homestead and couldn't take Pop with her.

Her chin came up. "I manage."

And she gave a slap with the reins. He was forced to move aside or have his foot caught in the plow as the mule lurched forward.

He stood at the edge of her plot for long enough that she grew uncomfortable under his scrutiny.

She fumed as she halted the mule and turned the plow in the rutted dirt. What did he think, that she wanted him near, asking questions? Forcing her to remember that she was a woman, not just a worker, trying to keep the homestead afloat.

It was uncomfortable. She was happy here on the homestead with Pop. Her mama had been practically shunned by Bear Creek. How could she expect different?

Nor did she have anyone else to turn to. She'd lived here all her life, wasn't comfortable in town, had never wanted anything else.

Finally, he disappeared through a copse of trees, back toward the soddy, and she felt she could breathe again.

And…if she was being totally truthful with herself, there was a time she *had* wanted something different. She'd dreamed of more education for herself. Hearing that Matty had a sister-in-law who had gone to medical school—*medical school!*—was like a crawly itch. Like the time she'd gotten into a poison oak patch. What would it be like to have that freedom? To go to college herself?

She would never know, she reminded herself. When her mama had died, Pop had been all she'd had. He'd given years of his life to take care of her. She could do no less for him, in these last years of his life. She owed him, in the sense of family duty.

No matter what old dreams she would sacrifice to do so.

Chapter Five

Matty should've gone directly to the dugout. Fire streaked across his chest. But he was intensely curious about these people whose lives he'd dropped into. And Catherine was terribly tight-lipped.

He went to the barn instead.

The structure was too near the stream. In worse shape than the house. Birds chirped in a tall pine across the creek. Afternoon sunlight slanted through a grove of larches, dappling him with shade. It should've been a peaceful setting, but he was too antsy for it to soak in.

He set the water bucket and dipper down near the corner of the building and stepped across the threshold. Inside, the area was split into two sections, separated by crudely constructed walls.

Along one wall there were rows of shelves with nesting chickens. Beside that were two neat and orderly stalls. One where she must keep the mule. A placid milk cow stood in the other. The hay was clean and sweet smelling. Obviously Catherine took good care of her animals.

But on the opposite side of the dividing wall was chaos. A jumble of belongings lay scattered on the floor.

A broken plow, harness, wooden pieces, metal pieces. He couldn't even tell what all was there. It was as if this was where they had collected all of the junk they accumulated since 1871.

Beneath the sweet smell of hay was a strong scent of damp earth, as if the driving rains had soaked into the entire structure.

He chose his steps carefully, curiosity driving him farther inside.

In the back corner behind the jumbled items, the storm must've washed away part of the grass and dirt that made up the roof. Sunlight filtered in, highlighting dust motes.

Would his weapon and tin star be hidden somewhere in this mess? Catherine could've easily stashed it here.

He could barely find the floor beneath the items scattered at his feet. It would take forever to go through all of those pieces, so he did the next obvious thing and began to examine the walls. There were some exposed boards that they used to prop up the roof. The back wall seemed to be the newest; maybe they'd had some kind of a cave-in or just wanted to reinforce the structure. Those newer boards were wedged tightly together, and he spared a thought wondering if Catherine had done it, too.

Along the outside wall there was a shelf where he found a rusty pocketknife and some old tin cans and other odds and ends. But no tin star and no gun.

A little deflated and a lot exhausted just from the short walk out to the field, he turned to go back to the house.

Something swung at him.

He reacted instantly, twisting his upper body to escape the intruder's attack. Pain ripped through him.

At the same time, he registered that it wasn't a person reaching out to grab him but instead an L-shaped construct of two connected wooden boards, swinging out from the corner.

He must have dislodged it when he came inside. Now it dangled over the open doorway.

Gasping with pain, adrenaline surging through him even though nothing was actually wrong, he hobbled to the doorway and ducked beneath the piece of wood.

The bright sunlight made his eyes water. Or maybe that was the pain.

Bending over to pick up the water pail had him gasping anew, and he had to brace himself with one hand on the side of the barn. This pain was as bad as it had been when he woke that very first day. It streaked through him, not only centered on his chest, but radiating down to the very tips of his fingers and toes.

He hobbled back to the sod house one step at a time. The pain made him loopy, and he was sure he wobbled several times, but somehow he managed to stay upright.

Neither Catherine nor her Pop were anywhere in sight when he pushed open the soddy door. Unable to bear it any longer, he dropped the pail and hoped there wasn't enough water left in the bottom to splash all over.

The sod house was so small that all he had to do was turn and flop backward onto the tiny cot.

More pain.

He couldn't help the cry that escaped his lips this time. The last rays of sunlight shone in the door he'd left open and speared his eyes. His head pounded.

Maybe he shouldn't have gotten out of bed at all. He hated to admit that Catherine might be right. He could only hope he hadn't made things worse for his healing collarbone.

The pain soared, and all he could do was pass out.

But just before he did, his hazy thoughts coalesced into one distinct fear.

If he had been out here alone, if Catherine hadn't found him, he could've died in that raging water. If Catherine wasn't helping him now, he would have no source of food.

It was just like what happened with his parents all over again. The familiar fear from so long ago crept over him, making it harder for him to bear the pain radiating everywhere.

He finally slipped into unconsciousness.

In the night, a rain shower passed over. Catherine woke to muddy drips hitting her cheek where she lay on a pallet on the floor.

The first storm, the one that had caused such bad flooding, must've washed away some of the soil and grass that made up their roof.

"Cath, you getting rained on?" Pop's low grumble met her ears.

She listened for the sound of the cowboy's even breathing but couldn't determine whether he was awake or asleep.

"I'll have to fix it tomorrow," she returned quietly.

Another day of work lost because of the storm.

She could hear Pop shifting in his cot, then finally his rustling stopped and his breathing evened out. The cowboy still hadn't spoken. Maybe he hadn't woken at all. He'd been laid out on the cot when she'd come in from plowing. Something had happened, because he'd been pale and covered in sickly sweat again, as if he'd reinjured his collarbone, but he hadn't volunteered any information.

While the cowboy had dozed in a state of pain, Pop

had quizzed her over supper, demanding to know what had her shaken up. She'd attempted to divert his attention but had been aware of his questioning gaze throughout the rest of the evening.

Months ago, when she'd told him of Ralph's pushy proposal, he'd been so angry that he'd threatened to go after the other man with a shotgun. She hadn't told him of any of the succeeding proposals and wouldn't tell him of this one.

Ralph would come to see that her rejection was final. He had to.

What man would continue pursuing a woman who was so adamant in her refusal?

Everything was still soggy and muddy the next morning as she climbed carefully atop the dugout roof. The roof likely wouldn't hold her weight, and the last thing she needed was to fall through, right on top of the cowboy slumbering inside.

Pop had disappeared on one of his rambles. If he kept to his normal pattern, he would be back by lunchtime.

She carefully placed a long flat board across the rooftop, ensuring it stretched from solid ground on one side to the other.

On her hands and knees, she scooted across the board, looking for places where the soil had washed away, clumps of grass or depressions where water was seeping in.

It was tedious work and by midmorning her back and shoulders ached. She squinted against the morning sun even as it warmed her head and shoulders.

"You okay up there?" The cowboy's casual question made her jump.

It had been muffled through the soil and grass between them, but sounded as if he spoke directly to the room.

She considered not answering, but the last thing she wanted was for him to come outside and watch her as he had yesterday at the field.

"I'm fine. Just trying to do a little patchwork here."

"I thought you were splashing me in the night." His voice held the teasing note, one that she didn't know what to do with.

So she said nothing.

"Actually, it would've made me feel right at home, like my brothers were playing pranks on me."

"Are you the worst of the pranksters?" she asked.

He laughed, a warm sound that made a feeling like hot molasses swirl through her stomach. She braced herself against it. She didn't even know where the question had come from. She wasn't curious about him, didn't want to know more about his life.

"No, that honor goes to my brother Ricky."

There was a short pause.

"Although Ricky has settled down since he got married. He lives away from the rest of us—his wife's family has a ranch up north. So now it's just me and Seb and Breanna left at home to play pranks. Unless one of my older brothers gets an ornery idea. Breanna might be the worst of us left at home."

She hesitated. She wasn't going to ask but was unable to stop the words from spilling over her lips. "What kinds of things does she do?"

"My ma was pushing her to put a pie in the Ladies' Society bake sale, and Breanna filled the thing with salt instead of sugar. She said it was on purpose, but it could've just been a mishap. She ain't the best of cooks. Of course she also has an aversion to anything Ma might do that has to do with matchmaking. Then there was the time…"

His voice trailed off, almost as if he was chuckling to himself, but she couldn't be sure, not with the roof between them.

"Seb is the youngest of us adopted boys," he explained. "He's real sensitive about being outpranked. So one night Breanna gets all these crickets and lets them loose in the bunkhouse. Those things were chirping away, none of us could get any sleep for about a week."

He grumbled something low she couldn't make out.

Her fingers located a soft spot in the ground, and she pressed. Soil shifted, loosening beneath her fingers.

"Hey!"

His exclamation told her she must have found a place where the dirt was dropping in.

"I'll need that dirt to mark where I need to patch," she called out to him.

A grumble she couldn't quite make out was his only response.

"I can show you exactly where it's coming in," he finally said. Then, "For a minute there I thought talking about pranks turned *you* a little ornery."

She packed dirt in as best she could without pushing more down onto him, but at his words something grabbed ahold of her middle and she mashed dirt down with both hands.

She heard him exclaim, heard him spluttering and spitting as if maybe he got the dirt right in his mouth.

Her voice wobbled just slightly as she asked, "Are you all right?"

She could practically feel the steam rising out of his ears from up here.

If it had been Mama down there, she would have tanned Catherine's hide. Even Pop wouldn't have understood what made her do that. She didn't quite understand it herself.

Would the cowboy get angry? Even in pain, he hadn't lost his temper other than the flash of his eyes when she told him she'd taken his weapon.

But then this really was her fault.

Matty stared up at the underside of the roof, still flat on his back. Still laid out.

This morning his chest felt as if a thousand-pound horse sat on it and refused to budge.

He was furious with himself for making his injury worse. He needed to heal up. To get out of here and home.

But for some reason he couldn't keep the silly grin from stretching across his face. Catherine was teasing.

This was the most she'd said since he'd arrived in her life.

"You'd better watch out next time you come in to have a cup of coffee," he said. "You might find it filled with mud." His words tasted gritty from the dirt that had fallen in his mouth.

Light streaming in the window highlighted the dust motes floating through the air.

She didn't respond, but a trickle of dirt rained down on the pillow where his head had been moments ago. She could make a fool of him once, but he knew how to move.

It chafed knowing she was out there working hard and he was laid up in bed. At least his brothers weren't here to see his humiliation.

But those same thoughts that had snuck up on him yesterday tickled the back of his brain all over again. If Catherine and her Pop hadn't been here, he would already be dead.

How could she stand to live out here so far from other people? Just the thought of what could happen—grave injuries, even death—made him shudder, and he was a grown man.

Out here, there was no one to depend on.

"How often do you get to town?" he called up to her. "I mean when it's not the busiest part of spring?"

"Never."

Her one-word response was a shock. "You mean you haven't been in a while? This year?"

"I haven't been since I was eight years old."

It couldn't be true. But he thought to the state of her clothes, the buckskin trousers and homespun shirt.

How did folks survive without going to town?

"But what about—" His mind spun as he searched for the right thing to ask. "What about the tools I saw in the barn?"

She must've heard the incredulousness in his voice, because her answer emerged sharp. "Traded a neighbor."

"What if you run short on crops one year?"

He could almost sense her shrug those slender shoulders.

"We make do."

"But what about friends—"

"I don't need a friend," she said. She sounded matter-of-fact, but something—maybe it was just being stuck in this situation—made him question whether she could be telling the truth.

"Everybody needs a friend."

"Not me."

His sister was one of the most tomboyish females he knew, but even she had friends in Oscar and Sarah's girls, Cecilia and Susie, and Emma, Fran's sister. It just didn't sit right with him that Catherine was out here alone without a soul to talk to except Pop.

She got real quiet. He could still hear her movements and sometimes see dust raining down inside the sod house. His eyes roamed around the place, his innate curiosity going crazy because he was stuck here lying on the cot.

The place was clean and neat, as if she took pride in having organized surroundings. Everything in its place.

But he could also see small things that had been left undone, probably due to lack of time.

The stove could use another coat of polish. The rag rug on the floor was badly worn.

His eyes were drawn to the wall right next to the bed. The panels were slightly uneven, making a slight pocket right next to his side. Between the two uneven boards, he could see the smallest corner of something.

He reached for it. As long as he kept his torso still, the pain was manageable. His fingertips brushed against something, but he couldn't quite grasp it.

He shifted, biting back a gasp when pain fired across his chest. But his fingers closed around it. Holding it up, he saw it appeared to be a leather pouch, brown with age. Medium-size. And something was inside it.

He set it on his stomach and wiggled the pull cord, finally drawing out what looked like...schoolbooks.

His fingers tracked idly over the long-ago familiar title of the book in front. A reader. The cover was intact, though badly worn as if someone had opened it over and over again.

Were these the same ones that Catherine had owned back when she'd been at the schoolhouse?

If so, why had she kept them?

It seemed such a simple and whimsical thing to hold on to.

And somehow he knew Catherine was an infinitely practical person.

Did the primer have a deeper meaning to her?

He heard scuffling above. Was she finishing with her patching job on the outside?

He doubted she would like to know that he found her hidden books. He carefully slid them back into the leather pouch and pushed it with the tips of his fingertips back into its hiding place.

Catherine entered the soddy, squinting a little as she came out of the bright sunlight into the dim interior. As her eyes adjusted, she saw the cowboy was still laid out flat on his back, his hair tousled against the pillow.

"Still in pain?" she asked.

In all his conversation, he hadn't offered up what he had been doing when he'd reinjured himself yesterday.

"Only when I move." He'd obviously wiped his face clean, but there was dirt along his hairline and she felt a moment of uncertainty at seeing it. Maybe she shouldn't have played the joke.

There were small piles of dirt also at the foot of the bed and on the table. Above each pile, those were the places she needed to patch.

She would deal with the dirt that had landed on the cowboy's pillow last; that way he didn't have to move quite yet.

After she'd climbed off the roof, she'd filled a pail

with mud down from the creek, a gray shale that dried to a stiff clay.

She carefully stood on the little stool between the table and Pop's cot, balancing when it wobbled. She wiggled her fingers into the small crack between two of the wooden slats and wedged them apart.

It was awkward work with her hands above her head and balancing on the stool. Made worse because the cowboy was watching.

"Do you have to replace the roof often?"

"Every few years."

She stood on tiptoe, stretching to push a clump of mud into the opening she'd created between the two slats.

"That must be hard work."

Backbreaking. The last time she'd had to cut squares of earth and grass and haul them where she needed them had taken a week and she'd been sore for another week after that.

"Haven't you ever wanted…well, things that normal girls might want? Friends? Frocks? A family?"

"I have a family," she snapped. Her arms were beginning to ache as she held them above her head. She kept her eyes on what she was doing, but the cowboy was sorely testing her focus.

"That's not what I meant," he backtracked. "I meant… like a husband someday. Babies. That kind of family."

Her ears grew hot. She knew her face must be red, but she hoped he would attribute it to the exertion and not his words.

"Those kinds of things aren't important to me." She meant more the former than the latter. The truth was, she did want to have a family someday. She'd always held a secret longing for it. And after Pop passed away, who would she have left?

"I didn't mean any offense," he said.

She didn't respond to that. His entire presence here bothered her, made her ask questions of herself. Made her think things that were dangerous.

She finished her patch and rubbed a muddy hand against her pant leg. Now the only place she had left to patch was right above the cowboy's head.

He must've known where her next target was because even as she stepped off the stool, he was attempting to struggle up onto his elbows. And having a hard time of it.

"Here, let me—" She braced one hand beneath his elbow. The muscles in his arms flexed under her hand as she tugged until he was sitting up. Sweat poured off his brow, and he panted with pain.

"There," he said. "It's only the getting upright that's bad. I'm all right now." He edged off the bed and onto the stool, far enough out of her way that she could stand on the bed and finish with the ceiling.

His nosy questions made her want to escape. It was safer in the field with the mule.

She worked quicker than she normally would, arms still aching, unused to working above her head for so long. When she attempted to shove the slats back in place, she cut her finger on a ragged edge.

She hissed but made sure the panels were secure before bringing her hands down in front of her. She examined the splinter sticking out of her finger and the blood welling around it.

"You need some help?"

It was as if he had to stick his nose into everything. He couldn't help himself.

She was irritated with his presence and with herself

for being unable to ignore those things that she wanted in the deepest parts of her heart.

"It's just a splinter," she growled at him.

Her hands were too muddy to stick her finger in her mouth. She'd have to wash off in the creek before she could do anything about the splinter.

But when she stepped off the bed, her foot went into the bucket and she lost her balance, falling onto the edge of the bed with a *whuff!* of air expelling from her chest.

It put her face-to-face with the unnerving cowboy. His eyes seemed to see right into her.

He didn't say anything.

She hiked her chin.

And then he did. "You say you don't need a friend. But I don't believe you. For as long as I'm here, I'm praying I can be that friend."

Chapter Six

A day and a half after Matty had made his declaration that he wanted to be Catherine's friend, he'd barely seen her since. She'd lit out of the soddy as if her pants were on fire. At the time he couldn't help but smile, but after thirty-six hours of boredom, he didn't find it funny anymore.

He'd pushed himself to get out of bed this morning, gritting his teeth against the pain. Catherine was nowhere in sight when he stood outside the dugout squinting against the early-morning sun.

The field she'd been plowing the other day was empty, and there was no movement near the barn, though the cow mooed. Had he scared her that badly?

Pop appeared from the nearby woods, muttering to himself. He didn't seem to see Matty yet. The older man had remained coherent, if quiet, for the past day.

And maybe Matty was desperate for human contact or maybe he was just crazy, but he called out, "You need any help this morning?"

Pop looked up at him, face drawn.

"It's me. Matty."

Recognition flashed in Pop's eyes, and Matty again

felt a stirring of unease. What if the old man woke up one morning and didn't recognize Catherine?

"I've been trying to think of ways I might help around here, in exchange for my keep."

Pop squinted at him.

"But it's hard without being able to move much. I thought maybe we could go fishing this morning, if you'll show me the creek."

He didn't really need the old man to show him the creek. He was capable of going by himself. But maybe it would keep Pop out of trouble and out of Catherine's way if they went together.

"Fine," the older man growled. "But don't lag behind."

Matty trailed Pop through the woods along the creek bank. A black-and-white chickadee chirruped, hopping from branch to branch. Underbrush tugged at his boots; silver ripples reflected sunlight off the water.

They settled under the dappled shade of a gnarled oak in a place where the stream made a natural bend. With all the fishing he'd done with his brothers, he knew that the big clump of roots that must protrude out into the water would be a natural spot for fish to congregate.

Maybe this hadn't been such a great idea.

Sitting at the water's edge, the large tree trunk behind him, he was only a little out of breath from the hike. Adrenaline pumped through him, along with memories of what had happened the last time he'd been near the water. For moments he was lost in memories of tumbling loose limbed in the creek, being unable to get his head above the murky water.

He blinked the images away.

The lazy trickle of water in the stream would have been comforting before the day he'd nearly died. The water level had gone down, though moss and branches and other debris left behind showed where the water had risen during the flooding.

He dropped his line in with a soft *plunk*, breathing in deep of woods and moss and brook.

Pop was silent a few feet away, his gaze focused on the water.

"Good trout fishing?" Matty asked. His voice was slightly hoarse as he fought back the memories.

"Most days."

Pop returned to his silence.

Matty was so used to having his brothers or *someone* around that the days of silence grated. He didn't like where his thoughts went without the distraction of his family. He didn't particularly like thinking about those three days when he'd been completely on his own, after his parents had passed away. He'd been stricken with fever, too, and when he'd come out of it, his parents had been gone.

He remembered the desperate fear that had filled him when he'd realized he was all alone.

They lived a fair piece from town, and he'd thought about riding one of the horses in to try to find help—he was only a boy, and while he could do chores around the farm, he didn't know how to cook or take care of himself. And there were certain chores that a boy just couldn't perform.

But a bigger part of him had been afraid to leave the farm. He knew the way to town. But what if he got lost? What if someone accosted him? He knew it was far-fetched, but he'd lost the two people closest to him and wasn't thinking completely rationally.

And then two days later a neighbor had stopped by to chat with his pa and found Matty on his own. He'd been taken into their home but told it wouldn't be permanent.

And his fears had simply shifted. What if no one wanted to adopt a boy of his age? Would he be sent to an orphanage? Would he be made to work?

For almost two weeks the town and the church had discussed his fate, until Jonas had been asked to take him in.

And everything had changed.

He wanted to break free of the memories. And so he blurted out a question. "How old were you when you went into the war?"

Pop looked up, skewering him with a gaze.

Matty met his gaze levelly. "I'm just making conversation."

Pop went back to looking at his line in the water without making a response.

"How long were you in?"

Still nothing.

Matty's line tugged and he pulled it in. Nothing on it. Fish had taken his bait.

"Anybody ever tell you you talk too much?" Pop asked in his gravelly voice.

Thinking about Breanna and his ma, a smile spread across Matty's lips. "Yeah."

Pop harrumphed, and for a moment Matty thought that was the end of it, but then the older man popped a pretty little trout onto the bank. "Had a good friend, John. He and I joined up together," Pop said quietly.

Matty kept his eyes on the water where his line disappeared. "Did you serve in the infantry? Cavalry?"

"We were sharpshooters. All those days we'd spent hunting together. He was better'n me—could hit a squirrel at a hundred yards."

"Did he survive the war?"

Pop was silent for so long that Matty thought he

wouldn't answer. Then, finally, "No. He was like a brother to me. And then one day, we were ambushed and he got hit… I watched him die."

Matty tried to imagine what it would be like going into something like that with one of his brothers at his side—and watching him die. He quickly blinked away the morbid thoughts.

"That must've been real hard on you. I'm sorry."

Matty pulled in a fat perch without tweaking his collarbone too badly and tucked it into the basket with Pop's trout, silence stretching between the two.

It was after he'd gotten his line back in the water that Pop said offhandedly, "You remind me of John—a bit."

Surprised, Matty jerked his gaze to the older man. "In what way?"

But Pop's gaze had gone far off—probably back into the past when John was still alive. And he didn't answer.

"Evening," the cowboy greeted.

Catherine stepped into the soddy and shut the door, closing out the thunder rolling in the distance. Rain pattered against the roof. Hopefully her patch job would hold.

She took off her hat and hung it on a peg next to the door. Water rolled down the back of her collar, chilling her.

The cowboy sat near the stove again, wooden spoon in hand, while Pop sat catty-corner on his bed.

Frying fish. The cowboy was frying fish.

Her stomach growled in appreciation. She had seen the storm clouds rolling in on the horizon as early as lunchtime and hadn't stopped working the garden plot. She'd wanted to get as much done before the rains started as possible.

And returned home, as bedraggled as a soaked puppy, to find this.

She'd been covered in dust from the field, but when the rain started it had likely turned to mud. Normally she'd have washed up in the creek, but it was really starting to come down now.

Her shirt was stuck to her like a second skin. Outdoors, it hadn't bothered her, but in the closed warmth of the soddy, she would soon begin to chafe beneath the wet cloth.

"If you want to change your shirt, we'll turn our backs, won't we, Pop?" The cowboy clapped a hand on Pop's shoulder, and to Catherine's amazement, Pop allowed the friendly gesture.

What had happened between the two men today? Did it have anything to do with the fish frying on the stovetop?

Not wanting to miss the opportunity to get into something dry, she gave a terse, "Fine."

The cowboy turned his back with some effort, Pop following suit. Catherine quickly shucked her soaked-through shirt and pulled a dry one on.

"Okay." Her stomach gurgled again as she crouched over the washbowl near the door. She needed to get rid of some of the mud that coated her.

Matty chuckled, even as he returned to stirring what was in the pan.

With so little experience with people in general, and with the long-ago memories of Matty's childhood cruelty, she didn't know how to respond. Was he laughing at her?

"Let me get you a plate," the cowboy said, not noticing or not caring about her discomfort. "We'll attend to that stomach of yours."

She splashed her face with water from the washbowl and washed her hands, then patted dry with the well-worn towel.

The cowboy was waiting when she perched on the end of the bed, a plate heaped high with flour-battered fish and golden fried potatoes and onion resting on the table before him. He slid it across to her, moving only his arm, she noticed. Probably so he wouldn't tweak his collarbone. She took it with both hands, but he didn't release it.

When he tugged slightly, her eyes flew to his face. Something of her uncertainty about his motives must've shown on her face because his expression softened the slightest amount.

"You're welcome," he said softly.

He let go of the plate and it scraped the table as her pull lost its counterpoint.

Her insides twisted. Was he making fun of her?

"You've got—" And then he reached one hand and touched her cheek. "Mud."

She jerked away from the unexpected touch but that didn't stop him from coming away with a clump of brown mud on his fingertip. She swiped the back of her wrist against her cheek, but it came away clean.

Shaken, she scooted back on the bed, until her back hit the wall and she was able to pull her knees up in front of her. She balanced her plate there, aware of the cowboy's continued attention.

Until Pop gruffed, "Got me a plate yet, boy? I'm hungry, too."

Matty scooped fish and potatoes from the pan onto Pop's plate, smiling a little and shaking his head.

Pop shoveled in a heaping bite, pushing it off the

plate and into his mouth, before the cowboy had made his own plate.

Pop groaned. For a moment, a frisson of worry arced through Catherine, but then her own forkful hit her tongue and she realized that Pop had made the noise out of pure enjoyment.

"Not bad, right?" The words could have been arrogant, but the cowboy didn't seem to be looking for praise. He was too busy eating. "Better than anything you ate out there on the battlefields?"

Her breath caught in her chest; she opened her mouth to interrupt, but Pop just shook his head, unperturbed. "Miles better."

Gaping a little, Catherine's eyes darted between the two men. They both ate with abandon, focused on their plates. Men.

The cowboy looked up, his eyes landing directly on her. "What's a matter?"

She returned to her own plate, shrugging, but the cowboy's gaze didn't move off. Finally, she gave in. Stubborn man. "Pop doesn't usually talk about his time in the war."

"Hmm," Matty said over a bite. He glanced at Pop, who was still engrossed in his plate. "Well, it wasn't like he opened up and shared every detail."

Pop grunted.

Matty grinned up at her and her stomach gave a funny little flip. "I told you about my family the other night. I figure it's your turn. Tell me about your parents."

This time she choked on a chunk of potato.

She coughed and gasped, and the cowboy pressed a mug of coffee into her hands. She sipped as soon as she had the potato dislodged. Eyes still watering, she asked, "What?"

* * *

Catherine went silent. That wasn't what he'd intended.

He would do anything in his power to distract the both of them from the powerful bolt of attraction that had flared through him when he'd touched her. The clump of mud had been sliding down her cheek and it had been a natural thing to do. He'd meant it in a perfectly innocent way, but the shock of his fingers against her petal-soft skin had arced through him like one of the lightning bolts striking outside.

He hadn't been expecting the attraction that had rumbled through him like too-close thunder.

Catherine was pretty enough, even though she was nothing like Luella. Luella enjoyed being the life of the party, a lot like him. At socials, she was always flitting from one group of friends to another, like some kind of butterfly or something.

But quiet Catherine, with her hair chopped short… Well, the cut actually made the structure of her face stand out more—made him notice the curve of her cheekbones and point of her chin. Catherine made him curious.

And he needed to be worrying about getting back to civilization, back to his life, not sparking the independent young woman he was stuck with.

"I'd like to hear more about your parents. If you'd be willing to tell me." He said it with his eyes on his now-empty plate, knowing that Catherine was so gun-shy that if she sensed his interest, she'd clam up.

But tonight she'd had to come in early thanks to the rain, and after days of being subjected to the quiet, he couldn't face another evening without some communication.

And she was silent for a long moment, finally asking, "Why?"

He should've known she wouldn't just talk to him. "Because I'd like to know you." He couldn't help the irritation leaking into his words.

He pulled a pail of water he'd asked Pop to bring in earlier and set it on the stove to heat, ignoring the pull of pain across his chest.

She questioned every motive. If he brought her a cup of water while she worked the fields, she squinted into the cup as if to see whether he'd poisoned her.

Now he held up the spoon, using the gesture to ask if Catherine and Pop wanted seconds. They both held out their plates. Silently, of course.

He sighed as he dished out the last of the flaky pieces of fish and crumbly potatoes. And then as his eyes flicked over Catherine's head, an idea coalesced.

"Let's play a game," he said.

Catherine's skeptical gaze skewered him, but he poured the warming water from the pail into the now-empty skillet, then grabbed the bar of soap from the nearby shelf and shaved some off into the water.

"My sister loves this one," he said. "It's called Eye Spy."

Pop grunted, and that meant either he wanted to play or he was done with his food.

Matty went on as he dunked his plate and utensils in the soapy water. "My family plays our own house rules. I'll choose something visible to all of us and tell you what color it is. You've got five chances to guess what it is. If you guess the item, you win, and it's your turn to 'spy' something. If you don't guess my item in the five chances, you owe me a boon. In this case, you answer one question."

Her eyes sparkled with interest, but she bit her lip. "And if you don't guess the thing I've 'spied'?"

"Same."

He had her interest. But he couldn't let her know. He pretended that he needed his full focus on scrubbing out the frying pan.

"Fine," she agreed hesitantly. "Since we're stuck inside anyway…"

Yes. At least for tonight, he wouldn't have to bear the silence.

"Do you want to go first?" he asked.

"You go ahead. That way I'll make sure I understand the rules as you've laid them out."

"All right." He allowed himself to gaze around the room once, for a few seconds, even though he already knew what he was going to choose. "Eye spy something red."

Her eyes darted quickly around the room, but she hesitated before saying, "The radishes."

He glanced up at the two withered vegetables in a basket above their heads, then shook his head with a grin.

"Your bandanna," she said, much more quickly this time.

"No, ma'am."

He was starting to enjoy this. Catherine's eyes had narrowed slightly. She was competitive. He filed the information away.

It wasn't her Pop's faded shirt on a shelf, or the jar of strawberry preserves, either, and he'd finished scrubbing all three plates and forks in the cooling dishwater as she hesitated over the last guess.

Her lips pinched slightly. What exactly did she think he was going to demand for his boon?

"Do you give up?" he asked, teasing quietly. "Or you'll have to take your guess."

"There's a cardinal that lives in the pine tree." She nodded out the window, streaking with rain. "Did it flit past the window?"

He shook his head. "It only counts if it's something we can all see."

She ducked her head. "So I owe you an answer? What was your red thing?"

"If you don't guess it, I don't have to tell you." He winked at her. "How did your parents meet?"

A flash of emotion crossed her expressive features before her eyes shuttered. Had she expected a more difficult question?

She laid her cheek on her knee, turning her gaze to the wall. When she spoke, her words were stiff. "They met at a social. My father asked her for an introduction and then to dance."

So her family hadn't always been antisocial. If her parents had attended a social, they mustn't have had a total aversion to being around people. What had happened since Catherine and Pop had been on their own?

She turned her head in his direction, again resting her cheek against her knee. "Eye spy something black."

The obvious answer was the skillet, so he knew she wouldn't have chosen that, not with the flash of competitiveness he'd seen in her eyes.

"The soles of my boots," he guessed.

"No."

"The inner circle of my eyes." He waggled his eyebrows at her flirtatiously and she flushed, a beautiful pink rising in her cheeks.

"Definitely not," she said firmly.

"The stovepipe."

"No."

He let a smile pull up one side of his mouth. "I give up." Her lips pursed.

"You've won your boon. What do you want to know?"

She opened her mouth, but then hesitated on a breath. "How did *your* parents meet?"

That hadn't been her original question. He knew it in his gut. Why had she changed her question?

"My ma was the preacher's daughter, and my pa was a lowly cowboy riding for a rancher in the area. She had a lot of beaus, but he was a stubborn cowpoke and won her over."

Her lashes fluttered as she lowered her eyes.

They played two more rounds where she correctly guessed the buttons on Pop's shirt and Matty gave up his middle name—Patrick—before she stood up. "I should dump the dishwater out."

He envied the ease of her movements as she shrugged into a long leather coat that would prevent her from being drenched again and moved to pick up the frying pan and then ducked outside.

Pop had been quiet while they'd played their rounds of Eye Spy, but now Matty asked, "You wanna enlighten me why she doesn't like talking about her parents?"

Pop's eyes flicked to Matty and then away, but he didn't acknowledge the question. Even Catherine's answer had been factual and short.

What didn't they want him to know?

As Catherine reentered the room, Pop grunted and poked a grizzled finger at Matty. "You need a shave, boy."

Matty made to raise a hand and rub a palm against

the bristle on his face, but just the action of crossing his arm over his chest made him wince. There was no way he could reach up to his jaw, not without pulling the injury and paining himself fiercely. "Don't think that's gonna happen anytime soon."

"Catherine can help ya out."

Matty's eyes flew to Catherine's, and she shook her head frantically, eyes almost panicked.

If that was her reaction, he didn't want her anywhere near his throat with a razor. "Maybe not tonight."

Later that night, Matty lay flat on his back, staring up at the ceiling where Catherine had forced dirt down on his head. Remembering it had a smile twitching at his lips.

Soft rain still fell outside, but so far Catherine's patches kept the soddy dry.

He couldn't get a good read on her, and it irritated him. Enough to cost him his sleep.

Folks in Bear Creek trusted him. Maybe because of his badge or maybe because his family was well established and held a good reputation.

So facing off with Catherine's continued mistrust rubbed him the wrong way. He'd been polite since he'd landed here. Even helped out, cooking supper.

If it took him two or three weeks to heal up enough to get out of here, he didn't want to live in silence. He'd go crazy!

What did it take to make a friend out of Catherine Poole?

And why did it matter so much?

Though he stared up at the dark ceiling, an image of

an eight-year-old Catherine staring up at him with tear-washed eyes flitted through his mind.

That was why. He needed to make up for the past before he went home.

Chapter Seven

Early the next morning, Catherine stood on the bank of the little stream, just around the bend from home. A patchy fog curled through the woods and made her feel isolated from everything and everyone.

She shivered in the chill air, craning her neck back and stretching to look at the pale gray expanse of sky. Elsie was no doubt waiting for her morning milking, but Catherine needed these moments to find her sense of balance again.

The cowboy's game last night, as simple and child-like as it was, had stirred up a whole hornet's nest of emotion in her chest.

His innocent questions over supper had brought her shame to the forefront. She was illegitimate. Born out of wedlock.

If she hadn't been so worried about him finding out, it might have been…fun.

Instead, she'd remembered how her mama had been treated on that last day in Bear Creek.

Mama had picked her up after school in the wagon, with their old plow horse in the harness.

"I've a surprise for you," Mama said as Catherine scrambled over the wheel and joined her in the bench seat.

Catherine sat her lunch pail at their feet with a clatter. "What is it?"

Mama flipped the reins and the plow horse began plodding away from the schoolhouse. "I raided my egg-money jar. We're going to the store and buying you some fabric for a new dress."

Catherine had been unable to hide her tears yesterday, after the other children had sung their awful rhyme at her. She'd tried to hide in the barn, but Mama had found her and demanded to know what was wrong.

"A new dress?" Catherine couldn't keep the hope and anticipation from her voice. If she had a dress made from *store-bought* material, surely the other girls would want to be friends with her!

A few minutes later, Mama set the brake and tied off the horse to the hitching post outside the mercantile. They didn't visit the store often—hardly ever—so this was a rare treat.

Catherine didn't know why they mostly stayed out of town. She'd never questioned Mama's statement that Pop didn't like most folks and just liked staying on the homestead.

But she'd begged to attend school, and now here they were. Surely a new dress would help her to fit in.

She followed slightly behind Mama, fingering a bolt of blue-sprigged calico when she heard the first whisper.

"There's Anna Poole. No, don't look at her!"

Catherine peeked around Mama's side and saw two women together standing behind a barrel of pickles. One had her fingers over her mouth. Both looked slightly horrified.

"Which do you like better, this darker blue or the

pink?" Mama drew her attention back to the bolts of fabric, but a glance at Mama's face showed pink high in her cheeks.

"The blue," Catherine answered. Her palms were moist; her pulse raced. She couldn't wait to have her new dress!

But there was a part of her that was conscious of the two women still whispering, though she couldn't make out their words.

Mama walked to the counter to fetch the proprietor, leaving Catherine for a moment. Her eyes went to the beautiful white lace gloves displayed on a shelf behind the fabric. They must be for decoration only—they would never last on the homestead.

Behind her, the whispers started again.

"That's the girl."

"Illegitimate."

Now her face burned. She knew what the word meant. Mama had explained it to her when they'd talked about why Catherine didn't have a papa.

Mama came back and the whispers stopped, but now Catherine's tummy hurt.

She'd thought the teasing at the schoolhouse had been cruel. But were these two grown women whispering about *her*?

The proprietor approached, the man's steps heavy on the boards of the floor. "I cain't sell to ya. I won't. Cain't besmirch the reputation of my store."

Mama's hand fell on her shoulder even as Catherine didn't understand his words.

"Come along, Catherine," Mama said. "We'd best go."

"But my dress—"

There had been no dress. Mama cried the whole way

home, driving their horse and wagon, though she'd tried to hide the tears from Catherine.

And Catherine had refused to go back to school. If the adults in Bear Creek were intentionally cruel, who would teach the children differently? How could she expect acceptance with a background like hers?

She'd deemed it safer to stay on the homestead, just like Mama.

And last night, she'd been afraid the friendly spark in the cowboy's eyes would disappear if he knew the truth.

She shouldn't care.

Because if she dared to open herself up to the cowboy further, she could expect the same thing to happen again.

A branch snapping and the crunch of fallen, desiccated leaves brought her head up. That hadn't come from the direction of the homestead.

Slowly, a shadowy form separated from the fog. Taller than the cowboy, with stringy black hair falling below a floppy hat.

Ralph again.

Why must he continue his unwanted pursuit?

She stood straight, aware that she was out of shouting distance from the soddy, and that she had nothing in hand that could be used as a weapon, if needed. No spade, no pitchfork. Nothing.

She could only pray she wouldn't need defending.

"Good seein' you again so soon," he said.

His leer erased any welcome she might've felt. Didn't he have work to do around his own place?

"Ain't you gonna say a nice, neighborly hello?"

His words and intent gaze sent a shiver of unease through her.

"What do you want today?" She considered turning and bolting. There was a chance she could melt into the underbrush and evade him, or even make it back to the soddy.

His eyes glinted. "Lots o' things. Still have a hankerin' to get married. We put our land together and we've got a nice spread."

He'd told her before that the creek winding through her and Pop's property would support a nice herd, if they had a mind to raise cattle.

"Floyd happened to be out for a walk yesterday and saw ya plowing up the wheat field."

His words sent a cold feather down her spine. His brother had been watching her?

"We figure you must got some extry seed wheat stashed somewhere, and since the hailstorm crushed our field, too, it would be a mighty neighborly thing for you to share it. Unless you're ready to get to the altar."

She brushed moist palms against her trouser legs. Could she outrun him? "Spying doesn't seem very neighborly."

He grinned, but there wasn't anything kind about his expression. "Y'all have always been so secretive over here. Never make social calls. Makes a body curious, is what it does."

She knew better.

"I'm sure you can purchase what you need in town." She said the words firmly, intending them as a dismissal, but instead of leaving, he stepped closer. The creek was still between them, but he could cross it in one wide stride.

"That bad winter storm took our cows, and we cain't afford to buy anything outright."

"I wish we could help you," she said. She edged backward, her foot catching on a loose root on the bank. She stumbled, her breath ratcheting in her chest as Chesterton strode to the edge of the stream.

"I know you've got seed—"

"Catherine?"

Matty's voice rang out from behind her, disjointed in the still-lifting fog. Relief rushed through her.

"Who's that?" Ralph asked, his voice changing from slightly wheedling to something more menacing.

Boots crunched in the underbrush, and then as she glanced over her shoulder, the cowboy appeared out of the fog. He had something in his right hand, but it was slightly obscured by the fog and shadows, and she couldn't tell what it was.

"Ralph Chesterton. Morning." Matty's easy greeting had her gritting her back teeth.

She wanted Chesterton out of here, not to have a morning chat.

"Deputy. What're you still doing in these parts?" Ralph's voice had changed again—he was like a chameleon Mama had read about once long ago. He was play-acting at being a friendly neighbor and nothing more.

Her breath still sawed in her chest. She opened her mouth to tell Matty off, tell him that he shouldn't believe anything Chesterton said, but then snapped it closed. Why should the cowboy believe her, when she'd barely tolerated him?

They weren't friends, any more than she was friends with Chesterton.

"Had a little accident and found myself horseless," Matty said. He'd moved until he was beside her, their shoulders almost brushing. "The Pooles were kind enough to take me in."

Ralph's eyes bugged out.

At her side, she registered the cowboy's size. She'd

done so when she'd pulled him from the creek, but since then he'd been mostly laid out. His height, his strength, somehow comforted her in light of Ralph's presence.

Matty hadn't mentioned his injury. Was he purposely keeping it to himself?

"They *what*?"

The disbelief in Ralph's voice was clear, and she thought she heard an exhale as if the cowboy found it humorous.

"You and your brother recovering from the storm all right?"

"Fine." Ralph's gaze had narrowed and she could almost see his thoughts churning behind his eyes. "I was just checking on Catherine. You know, doing the neighborly thing."

But when his gaze cut to her, his smile morphed into a sneer that sent a shiver through her.

"I'd better get home and make sure Floyd doesn't burn the bacon. Catherine." He nodded to her, but the intensity of his gaze told her this wasn't over.

He nodded to the cowboy. "Iff'n you want a ride into town, you know where to find me 'n Floyd."

He disappeared into the woods, and as the fog burned off, she watched until she couldn't see him anymore and her eyes burned.

She blinked away the moisture, not wanting the cowboy to see a weak moment.

"What did he really want?" Matty asked quietly, still staring after Ralph.

She glanced up, and he looked down at her. This close, she was unable to ignore his presence.

"He came to find out if Pop and I had stockpiled any seed wheat." She didn't mention the marriage proposals.

His eyes scanned her face and the discomfort his scrutiny prompted made her raise her chin.

"You all right?"

"Fine." She let her gaze slide past his ear. It was easier to affect a tone as if she *was* fine without looking him straight in the eye. It wasn't a lie, not exactly. Ralph had made advances toward her before, and she'd learned to be careful.

If only she could tell her galloping heart that everything would be all right.

Matty watched the pulse jumping at the base of Catherine's neck. If she'd been his sister, he would have pulled her into a reassuring hug.

She might not admit that Chesterton had scared her, but Matty wasn't just any man. He was a deputy, trained to recognize the slight tremble in her hands, the white lines around her mouth.

"You know if there's trouble that I'm honor-bound to protect you," he reminded her. "It comes with the badge."

Her eyes flicked to his face and then away again before she nodded tightly. "There's no trouble."

But there was no way he'd missed the tense undertones between her and Chesterton when he'd interrupted their conversation. Something was going on.

She didn't want his help, that was clear. Too bad he needed hers until he healed up.

When he'd heard the male voice—Chesterton's—from a distance, he'd rushed forward, almost losing his footing in the damp, crushed leaves at the stream's edge. He'd thought to ask Chesterton to take him to town, or at least to get a message to his family that he was all right and to come get him, but the moment he'd seen Catherine from behind, seen her shoulders tensed up to her ears, his intuition had kicked in and urged him to tread carefully.

He hadn't missed the intent way Chesterton's gaze had tracked Catherine, or the way it had twisted Matty's gut up inside. Catherine was barely an acquaintance, but the protector in Matty had bristled.

Catherine was virtually alone out here. If Chesterton was making unwanted advances, who would protect her? *Pop?*

And she hadn't seemed happy to see the other man. She'd been wound tight as an unbroken horse beneath its first saddle.

How could he ask Chesterton to send word to his family when it would leave Catherine unprotected?

Catherine shifted slightly, her sleeve brushing against Matty's arm. "Were you looking for me?"

He held up the straight razor, towel and bar of soap he carried in his right hand. "Your Pop had a point last night. This scruff is starting to itch. I thought I'd beg you to help me out or follow you around until you gave in."

He saw a flash of her white teeth as she bit her lip briefly. "I suppose I could. You don't want Pop…?"

"Your Pop's hands are about as steady as his memory." Which continued to be a worry as the man grew quiet at times and sometimes called Matty by another name.

She nodded, glancing around. "Where—"

"There's a stump back this way, right next to the stream bank. I think it'll work if I lean against it…"

She followed him as he maneuvered through the brush to an area bare of underbrush but still within arm's reach of the stream.

He awkwardly lowered himself to the ground, leaning his upper half against the stump. It was about the right

height. He could lean his head back against the wood
without much discomfort.

"What should I…do?" She sounded so hesitant, as if
he was a coiled rattlesnake instead of a man who just
needed assistance shaving.

"Work up some lather with the soap first. Then you'll
use the razor to scrape off the whiskers." He kept the
towel as he handed her the soap.

She recoiled a tiny bit. "What if I cut you?"

"You ever sit and watch your pa shave?" He didn't ask
about Pop. From the man's scraggly, unkempt beard, the
older man undoubtedly hadn't shaved in years.

Her expression changed. Closed off. She shook her
head.

"Come here." He used his hand to beckon her closer.
She complied, crouching at his side. He took the razor
from her and stretched his opposite palm flat.

"You're not cutting into the skin," he told her, dem-
onstrating by dragging the razor across his palm slowly.
"Just scraping the surface. You try."

Her hand trembled when she brought the razor to his
exposed palm.

"I—"

"Here." He closed his free hand over her smaller one,
immediately noticing the difference in size. His pulse
jumped. He guided her hand as if he was shaving his
palm, unable to keep from noticing how close their proximity had brought her cheek to his. Wayward strands of
her short hair tickled his skin. A beam of dappled sunlight angled just so and illuminated freckles across the
bridge of her nose.

He swallowed in a throat that suddenly felt like sand-
paper.

"Do you feel the contours?" he asked, voice gone hoarse. "The different planes?"

She nodded, wisps of her hair again tickling him, and he released her. She stood, moving several paces away.

His heart beat in his head and throat, choking him.

She didn't seem to be affected at all, now kneeling on the stream bank and lathering the soap.

He unbuttoned the top two buttons of his shirt and wrapped the towel around his shoulders and neck, then leaned his head back against the stump and waited.

She appeared above him, blocking out the clouds and bright blue sky behind. Her hands full of lathered soap, she smeared it across his cheeks and jaw, then down his neck.

"Stand behind—" He started to talk, but her hand brushed his lip and he got a taste of strong soap.

He wrinkled his nose and a wide, unguarded smile crossed her lips. Her eyes crinkled at the corners, and her entire expression changed, taking her from *pretty* to something far more. Until she hid her smile behind her wrist.

He was so unnerved that he had to clear his throat before he could speak. He let his head fall back against the wood with a soft thunk. "If you stand behind me, you'll be at a better angle to wield the blade."

She did, and unfortunately the position put her lips— pursed with concentration—directly in his line of sight.

She took the first stroke with the blade, and the metal moved smoothly along his neck to just below his jaw. Her lips parted in a silent exhale.

The bottom of his stomach dropped out. He needed a distraction.

She moved to wipe the blade against the towel and

he blurted the only thing he could think of. "Eye spy something green."

One of her eyebrows crooked up as if she thought he was a little crazy to want to play at this very moment.

"We're surrounded by green," she murmured as she leaned close again. Her breath fanned his forehead and he closed his eyes against the sensation.

The blade scraped his neck again.

With his eyes closed, the smell of the soap stung his nostrils. He heard the distant caw of a crow. Still felt the moist warmth of Catherine's breath on his face.

"Is it the budding leaves on the trees?"

"No." He barely opened his lips to whisper the answer, not wanting to move and get nicked.

Then she touched him. The barest brush of her fingers beneath his jaw as she guided him to tilt his head.

His eyes flew open.

"The grass?"

"No," he whispered.

Their eyes connected, though she was upside down in his line of vision. Something tenuous and unfathomable passed between them before her eyes flicked away. "The finch over there."

"It's yellow," he breathed.

When she still hadn't guessed the moss on the side of a nearby tree, he asked for his boon, "Have you ever had a beau?"

A flush appeared high on her cheeks. "No."

He did his best to ignore every sensation as she took her turn at the game and stumped him with the gray squirrel playing among the branches of a high tree.

"Are you sparking anyone?" she asked him in return.

He was completely surprised by the question. It was the first personal thing she'd asked him since his arrival.

"I...don't know."

There was a long stretch of silence as she shaved the point of his chin. Then, "How can you not know?"

Because as of yesterday, he was confused by the attraction he felt toward Catherine. Since he'd been here, he'd hardly though of Luella at all. And how could he want to fight for her when he was becoming interested in Catherine?

"It's complicated," was all he said.

An adorable crinkle appeared between her eyebrows. "Complicated."

"Like you and your seed wheat," he said. "You do have a stockpile, don't you?"

"If I do, that's my own business."

He forced himself not to smile, not wanting to get nicked. She was hiding something, he was almost sure of it. Whether it was grain or not, he didn't know. But it gave him one more thing to find out about the enigmatic girl he was stuck with. Suddenly, he wasn't so eager to head home to his family.

Catherine used the only unsoiled corner of the towel to wipe the cowboy's face. "Finished."

He sat up straight, one hand reaching for his chin as if he was going to check her work before it pulled at his injury and he dropped it to his lap. "Thank you," he said.

She backed up as he stood, almost unable to tear her eyes from his face. Clean shaven, he was even more handsome. How was that possible?

She was still shaken from the run-in with Ralph. That had to be causing her reaction to the cowboy.

"I'll return these where they go. Then I've got to get to work." She held up the razor, soap and towel. She was surprised the cowboy had located the razor, tucked back on a high shelf. Pop hadn't used it in years. The square of homemade soap was the same one they used for household purposes.

He followed her back toward the dugout. She ducked inside and quickly settled the shaving supplies, and emerged back into the sunlight to see the cowboy standing halfway between the soddy and the barn, looking curiously between the two.

"I'd like to help," he said. "Only, I'm not much for heavy lifting these days."

"It's fine." The less she saw of him, the less he could discombobulate her.

He sighed. "I owe you and your Pop a lot for putting up with me." There was another pause. "Please."

She looked away from him, let her eyes go to the horizon. "There are some tools in the barn that need repairing."

She didn't particularly want him spending more time in the barn, not after the events of this morning and his curiosity. But her secret was well hidden.

"My brother Ricky is the fixer of the family, but I can give it a try."

She nodded and made her escape.

Chapter Eight

Matty spent the afternoon sorting out the mess in the shed. With the jumble of broken farm implements mixed up with odds and ends and some items that were whole, it was hard to tell what pieces went where.

His feelings for Catherine weren't so easily sorted.

He sneezed yet again as his task disturbed the dust in a cloud. Catherine's cow mooed its displeasure at him.

It must've taken years of collecting to get this much junk accumulated. How did Catherine and Pop find the tools they actually needed?

He finally got the shed emptied, to where he could see the dirt-packed floor. He'd matched up what odds and ends he could and ended up with several hoe heads, a potato planter and malt fork that were in decent shape.

He'd piled the broken implements together. Among them were a scythe, milking stool, washboard, ax and what might be a turnip chopper.

And then odds and ends were spread across the grass. Wood and metal pieces that he couldn't match to anything else, plenty enough to trip over if he wasn't careful.

"What're you doing, thief?"

The growled words from behind him had Matty

whirling. He tried to raise his hands in a defensive posture, but pain ripped across his chest at the movement and he couldn't get them higher than his waist. He was acutely aware of the gun belt that Catherine still hadn't returned to him.

It was Pop, standing between the house and barn with a frying pan cocked as if he was ready to bean Matty with it.

Matty was fairly sure he could outrun the old man, but he was more concerned with the wild light in Pop's eye. "Pop, you all right?"

Pop's eyes narrowed. "Who are you?"

Mind spinning, Matty eyed the implements on the ground closest to him. He didn't want to have to defend himself against Pop, but if the older man was so confused that he didn't recognize Matty, he could be a danger to himself or Catherine if she came upon them suddenly.

"Matty. Remember, I've been staying at your place. We went fishing together yesterday."

"You're trying to trick me. Whatever you're thinking to steal, you'd better get offa my land right now. I ain't got no patience for thieves."

Matty knew better than to let his guard down; he was frustrated that Pop had surprised him. Things had been peaceful the past several days. Pop hadn't had any middle-of-the-night episodes and Matty even thought they were on their way to becoming friends after the fishing trip yesterday.

"I don't want to steal anything," Matty said, still trying to figure out the best way to placate Pop. There wasn't anything of value here to steal. "And I can't... exactly leave."

Pop's brow furrowed, his face turning an alarming

shade of red. Then he put a hand over his chest and Matty noticed how hard he was breathing.

"Calm down a little. I'm a friend of Catherine's." Maybe calling them friends was a stretch, but he was worried about Pop as a gray pallor crept up the man's face.

"Catherine?" Pop's expression crumpled in confusion and his shoulders slumped slightly.

Matty still held his hands up in front of him as he stepped toward the older man. "Do you need to sit down?"

"I...I don't know."

Matty kept an eye on that cast-iron skillet as he took another two steps until he was within arm's reach of Pop.

The older man's eyes flickered and then cleared. "Matty?" The skillet clunked to the ground. It would need to be washed. Later.

Matty exhaled his relief. "You all right?"

"Chest is kinda tight."

"Why don't we sit over here?"

Matty guided the older man to the patch of shade thrown by the barn and settled him there. His breathing began to even out, but that sickly gray pallor remained. "You have attacks like that often?"

"Every now and then. Figure my heart'll go out one of these times."

"You ever think about having a doc check you over?"

Pop snorted derisively. "Don't trust any of 'em."

Matty raised an eyebrow. "Yeah." Because Pop didn't trust anyone. "My brother's a doctor. I'd trust him with my life."

Pop just grunted.

He sat with the older man until Pop's breathing eased completely and color returned to his face. Did Catherine know he had spells like this? Why wouldn't she insist on Pop seeing a doctor?

Looking around, he realized the tools were proof that the Pooles hadn't lived as isolated as he'd imagined.

Had something happened in the past few years that had made Catherine and Pop withdraw even more? Was it as simple as Pop's forgetfulness and distrust of just about everyone? Or was there more to it, like the situation with Ralph Chesterton? How could they not ask for help?

Matty didn't know. He hadn't intended to get involved in the Pooles' lives, but it had happened anyway. And knowing what Catherine faced out here alone, what kind of man would he be if he just walked away when the time came?

That night, Matty held supper until Pop started to grumble. It was well after dark when Catherine ducked through the door. Her hair was damp, as if she'd washed up in the creek. She gave him a sidelong glance, not looking directly at him.

Pop snored away on his cot in the corner. Matty greeted her with a nod.

"Everything all right? No more run-ins?"

"Fine. Just busy."

Her clipped words were the complete opposite of the wide, unguarded smile she'd gifted him with this morning. And there was a part of him that missed seeing it again.

He sat on the end of the bed with his back propped against the wall. He'd found and chopped a chunk of pretty oak into pieces and retrieved the pocketknife from the barn. Now he worked at whittling the chunks. He had a few finished rectangles piled next to him on the blanket.

"Your supper's probably cold."

She went to the stove and picked up the plate he'd covered for her earlier.

She inhaled deeply. "I'm so hungry, I don't care if it's cold."

She sat cross-legged on the floor, wedging herself between the bed and table, stuffing her mouth even on the way down. He worked to focus on his whittling and not the way the lamplight glinted off her damp hair.

"I finished plowing the field," she said between bites. "The moon came up, and I was so close that I just stayed with it."

She must be exhausted. He was used to the draining days spring work required, but how much worse must it be for a woman virtually alone?

"I thought you might be avoiding me."

After the bolt of attraction that had passed between them on the stream bank this morning, it was a valid guess.

He saw her face flush in the dim light thrown by the lamp and figured his guess was right.

Which did something funny to his insides.

He glanced over at Pop's figure huddled beneath the blanket. "You notice him having shortness of breath? Going real pale in the face?"

She looked up at him sharply, her fork clanking against her plate. "What happened?"

"He came out to the shed and didn't recognize me."

"Was he violent?"

That she asked told him enough to know the answer to his question, but he asked anyway. "He threatened it before he started losing his breath. Has he been violent with you before?"

She looked down, hiding her eyes from him. "Only once. I wasn't expecting him to be locked in the past, and he surprised me. He was very upset about it afterward."

"What will you do if he gets worse? Starts losing touch with reality every day?"

She went back to her food, her head down. She shook her head slightly. "I don't know."

"Is there no one…a long-lost aunt or…"

She shook her head again. "Just the two of us. Before Mama died, it was the three of us."

He hadn't known her father had died young.

She went silent so that it was just the scrape of his knife and the clink of her fork.

"Have you tried to talk him into seeing a doctor?" he asked.

"He won't."

"But—"

She shook her head again and then raised her wrist to wipe her face. He squinted in the low lamplight. Had he made her cry?

He doubted she would welcome it if he reached for her, but his hand clenched around the wooden piece in his hand with the wanting.

This upset was more the reaction he'd expected this morning after the confrontation with Ralph. How did she keep such a calm manner with so many stressors?

"If…if something ever happens, you can come to my family for help."

She sniffed once. She set her plate on the table. "What are you making?"

"Dominoes. You can play games with them. Like cards."

"You like games."

It wasn't a question, but he was happy for the conversation—the most they'd spoken yet. "There's always something going on in a family as big as mine. My brothers are competitive and I like the challenge of learning new games, new strategies. I'll teach you if you like."

She hummed and he took it for assent. "What kinds of things do you like to do? Read?" he asked, remembering the primers he'd found in her hiding spot two days ago.

She was quiet for too long. He lost concentration on the domino and looked up at her.

"I can't read," she admitted so softly that he barely heard her. "I never went to school, except for those few days..."

When he and Luella had been so awful to her.

"I'm sorry," he said again, and again it seemed so inadequate. He'd been so arrogant, and so innocent of the harsh reality that life could be—as it had been to him only short months later.

On the heels of his apology, he wondered again: Was their teasing so bad that it had caused such deep scars? Or did something else keep her from returning to the classroom?

She shrugged, and her voice was suspiciously casual when she went on. "We're a far piece from the schoolhouse anyway. It was too far for a child to walk, and my mama couldn't drive me every day. It was too much."

"I could teach you to read."

The words were out before he'd really thought about them.

Her head jerked up, her eyes sharp in the low light. "Why?"

He dropped the knife and domino. They landed with a soft clack against the other wood chunks on the quilt. "Why do you have to question my motive for every single thing?" He raised one hand to ruffle his fingers through his hair, ignoring the pull of pain across his chest at the action.

She glanced over her shoulder at Pop, still snoring away and oblivious to their conversation. "Maybe because my only interactions with you before this were four days of you torturing me."

"That's an exaggeration," he returned.

"Not by much."

"Maybe if you got off your homestead and into the real world, you'd find out that I'm someone you can trust."

She recoiled as if he'd struck her. Her eyes flashed as she reached for the quilt folded on the little stool nearby. "It's late. Let's turn in."

"Catherine—"

She lifted the covering and blew out the lantern, leaving them in darkness. He sighed.

Using Pop's snoring to orient himself in the darkness, he cupped both hands around the closed pocketknife and dominoes and tucked them on the small shelf above his pillow. He lay out flat on the bed, staring up into the blackness overhead.

He hadn't meant to offend her.

She was like a green broke filly. He didn't know all the things that spooked her, all the things that made her close off.

And what did it say about him that he wanted to know?

Chapter Nine

It was the middle of the night when Catherine woke, disoriented. What had startled her?

"The Johnny Rebs, they're sneaking up on us."

Pop's growl sent fear skittering through her even as she fought the sense of disorientation to try to come fully awake.

"Pop?" She reached for the stove door, opening it to provide some light. "It's just us—me and Matty."

The orange light illuminated the cowboy, hair tousled and struggling his way upright.

He grunted. In pain? "I heard something. Outside."

There was an audible thump from outdoors. Her heartbeat thrummed in her ears.

The cowboy's feet hit the floor just inches from her hand propping her up.

"Where's my gun?" he asked, and there was no mistaking the menacing tone of his voice.

"Not here."

He grumbled something below his breath as he pushed to his feet. "Can you light a lamp?"

She scrambled to her knees. "You're not going out there—"

But he was already on his feet, pushing open the door.

She used a twig from the basket beneath the table and lit the end of it in the glowing coals from the stove, then lit the lamp.

The cowboy took it from her grasp before she could protest and ducked out the door.

"Pop, stay inside," she said.

She tromped out after Matty, receiving a glare over his shoulder. This was *her* home. She could defend it.

The darkness was close, encompassing. The moon had waned in the sky, leaving only the stars overhead for illumination.

Matty held the lamp out in front of him, lighting the ground as he approached the barn. She followed a few steps behind.

Until he stopped, holding one arm out to the side to prevent her from passing by.

"Somebody's been out here."

At his words, fear rose in her throat, blocking her from breathing for a protracted moment. Someone had been *here*, on her property?

"I'd piled everything closer to the barn… It looks like they tripped on some of this junk in the dark."

"It's not junk." She barely breathed the words, terror crashing through her and muting her voice.

At her words, he threw a *look* over his shoulder and stepped into the doorway, flashing the lantern into the mule's stall and where the chickens roosted.

"Whoever it was, they're gone now. Animals are riled up, though."

It was a small comfort. Someone had been here, sneaking around. In *her* place.

She didn't feel safe, not at all. She had Pop's old hunting rifle and was a decent shot, but had to keep it put up because of his sudden spells of memory loss and aggression. She had a hatchet and a hunting knife, but with her small stature, how could she hope to overpower someone larger than her?

"I'm going to make a pass through the woods by the creek—it's the most logical place someone would hide if they were sneaking up. You all right?"

The cowboy turned his attention from where he knelt among the pieces of broken tools to her.

She clasped her elbows with both hands, folding her arms across her midsection. He stood up and took a step toward her. She took a step back.

"I'm fine. Just…just angry." Yes, that was one emotion she could grasp, that she could share.

"You okay if I make a pass through the woods?"

"Of course." She jerked her chin up, as if the force of that movement would make her words more true.

He held her gaze for a long moment, the lamplight softening his features. He opened his mouth as if to speak, then hesitated. Finally, he said, "I'd like to have my pistol returned."

She nodded jerkily. Maybe he was right. Now that he knew what a danger Pop could be, he could take precautions with the weapon.

She didn't like feeling unprotected, hated the feeling of violation that someone had been in her barn, spying on her belongings. Or worse, trying to steal something.

Matty disappeared into the darkness, taking the lantern with him. She let her eyes adjust to the low light before she slipped into the shed, where it was even darker.

"It's all right, girl. It's just me." She ran her hand over the mule's flank, felt the swish of its tail and the shifting of its feet.

The chickens clucked softly, a sign of their agitation when they would normally be sleeping.

The familiar barn smells were small comfort as the sense of violation sent continued shivers through her.

Catherine passed the mule completely and used her hands to feel her way to the inside wall of the stall. Her secret hiding place. The wood-paneled wall was made to look as if it backed up to the soil beneath the hill, but it was a false wall.

It was so dark in the barn that all she could use was the sensation of touch to move the top panel away. She ran her fingers along the flour sacks piled inside, exhaling a sigh of relief.

Whoever had been snooping in here hadn't found the seed wheat.

By touch, she found the cowboy's gun belt that she'd wound into a spiral, and the tin star and his pistol. She carried them pressed against her stomach with one arm while she used the other hand to replace the panel. She ran her hands over the smooth wood, making sure it was firmly in place and that no one would be able to notice a difference even if they looked closely.

It was all she could do.

And after tonight, it didn't feel like enough.

Matty made his way through the woods toward the stream—the same direction he'd come across Catherine and Ralph yesterday morning—on a hunch.

An owl hooted, but other than that, all he heard was the crunch of his boots against a twig on the ground and his own breathing.

He reached up to swat a low-hanging branch out of his way and his collarbone pulled, making him hiss.

He didn't like carrying the lantern—the flickering

light it cast made him a target. But he figured someone who didn't have the guts to make a known threat,
someone who would sneak around, wouldn't shoot him
outright. He hoped.

Catherine's white-faced fear remained front and center in his mind as he trekked through the dark.

She'd been shaking, as if the stiff night breeze might
carry her away, but she'd clasped her elbows tightly to
herself and he'd quashed any idea of reaching out to
offer her comfort.

Didn't mean he hadn't wanted to.

That she battled her emotions with the same intensity
as she faced replanting the fields and taking care of her
Pop made him admire her. He couldn't help it.

Who would be snooping around? The neighbor was
the obvious culprit after he'd confronted Catherine yesterday, but Sheriff Dunlop had taught Matty not to make
assumptions.

Matty squatted on the stream bank, finding tracks.
Big boots. Man-size tracks. Pop wore leather moccasins,
like Catherine, so they couldn't have been his.

Matty followed the tracks for a bit until he lost them
in some underbrush. He'd come out again tomorrow and
make a more thorough investigation.

He circled back to the shed, the lamp illuminating
Catherine's silhouette as he closed the distance between
them.

She had his gun belt and weapon in hand, and he took
it from her, trading for the lamp so he could wrap the
belt around his waist.

"Thank you, Catherine."

He threw open the cylinder and checked the cham-
bers. Empty. He thumbed out enough bullets from the
belt to load up and started sliding them into their spots.

"There were tracks down by the stream, crossing a little farther than where I met up with you this morning."

A visible tremor went through her.

And he couldn't resist his impulse. He holstered his gun and reached for her. He only clasped the bend of her elbow, barely breathing in hopes she would receive the comfort he offered her.

She looked up at him, eyes luminous and shadowed.

"It's going to be all right," he said. "I'm going to stay out here tonight. Keep watch."

He waited for her to push him away, to reject the kindness he offered, as she had earlier, but her eyes closed and her head tilted down. And she didn't move away.

He exhaled the tension he didn't know he was holding on to.

"Do you think it was Ralph?" she asked softly.

"I don't know. If it wasn't, someone wanted it to look like it was him, making tracks from down where we met at the stream."

He looked up at the stars overhead. "You want to tell me what Ralph might've been looking for?"

She shrugged slightly, finally dislodging his hand from beneath her elbow. She still didn't trust him enough to let him in on the secret.

Her distrust weighted the silence between them, dissolving the camaraderie he'd felt building moments ago.

Finally, she reached out and pressed the tin star into his palm. "You'll want this, too."

He rubbed his thumb over the face of the star, the metal cool against his skin. *This.* This was how he could prove to her that she could believe in him.

"You might not be able to trust in me as a friend. But you can trust in this." He pressed it back into her hands. "I'm honor-bound to do my job. And that includes protecting the people of Converse County. If you can't trust in my friendship, you can trust in that."

He left her with the star and the lantern and went back to the dugout. Inside, the stove door remained open, gilding the room with warm orange light from the coals inside. Pop had curled back into his blanket and was snoring once again. At least the older man hadn't followed them outside. Likely he would've chased the intruders out into the night, and then Matty would've spent hours chasing *him*.

He picked up the small stool and the quilt off the cot and met Catherine just outside the door.

"What are you doing?" she whispered, glancing over his shoulder inside the soddy.

"I'll stay out here tonight. Keep an eye on things in case whoever was here gets any ideas about coming back."

"But you won't get any rest."

He couldn't help the half smile that lifted the side of his mouth. She almost sounded as if she cared—as a friend, of course.

"I'll be fine. I may not be able to help you with replanting your garden, but I can do this."

She acquiesced with a single nod and he set up the stool around the natural curve in the sod house, several feet from the door but with a good line of sight on the shed.

Maybe it was a blessing that Catherine had asked him to fix some of the broken tools. If he hadn't spread all the Pooles' junk out in the yard, they may never have heard someone sneaking around.

Catherine didn't seem to want to trust him enough to let him know what the trespasser might have been looking for. But tonight... He couldn't shake the feeling that for once, he'd done the right thing. Started to build her trust, even if she couldn't open up and tell him what the intruder had been after.

He only hoped it lasted until the morning.

He settled in for a long night of keeping watch.

Catherine lay on the cot—with the cowboy outside there was no reason to sleep on the floor—and stared unseeing into the darkness.

Had Ralph snuck into her barn?

Ralph and Floyd were a lot like her—they rarely went into town, kept to themselves. They'd been homesteading nearby for years.

But over the past year, Ralph's attention had become more pointed. His marriage proposals and seeming desire for their land were a constant worry niggling at the back of her mind.

Had something happened on their homestead to make them desperate?

Was their desperation a danger to her and Pop?

If Pop found one of them sneaking around the property during one of his rambles, he was likely to get violent. Only, they were big enough and young enough to overpower her grandfather. No one except Matty knew about Pop's difficulties with fading into the past. If that happened, could Pop be hurt or, worse, killed for attacking one of their neighbors?

Matty had said she didn't trust him, but the truth was he knew more about her life than anyone else. He was closer, saw more than anyone who wasn't family. And maybe that was what frightened her.

She had no room for childhood dreams. She'd given them up when she'd witnessed her mama being ostracized by the *good* citizens in town.

She'd been safe here on the homestead with Pop ever since, until now. Now Pop's delusions were a threat, and so was whoever had come onto her property tonight.

She'd never been so grateful as she was to have Matty here to protect her, just for the night.

And that was dangerous thinking. If she got used to his assistance, then what happened after he left?

And he would leave. She knew he must be counting down the days until he was healed enough to walk away from here.

The fact that he could've asked Ralph to get a message to his folks and hadn't confused her. Since his injury, he'd asked every day for her to help him return home.

Until today.

There was a part of her, a very small part, that wondered what it would be like to open up to him. To confide her fears. To find a shoulder to lean on.

She couldn't. She didn't dare. He had such a strong sense of right and wrong…if she told him about her parentage, there was a good chance he'd shun her like everyone else.

Chapter Ten

Matty squinted in the bright midmorning light, squatting to examine the ground at his feet.

He'd spent the morning wandering the Pooles' property. Watching. And tracking. He'd walked alongside the meandering stream for a good long while, cut through the woods and walked bareheaded through Catherine's fields before circling back to the soddy.

Pop was nowhere in sight. Catherine bent over a washtub, scrubbing clothes on a washboard. Her face was flushed, her hair curling about her cheeks in that short cut that shouldn't look so feminine.

"Where's Pop?" he asked, approaching. He needed to explain what he'd found, but if the old man was around, it might be better to wait.

She shrugged. "He went wandering a while ago."

She shook out a men's shirt that had once been white and while wet was now nearly transparent in certain places. Matty took it from her before she could protest and ducked beneath the string she'd hung between the sod house and barn. There were several clothespins in varying states of wear clipped to the line.

She watched him with that adorable wrinkle above

her nose and he expected a protest, even as he pinned one shoulder and then the other to the makeshift clothesline with only a small twinge of pain across his chest.

The protest he waited for never came.

She went back to her washing, dunking a pair of trousers in the sudsy water.

He remained where he was. "How often does your Pop wander?"

"Most every day."

This time she handed him the trousers without him having to ask. Their eyes met across the clothesline before she quickly turned back to the tub.

"How far does he range? Does he often take the same path?"

"I…don't know. Why?"

Her eyes were shadowed as she handed him a pair of worn socks.

"I'm concerned about what I found. There's two trails, well-worn and recent."

He didn't sugarcoat what he'd found. By now, he knew that giving her the full, unvarnished truth was the best course of action.

She went still, her hands clutching the edge of the washtub.

"Either your Pop has been wandering so much that he's leaving a trail, or someone—maybe more than one someone—has been spying on you."

He saw the tremor in her hands as she passed him another white shirt, this one slightly smaller. Hers?

"I really thought last night was a fluke," she said. "I wanted it to be," she whispered.

This time when she handed him a smaller pair of trousers, he clasped the fingers of both her hands in his. With the line between their hands, it wasn't romantic;

he only hoped it to be comforting. Her hands were cool and moist.

"You wanna tell me what's going on?"

He saw her throat work as she swallowed. "Our neighbors…the Chestertons—erm, Ralph, in particular—have made some threats against me and Pop."

He let his gaze linger, long enough that she flushed and her eyes flicked down to the ground.

"At me. Mostly me."

"What kind of threats?" He had to work to keep his voice level as anger streaked through him. What kind of man threatened a woman?

She shrugged, her eyes still down and her voice low as she said, "He claims he wants to marry, that we can combine our homesteads and…have an easier time of it, I guess. Not have to struggle so much to live off the land, if we teamed up."

The disgust in her voice made it clear what she thought of that idea.

"And you've told him you're not interested?"

She nodded. Color rose high in her cheeks. She still didn't meet his eye.

"How many times?"

"One, that Pop knows about."

He waited.

"And five or six more times, after that."

He blew out a loud breath, startling her so that she finally glanced up at him and also jerked her hands away from his at the clothesline.

"Has he threatened you outright?"

She frowned. "It's mostly implied. Statements like, *You'll regret saying 'no' to me.* Things like that."

He'd been right not to ask the man for help yesterday. He hadn't known that he'd be leaving Catherine alone with a situation like this, had only that *zing* of intuition to rely on. But he'd apparently been right.

"How come you haven't told Pop? About the rest of the times he's accosted you."

She tilted her head to one side, giving him an expression as if to say, *You know why.*

And he did. Pop was likely to react with violence toward the other man, which wasn't a solution if no real threat had been made.

"I'd prefer you not tell him, either."

He shook his head. "He should know—"

"Not yet."

He blew out a breath but didn't argue further. "I'll be keeping watch tonight, and until we can figure a way to get Chesterton to leave you alone."

Her eyes met his for a brief moment and he found himself saying, "Eye spy something blue."

Her brow creased and she turned quickly back to the tub.

"The sky?"

He found himself flushing and scrambling for words as he clipped the trousers onto the line. "Yes, you've got it."

What had he been thinking? He hadn't. He'd been looking deeply into her beautiful eyes and almost gotten dizzy at the depth of emotion that had swirled through him, threatened to pull him under.

He wasn't like his brother Ricky, who was known for his silver tongue—although he'd reformed since even before he'd married. Matty's awkwardness was perhaps why Luella had broken things off.

Catherine didn't even seem to notice.

She bent farther toward the ground, using her arm to fish for anything that might be at the bottom of the tub. "Won't you become exhausted staying up all night, every night?"

"I'll make do. I'll catch some sleep during the day, if I can."

She didn't come up with any additional clothing, and he ducked beneath the line, his mind continuing to churn.

"Are there any other neighbors close? Other than the Chestertons?" If so, maybe one of them could help with the situation, or at least send word back to the sheriff.

"All the land north of us belongs to one rancher. He doesn't bother us, and we keep to ourselves."

"Maybe I should pay a call on both."

Her brow scrunched. "A social call?"

"Sometimes being friendly is the best way to get information."

She didn't look convinced.

Catherine trailed the cowboy as they crossed the field toward the Chestertons' place. Until he turned his head to look at her over his shoulder and raised his brows at her. She moved to catch up, walking at his elbow.

What had prompted her to do this?

This morning marked six days since the hailstorm and flood, and as of this morning, she'd discovered that the wheat crop wouldn't recover. The spikes had been too far developed and the crushing weight of the hail had destroyed them.

She needed to focus on replanting the fields and had noticed damage to the barn that needed repairing, too. But she didn't trust the Chestertons as far as she could throw them, and when Matty had said he was going to *talk to the men*, she'd been interested. This was her life.

She wanted to know what he was going to say, wanted to get a sense if Ralph would leave her alone.

So when the cowboy had asked if she wanted to come along, she'd found herself agreeing. She'd left a stew cooking over a low fire with Pop to tend it.

She'd vacillated whether to tell Pop about Matty's suspicions about how often someone had been coming onto their land, but ultimately she'd decided not to. There was no use in upsetting her grandfather, not when they didn't have definitive proof of Ralph or Floyd spying.

Why had she agreed to come? Matty hadn't pushed. He'd probably asked only to be polite, but here they were, trudging along together. As they crossed over the edge of the Pooles' property, she could see bluffs in the far distance.

They crossed over a shallow ditch and the landscape changed from field grass to dirt. They'd made it to the Chestertons' place.

The field was unevenly plowed. Pockets of murky brown water were dispersed throughout, but the job of plowing had been badly done in the first place. The hail had wreaked havoc here, as well. Their crop was beyond recovery, just like Catherine's.

She hadn't been here in years. Maybe not since before her mama had passed and another family had lived here. She didn't expect the dilapidated building—really just a shack. It was small; she guessed the inside would be as small as the soddy she shared with Pop.

But one side of the roof was falling in and the wood showed cracks clear through to the interior—some through to the other side.

Nearby, the barn was in just as bad shape. A large hole gaped black in the roof.

There was no sign of livestock, but Ralph stepped out of the shack.

"Afternoon," Matty said.

"This a social call?" Ralph asked. He stood with one hand propped on his hip, eating what looked like a biscuit. Crumbs littered his beard.

"House needs some repairs. Can't invite you in today. Could use a woman's touch to fancy it up." His eyes slid to Catherine and away.

Matty ignored his jab at Catherine. "We won't stay long. Not feeling particularly social. Your brother around?"

"No. Why?" Ralph's gaze narrowed.

The cowboy didn't answer immediately, letting his gaze roam. "The storm hit your barn hard, looks like. I didn't notice the other day when I passed through."

Ralph's expression was narrow and suspicious, but he shoved the biscuit into his mouth, taking a large, messy bite.

"We've fallen on some hard times." Crumbs sprayed from his mouth as he spoke.

"Our wheat crop suffered, too," Catherine said.

His attention shifted. She quailed beneath the hard light in his eyes.

"You gonna replant?"

She heard the deeper question behind his words. *Didn't she have a stockpile?*

"We'll need to do something to survive the winter."

"So will we." Ralph's words sounded like a threat. When he smiled, it was more of a sneer. She could almost hear his unspoken words, *It'll be easier to team up.*

A shiver snaked through her.

"When's your brother going to be back?" Matty asked.

Ralph's eyes slid to the side as he shrugged. Either he didn't know, or he wasn't telling.

Matty squared his shoulders, hoping the sunlight would glint off the badge pinned to his chest and remind Ralph of his position in the town. He had a vested interest in keeping Catherine safe, same as he did for any other resident of Bear Creek.

"Catherine mentioned you've been making some unwelcome advances."

He hadn't meant to just lay it out there, but he wasn't known for his subtlety. And sometimes a man needed the words said outright.

Ralph's face showed no surprise. And then his mouth split in an ugly smile. "I didn't know it was unwelcome."

She muttered something at Matty's side. Sounded like, *Yes, you did.*

"I certainly ain't the kind of man who pushes his affection on a woman who don't return it."

Beside him, Matty felt Catherine almost vibrating with tension, with the words she was no doubt holding back.

He touched her elbow, just a slight brush of his fingers, trying to let her know to stay calm and let him handle this. Maybe it hadn't been such a good idea to invite her along, but he'd been hoping to give her some comfort by confronting Ralph Chesterton outright and coming to a resolution.

"Now you know," Matty said, forcing a calm note. "I'm glad we got that resolved so easily. Now Catherine can rest easy that you won't be talking to her again about marriage or her property."

The other man wasn't smiling anymore. The slight narrowing of his eyes and the hard glint in their depths were warning signs that Matty knew well enough. But he nodded, a slow bob of his head.

"That's real good," Matty went on. "I'd hate to have to get the sheriff's office involved. *More* involved than me coming out here to talk to you."

"If that's all you came to say…I've got work to do." Ralph's lips parted, but his expression couldn't be called a smile.

They took their leave.

Catherine was quiet as she walked beside him. He didn't think this was her normal, pensive quiet.

"Something tells me that won't be the end of it," he said.

"You don't think so?"

She kept her head down. She didn't sound terribly surprised.

"I'll keep watch. I still think you should let Pop know. Have you changed your mind about talking to him about any of this?"

She shook her head. "He gets lost in his memories enough as it is. If he starts feeling threatened, it might make it worse."

He exhaled. The woman was stubborn, but he could also see her point.

He didn't like the way Ralph's eyes had turned hard when he looked at Catherine. Didn't like the thought of her alone out here with no protection.

"I'm still thinking of visiting the big ranch. Having someone else looking out for you would be smart once I head home."

Because he knew it couldn't be long until the sheriff's search party, or his brothers, would be coming for him. His time here with Catherine was short.

"I don't want anyone else around."

She might not, but he couldn't leave her here unprotected.

"If not someone from the big ranch, who's gonna protect you? Pop?"

She bristled at his words, and he scrambled to explain. "He said he was a sharpshooter in the war."

"Yes, and what if he shoots an innocent traveler passing across our land? The war was forty years ago, but to him, it's as if it happened yesterday."

"If you think he's that dangerous, how can you stay alone with him out here?"

She whirled on him. "Should I institutionalize the only person who's cared for me the past decade?" she demanded.

"That's not what I—"

She shook off his words and stomped ahead of him. She still mistrusted him.

But he was determined if the only thing he could do before he healed up enough to get home was ensure Catherine's safety, he would. Even if it meant protecting her from her own kin.

Chapter Eleven

Early the next morning, Sunday, Catherine slipped out of the soddy. She leaned against the closed door, breathing in the damp, earthy air. Pop remained inside, still sleeping.

The first rays of sunshine crept over the distant horizon, and she stood for several minutes just outside the door, breathing and soaking up the morning. A whip-poor-will called out softly in the distance. In these spare moments, she could pretend that there wasn't a threat hanging over her head, could pretend she was still a simple girl trying to survive on the homestead with Pop.

She wrapped her hands around her elbows to ward off the morning chill.

Movement came from feet away. The cowboy, shifting on his stool.

A quick glance revealed the pale oval of his face in the early-morning gray. Leaning back against the soddy's side, he tipped back his hat.

"Little early to be stirring for a Sunday, isn't it?"

She stiffened a bit, but forced out an exhale. He wasn't trying to offend her. He had been kind in the face of her mistrust.

The evening before had been uncomfortable. She probably owed him an apology for blowing up. His words had touched on her fears. And she'd hated that he saw them, this man who'd been dumped at her door.

She'd actually expected him to be snoozing, although with such an uncomfortable seat and the cool night air, maybe that had been asking too much. He did have a blanket wrapped around his shoulders.

"I just…" She let her voice trail off, eyes going to the horizon.

This was one of her favorite times of day. The quiet in between the night and day—animals both going to bed and waking. Those few moments when the sky turned beautiful colors and she could imagine…lots of things. That she wasn't stuck out here with Pop. That she'd finished her schooling. Traveled.

Sometimes she wondered if the sunrise looked the same from the other side of the continent. Or from *another* continent.

Would the cowboy laugh at her if she admitted to such frivolous thoughts? They had no place in her daily life of work, work, work. But just for these few moments…

"Beautiful, ain't it?" he whispered.

"Yes."

She didn't let her eyes slide over to him, afraid to see whether he judged her for needing these private moments.

"It's moments like these that make me remember to slow down and appreciate the beauty God's put around me."

That didn't sound like a man who would poke fun at her. She couldn't help her glance toward him and found his gaze on her, not on the sky.

Heat flushed her cheeks.

Would there ever come a time when she grew comfortable around the cowboy? He could discombobulate her with only a sentence and a look.

Maybe if she'd had more experience with people she would understand his cues. But the very reason she didn't have that experience was why she couldn't let her guard down.

She shored up her shoulders and squinted against the rising sun. "I suppose it's time to do the chores, at least the ones that can't be put off until tomorrow. Pop will read his Bible for us after breakfast."

He'd been unconscious a week ago and missed much of the quiet Sunday she and Pop had spent. Even if they'd lived closer to town and the little Bear Creek church, no doubt they would have had quiet worship time at home.

The cowboy pushed up off the stool, one hand coming to rub high on his chest. "I probably can't milk the cow for you, but I can gather eggs."

The cowboy followed her to the shed, whistling softly.

By the time they reached the shed, the cowboy had gone from whistling to singing a hymn she remembered her mother singing from years ago.

The cow gave a mournful moo as Catherine settled on the milking stool. She found herself hiding a smile in the animal's side as her hands warmed to the task.

The cowboy kept singing as he visited each hen's nest, and before she realized it, she was singing softly, too.

Matty heard Catherine's soft soprano, and something shifted beneath his breastbone.

Not his injury. Something more.

He'd had the same feeling when she'd come outside that morning to watch the sunrise. For someone who was constantly busy, always working, seeing Catherine take a moment for herself to appreciate the beauty of God's creation... Well, he'd been unable to look away from the beauty of *her*.

Now he sang to distract himself from the attraction. Even with the distance she'd put between them last night, it had simmered. He thought she felt it, too.

But after Luella's rejection, he found it hard to trust his gut, at least where women were concerned.

And besides, Catherine seemed determined to maintain her isolation on the homestead. He didn't understand why, and his curiosity ate at him.

Was her determination really a result of what had happened in the schoolroom?

Or because of Pop?

Or something else?

An hour later, they'd eaten the fresh eggs Matty had scrambled and the bacon he'd fried.

"Catherine and I were thinking we might pay a call on your other close neighbor this afternoon," he said to Pop.

"The Elliott ranch? What for?" Pop asked.

"To visit."

"Catherine don't visit."

Catherine's eyes remained on her plate. She was no help.

"We won't be gone long. I'm sure you can stick a pole in the creek, catch us some dinner."

Pop leaned back in his chair, crossed his arms over his chest. "You can visit all you want, but why's Catherine have to go? What's she got to visit about?"

"I'd like to go, Pop," Catherine said, though she kept her eyes down.

"Fine." The older man got up from the table, dishes rattling when his knee bumped the table. "Fine."

Pop stomped to the door and slammed out of the dugout.

"You think he's going to cause trouble?" Matty asked, concerned.

"I think he's going to go wandering. He might not even remember where we're going in a little while," Catherine said, voice low.

But that didn't erase the little worry crease between her eyebrows. "Maybe I should stay, just in case."

"I'd like you to go," he said. "Let this Elliott and his family see you. Realize that you're a vulnerable woman." And if they agreed to help watch over Catherine, maybe he could also ask them to send word back to his family.

She bristled and he held up his left hand—the one not holding the spoon to shovel food in his mouth—as if to placate her. "Not that you *are* vulnerable, exactly—" He stopped himself before he got in hotter water with his words. He *did* think she was vulnerable out here alone. Ralph was much larger than her, and if he surprised her... And Pop wasn't any real help. If anything, he was more work for her.

It all reminded Matty a little of waking up from that fever, alone and knowing no one was coming to help. Well, he wasn't going to let things go out here, not when he *could* help. Even if getting her to accept it was like breaking the stubbornest filly he'd ever met.

She seemed contemplative. That little line between her brows furrowing deeper. "I suppose it would help if I wore one of my mama's old dresses."

Catherine in a dress? "That'd be perfect."

If this played out the way he wanted it to, he wouldn't have to worry about Catherine after he headed home to Bear Creek.

Chapter Twelve

Catherine didn't know what had possessed her to offer to wear one of two dresses her mother had put away in a trunk far beneath the bed, but she'd done it.

She felt foolish.

Her feet kept getting caught in the long skirt. She wasn't used to the material blocking her way, and her stride was too long. She nearly tripped, sending a quail fluttering away through the long wild grasses.

She should've stayed behind with Pop.

Pop, who'd looked at her as if betrayed when Matty had revealed she was going with him on the visit.

Now she couldn't ignore the glances the cowboy kept sending her way.

"What?" she asked, the sharpness of her voice revealing her testiness.

This was uncomfortable. She didn't *do* social calls.

"Nothing."

She didn't believe him. She felt as she had back in the schoolroom, when she'd been *homemade Cathy*.

"Maybe this wasn't such a good idea." She started to turn back. She could return to the homestead and pretend she hadn't agreed to accompany him in the first place.

"Catherine—" He took two steps after her, taking her elbow in hand and urging her to turn back with him.

She didn't jerk away, but she did tug her arm back. After days of his presence, those casual touches—like when he'd clasped her hands in comfort at the clothesline yesterday—had stopped surprising her.

They stood there in the open field, facing each other. She couldn't quite meet his eyes.

"You don't have to come—but I'd like it if you did."

She remembered. So the Elliott family could see how *vulnerable* she was. Pity her.

Hadn't she had enough of being subjected to the whims of others as a child?

She ducked her head, squeezed her eyes tightly closed. What was the right thing to do in this situation?

Even after Matty's conversation with Ralph yesterday, she doubted her neighbor would leave off bothering her.

Without the deputy around, she would be forced to rely only on herself again.

And wouldn't it be good to have someone to watch out for her when Matty left?

Still undecided, she let her eyes slide to the horizon, but she fell into step beside him again.

"My sister Breanna would wear trousers every day if she could get away with it."

She didn't glance at Matty as he spoke. Maybe he meant the words to ease the awkwardness between them. Or maybe he'd sensed how much she liked hearing about his family.

"My ma drags her to a quilting bee or to have tea with Ma's friends every once in a while, and Breanna digs in her heels each and every time."

His affection for his sister came through every word

even though his comment wasn't particularly complimentary toward her.

"You miss her," Catherine stated.

"Yes. She and my brother Seb are the only ones of marrying age who aren't hitched, so we've sort of banded together. My nieces Cecilia and Susie are about the same age, but Breanna has her own mind and often prefers to stay in the bunkhouse with us boys."

"How old are your siblings?"

"Seb is twenty and Breanna seventeen."

There were a few beats of silence, and then he spoke again. "Eye spy something…"

She didn't guess and his boon question was, "It seems like there's something more than what happened back in school. I'd like to know why you won't go back to town."

Blood rushed to her face, pounding in her ears. Had he guessed the truth?

"That wasn't a question," she hedged.

"Will you tell me why you refuse to go to town?"

She could tell him. Maybe if he knew about her parentage, he'd stop pushing her to seek help for Pop. But there was a part of her that hesitated.

If she told him, everything would change. He'd look at her as the women in town had.

And for some unfathomable reason, she couldn't bear that.

"My mother and I were not always treated kindly when we visited town. Things were difficult without my father around."

It was all she could give him. She couldn't say *born out of wedlock* or *illegitimate*.

Instead of judgment, his eyes softened with…understanding?

And she remembered that he'd lost his parents, too.

He hadn't understood what she was really telling him. And she couldn't say more.

When she didn't take a turn at the game, the cowboy kept sending sidelong glances her way. Afternoon sun beat down on her head, but it was the cowboy's glances that warmed her from the inside out.

"Do I look so awful?" she asked after the fifteenth time he'd glanced her direction. She kept her eyes on the mountains against the far horizon, afraid to see the answer in his face.

"You don't look awful at all."

She glanced sharply at him, in time to catch him looking at her again. They made their way through the field thick with wildflowers. In the distance, cattle grazed, content to ignore them.

"Then why are you looking at me?" she demanded.

"I was trying to decide whether you'd slug me if I said you looked pretty in that dress."

Her eyes slid down to her feet, where the dress kicked out in front once and then again. Was he teasing her again? She wished she knew.

"Or if you'd go all shy again."

He bumped her shoulder with his arm. When had he crept close enough to touch her? She angled slightly away, but they were already close enough to the main ranch house that moving away farther would be noticeable.

The low, sprawling building was made from natural rock and some timber, with large, expensive glass windows across the front. Where the Chestertons' place had been dilapidated, this ranch house was well built and well maintained. The corral fence was in good shape, and a fine mare stood placidly near, her ears twitching in their direction. Farther away, behind the corral, the barn was large. And painted.

Her discomfort grew as Matty took the two front steps confidently and knocked on the door.

"What if they don't want us to come calling? How do we know anyone is even home?"

"We don't." He grinned at her over his shoulder, but the flash of teeth against his tanned skin didn't offer any reassurance. What had she been thinking, accompanying him?

She fervently hoped that the family inside had gone to church and not returned yet.

But to her chagrin, a young woman opened the door.

Matty introduced her as a neighbor and himself as a friend and a deputy from town. They were ushered into a parlor and plied with warm slices of rhubarb pie and introduced to Mr. Harold Elliott and his wife by their daughter, Michaela.

Catherine's terrified expression as she settled on the parlor sofa beside him might've made him laugh in another circumstance, but he needed to stay focused on his mission to find help for Catherine.

He touched her shoulder lightly, settling his arm on the back of the sofa, his calloused fingers catching in a crochet doily. The frilly things covered almost every surface.

Catherine's chin jerked toward him and he hitched what he hoped was a reassuring smile. She looked like a filly about to bolt under its first saddle. She didn't seem to know what to do with her skirt. She fiddled with the folds of fabric, showing an uncharacteristic nervousness.

He felt right at home. The horsehair sofa and wingback chair could've been from his ma's parlor. He told himself not to get too comfortable—he had a job to do here today. But it sure was nice to sit in a civilized room again, not the rough furniture and tight confines of the dugout.

"I'm so glad to know there's another woman nearby," said Mrs. Elliott. Her smile was welcoming and encompassed both Matty and Catherine.

Harold wasn't so quick in his welcome. "I've come calling at your place a coupla times since we moved up this way two years ago. The little soddy just south, right?" he asked Catherine.

She nodded, but her posture had gone stiff.

"Never seen anybody there. Almost like folks had disappeared when they saw me comin'."

The fingers of Catherine's near hand clenched in her skirt.

From what he'd gleaned over these past days with Catherine and Pop, as Pop's paranoia had worsened, Catherine had left off visiting with and trading with neighbors the past few years.

Maybe it was proprietary and maybe she would shake him off, but he settled his hand loosely over hers.

"Catherine's granddad is…distrustful of strangers. With such a pretty granddaughter to protect, who can blame him?"

She didn't shake off his hand, but she did shoot him a glare.

"No company? That would drive me batty." Mrs. Elliott and Michaela shared a glance. "I'm afraid we're in town as often as we can persuade Harold to drive us."

The young woman bobbled her fork. It rattled against her pie plate. "I like the quilting bees the best."

It was a perfect opening for Catherine to speak up, but she remained silent at his side. He squeezed her hand, hoping to urge her to join the conversation.

"My…my mama liked to quilt. She's been gone now for several years."

"I'm sorry to hear that, dear," said Mrs. Elliott. "You're welcome to come and visit—and quilt—anytime you like."

He heard Catherine's soft exhale. "Thank you for the invitation. It is hard to…step away from the duties of running the homestead at times."

"Did you have much damage from the recent storm?" Matty asked when the conversation stalled.

"Not much." Harold nodded toward the window overlooking a wide green pasture. "Part of the barn roof blew off, but our hands already fixed it."

Matty mentioned the fine specimen of horseflesh he'd seen out in the corral, which opened the door for Harold to talk about his operation and his animals. Although horses were Matty's brother Oscar's passion, his pa's ranch ran cattle and he could talk enough about both types of animals to sound knowledgeable.

Harold invited Matty to visit the barn and he took his chance to converse with the man one-on-one.

"I'll be back."

A panicked look crossed Catherine's face. "But—"

He smiled at her. "Soon."

He walked with Harold through the yard toward the barn. Chickens squawked and clucked, parting for their approach. A black-and-white farm dog lay in the shade of the porch, tongue lolling out of its mouth. In the distance, a man rode horseback.

Matty took a deep breath of the fresh air. "You've got a nice spread. That mare in the corral is good stock."

"I don't think you dragged your gal out here to talk about my spread. What's your real purpose here?"

The direct question was unexpected. Matty had thought the older man would want to chitchat for a while.

He leaned against the corral railing, putting off a casual air, though Harold's direct stare had his hackles up. After the confrontation with Ralph Chesterton, even Harold's direct manner seemed suspicious. "I appreciate you shooting straight with me. I didn't mention it inside, but my duties as deputy brought me this direction after the storms to check on folks. Catherine's place has had some funny happenings."

"What kind of happenings?"

"Somebody sneaking around at night. Neighbor on her other side has been making some unwanted advances."

Harold crossed his arms over his chest. "It's a shame. At least she's got her grandfather to look out for her, though."

Matty shook his head. This was where he needed to tread carefully. "The grandfather is getting up there in years. Catherine bears most of the work on the homestead."

Harold's stark posture with his arms still crossed over his chest didn't bode well for what Matty was going to ask.

"You said you have two hands. I'd like to ask you to send them over to Catherine's place and patrol every once in a while." It didn't have to be every day. But if Ralph Chesterton knew someone else was watching out for Catherine, he'd have to see she wasn't easy pickings. A coward like him would give up when faced with opposition.

"I can't do that. My men work hard for their pay. They ain't got time for running all over tarnation. And besides, what if this other neighbor turns violent? I ain't gonna risk my hands."

Matty's back teeth ground together. Harold would prefer to leave Catherine to the devices of a violent man?

"Besides, ain't protecting folks what the sheriff and his deputies are charged with?"

The pain in Matty's jaw only got worse as he bit back the words that desperately wanted to emerge. "Of course it is, but with Catherine being so far from town, it's not feasible for someone to ride out every day and check on her."

Harold shrugged. "Maybe she should move closer to town, then."

Matty nodded to where the men worked just barely in eyesight. "Mind if I talk to your men? They might be willing to help a woman on their own time."

Harold remained in his closed-off posture. "You can ask, but they both get one day off every two weeks and usually like to spend it in town with a little comp'ny."

Where the man had been open and friendly inside with the women, his shuttered expression warned Matty off. He'd expected to find help in Harold Elliott, but he couldn't have been more wrong.

Now how would he protect Catherine, once he'd gone back to his life in Bear Creek?

Catherine sat in the parlor with Michaela. Mrs. Elliott had excused herself into the kitchen after the men had gone outdoors.

She knew it would be rude to reject the piece of pie she'd been offered, rude not to sit down with her cup of coffee and chat.

That didn't stop her hands from shaking.

The cowboy had abandoned her. She could see him through a large glass-paned window, standing with one foot up on the corral railing. Relaxed as could be. Talking, of course.

But inside, the silence stretched awkwardly. Catherine's face heated and she cleared her throat. She cast about for anything to talk about. What did one speak of in a social setting like this?

Michaela only looked bored.

"Do you...have any brothers or sisters?" Catherine asked finally. Surely family must be a safe topic.

"One brother. He lives in Sheridan with his wife. I've begged and begged Mama to let me stay with them over the summer, but she won't agree."

An expression that might've been a pout crossed her face. "Sheridan has much better shops than Bear Creek. I'd just love to purchase a new dress, don't—"

Michaela cut herself off. She smirked slightly—Catherine could well imagine what she was thinking. Catherine's dress was old and had been a simple style when her mama had made it years ago.

Too different. You don't fit, her mind whispered.

Catherine worked at showing no emotion. She sipped her cooling coffee.

Michaela seemed to grow bored with Catherine's silent response. She glanced out the window. "Your beau is handsome. Is it serious?"

Catherine choked on a bite of pie. Coughed. Her eyes watered. "He's not my beau."

"No?" Michaela's eyes sparkled with interest as she looked out the window again, this time leaning slightly forward. "Then I hope he'll come back inside and continue the visit."

A hot knot lodged in Catherine's chest at the words. Why shouldn't Michaela flirt with Matty if she wanted? She was pretty. Wore clothes fashionable enough to make Catherine seem like a brown sparrow compared to a brightly colored finch.

Catherine had no claim on the cowboy.

But the hot knot behind her sternum remained.

Apparently bored with Catherine's lack of conversational skills, Michaela excused herself and disappeared into the kitchen.

Catherine's edginess prompted her to her feet. She left the coffee behind on a fine-looking little table next to the sofa and moved to the window. Matty and the landowner stood near a corral. Matty's body language confused her. The set of his shoulders seemed tense, but he had his hands out, as if he was pleading for something.

Soft voices from the kitchen filtered to her, now that she was standing closer to the doorway, instead of sitting in her seat.

"Did you see her *hair*?" Michaela's voice carried clearly to Catherine's ears. The disdain in her tone was easy to discern.

Intense heat crawled into her cheeks. Without her consent, her hand climbed into the curls at the nape of her neck.

The women were still speaking, but Catherine could no longer make out the words. She blinked back hot moisture that stung her eyes.

The only thing worse than overhearing the insult would be if the women came back and witnessed Catherine eavesdropping.

So she carefully made her way back to her seat on the sofa, blinking rapidly to clear the moisture from her eyes.

And none too soon. Michaela reentered from the kitchen, moving to sit in her chair in a graceful movement. She didn't fumble with her skirt. She was perfectly at ease in her role as a woman.

Nothing like Catherine.

Several more interminable minutes passed in unimportant chatter before the men returned.

Shortly thereafter, Matty excused them.

"That was a pointless waste of time," he grumbled as they trudged back the way they had come. "But at least we got to have a nice cup of coffee and that pie, hmm?"

She swallowed hard, unable to tell him what had happened with the womenfolk. Wouldn't he think it was her fault for being too different?

"There's no help coming from them."

She raised her chin.

"Not," he said quickly, "that you needed their help anyway."

He quirked a sideways grin at her.

He did have *some* redeeming qualities, she ruminated as they walked home in contemplative silence. One of which was that, unlike in their school days, the Matty she was coming to know now never made her feel lessthan.

Chapter Thirteen

Dawn was breaking as Matty crept through the woods just south of the Pooles' soddy.

He stepped on a twig and it cracked loudly. He muttered under his breath. If someone was out here, surely they would've heard that.

He'd woken from a light doze, his back against the barn, and smelled woodsmoke. Nothing had been stirring in the dugout—Catherine and Pop must've still been sleeping—so he'd begun a slow, quiet circuit around the perimeter of the property.

He hadn't been sleeping much out-of-doors and his thoughts were slow to clear, but one question kept bumping loudly around his head. If someone were spying, why would they start a fire that could get them discovered?

He had no proof that the person snooping around three nights ago had been Ralph Chesterton. He had his suspicions, but he couldn't take action unless he caught the man actively threatening Catherine.

And as he healed, he had less and less time to keep watch.

A murmur of voices had Matty ducking behind a tree. That sounded like two men, speaking in low tones. He slipped his revolver out of its holster, though he kept it pointed at the ground—for now.

He didn't want to think about what the recoil would do to his collarbone if he had to fire the weapon.

He edged slightly around the tree, trying to get a glimpse of what and who he was up against. Two horses. Was that...?

Matty squinted in the growing light. That looked like his brother Seb's horse. And behind the palomino... Edgar's head rose above the horse's flank from where he'd been crouched between the two animals. He caught sight of Matty and dropped the horse's hoof from where he'd been examining it.

"What are you doing here?" Matty asked, holstering his weapon and moving out from behind the tree.

Edgar's face brightened. Seb's head came up from where he squatted beside a small campfire.

"Looking for you." Edgar rounded the horse toward Matty. "You look like something the cat would've left on the doorstep. Why didn't you send word where you were?"

"Your horse came home without you the day after you'd ridden out," Seb added. "Ma's been worried sick." He stood.

"It's complicated. I—" Matty's words cut off in a grunt of pain when Edgar embraced him enthusiastically.

Edgar let go immediately. "What's wrong?"

"You hurt?" Seb echoed as he joined them near the horses.

"Collarbone. Probably broken."

"Can you ride?"

Matty shook his head in the negative. "The Pooles have been putting me up. As long as I watch my movements, I can get around."

"Who?" Seb asked. "Never heard of 'em."

The horses stamped and swished their tails, reading the human excitement.

"They're a family homesteading out here. They... don't get to town much. How'd you find me, anyway?"

Seb shifted his feet, his excitement palpable. "We've been riding from house to house, asking folks if they'd seen you and searching every little copse and ravine. The sheriff didn't think you'd have made it this far out from town. We've spent all week on your trail."

"Until yesterday," Edgar said. "Floyd Chesterton rode out to tell us he'd seen you."

Chesterton. It shouldn't have been a surprise, but Matty felt a surge of unease. Had Ralph's brother purposely gone to Matty's family? Suspicion flared anew. Once Matty returned home, there would be no one to watch over Catherine.

He moved to squat next to the fire, his brothers joining him there. Accepted a cup of his brother's sludgy coffee. Breathed in the scent that reminded him of home.

He wasn't ashamed that his eyes stung a little.

"What's going on?" Seb asked.

Matty took off his hat, ran a hand through his hair. "Three days ago, I would've been thrilled to see you, would've sent you home to fetch a wagon."

"But not today," Edgar surmised.

Matty shook his head. "Catherine's neighbor has been making untoward advances...enough that she's shook up about it."

"Catherine?" the brothers echoed unanimously.

Heat flared in Matty's face, and it wasn't from being so close to the campfire. "Catherine Poole. She lives out here with her granddad, basically runs the whole place herself."

Edgar and Seb shared a glance.

"A woman?"

The heat in Matty's face intensified.

"Someone threatening her?" Seb bristled, and Matty had never been so appreciative of his brothers' protective natures toward womenfolk.

"She barely admitted to it, but a few days ago, I came upon Ralph Chesterton and it sure sounded like he was threatening her. Then someone was out in the barn later that night, made some noise and woke up the household."

"You sure it wasn't an animal?" Edgar asked skeptically.

Matty leveled a glance at him. "Once I started looking, it was hard to miss the perimeter someone has worn into the grass. That's not an animal."

"What's he want?"

"She says he's after the land. She's got a nice creek. It'd make a nice watering hole if he's of a mind to raise cattle. There might also be a stockpile of grain, though she hasn't told me outright about that. Not much else of value around the place." Unless you counted Catherine herself. Thinking about someone targeting Catherine in particular twisted a fist in Matty's gut.

His brothers were silent for a long moment. Seb sifted through the coals with a long, slender stick.

"I'm guessing you don't want us to rush home and bring the wagon," Edgar finally said.

Matty rubbed a hand up the back of his neck. "I can't just leave her here without protection."

"What about the granddad?" Edgar asked.

"I can stay with ya. I've got my bedroll," Seb said before Matty could answer. Matty read the excitement in his brother's sparkling eyes and the roll of his shoulders.

But Matty shook his head. "You know I'd love to have you at my side, but Catherine's grandpop has some…

Well, he's getting up in years and he sorta has this… memory lapse. Makes him real wary of strangers. And doesn't make him much for protecting the place, either," Matty said with a nod to let Edgar know he hadn't just ignored his question.

Matty let his eyes slide to the horizon. He couldn't forget Catherine's sweet singing voice yesterday morning, or the pang of attraction that kept rearing its head between them.

In addition to the possible danger for Catherine and Pop, he also couldn't forget the question that kept bumping around inside his head. If he left now, when would he see Catherine again?

Somehow he knew that if he left now, the tentative friendship building between him and Catherine would be over.

He'd go back to his life working with the sheriff and working the family ranch. If he had a hankering to see Catherine, it would be an entire day's trip to ride out here and back, just for a short visit. If he could count on seeing her at Sunday worship or other social events like the town picnic, deepening their friendship wouldn't seem so daunting…

He needed more time for more than one reason.

"I need a few more days," he said. "Can you go home and tell Ma and Pa that I'm all right, that I'll be home when I can?"

Seb scattered ashes, disappointment obvious in his frown. And Edgar held Matty's gaze long enough to make him uncomfortable. Could his brother see just how much he needed to make sure Catherine was taken care of?

He couldn't explain the need. It didn't make sense for him to be so attached to her, not when he couldn't read her well enough to know if she wanted his friendship or wished he'd leave. But the attachment was there. He couldn't walk away, not when she needed someone on her side.

"I don't know how long we can put off Ma," Edgar said. "Doubt she'll go another week without getting out here to see for herself that you're all right. And the sheriff's been real concerned, too. He sent out riders that first day, but lotta folks been needed in town to see to the repairs. If you don't show up at the ranch by Sunday, we'll come back for ya."

Matty nodded. It would have to do.

Six days to figure a way to keep her safe from Chesterton. Six days to get her to open up about what valuables she might have hidden on the place, in case that's what Chesterton was after—though Matty doubted it.

Six days to get her to open up to him, to find out if she felt anything more for him than friendship.

Catherine moved through the woods as silently as possible. She carried a pail of early-season blackberries. She'd visited the patch for the past several years and somehow the conditions of the little pocket of woods always made the berries ripen a month before the rest of the berries in this area would ripen.

And if she missed out on collecting them, the wild birds would take them all.

The blackberries along with the syrup she'd made from the maple sap earlier this year would make a nice complement to Pop's biscuits tomorrow morning.

She was nearing the dugout when she caught sight of something suspicious and ducked behind a wide oak.

Heart hammering, she peeked out around the oak. Ralph was skulking, half hidden behind a knocked-down tree that angled up from the earth, propped up by another, smaller tree. His attention was on the homestead.

Catherine looked beyond him, without moving from her hiding place behind the tree. From this distance, she couldn't see activity in the barnyard, but likely he could.

It disgusted her to know that he might regularly be spying on her. No wonder his place was in such disrepair, if this was where he spent his time.

And…knowing that he was watching sent chills down her spine. How often?

How…vile.

As she watched, he ducked behind the windbreak tree. She edged back behind her own cover, in case he turned where he could see her.

Noise of oncoming footsteps crunching through the underbrush held her attention. Coming from the direction of the homestead. She could only pray it wasn't Pop.

"I can see your boots," came Matty's voice. He sounded casual, but there was an edge to his words.

"Deputy." Ralph stood tall. He raised both hands in front of himself briefly. Maybe to show that he had no weapon. "Didn't expect to see you still hanging around these parts."

What did that mean? Then she remembered that Matty hadn't revealed his injury to Ralph. If Ralph thought he was in good health, perhaps he'd expected the cowboy to have moved on by now.

"Thought we talked about you leaving Catherine alone," the cowboy countered, voice dangerously low.

Then, without warning, Matty's gaze traveled to her in a direct line, almost as if he'd sensed her here.

Ralph turned to follow Matty's gaze, and by now it would be pointless to continue to hide, so Catherine stepped out from behind the tree.

Ralph's eyes still had a hard light to them as his eyes followed her movements to join Matty. "Afternoon, Catherine."

"You're trespassing," she said.

"I was simply checking on a neighbor."

"Shouldn't you be worrying about your own property?" She came even with Matty and he touched the back of her wrist. Just a simple touch, but knowing he stood with her helped calm the fear that had risen in her throat at seeing Ralph sneaking about and spying.

"I warned you to stay away from Catherine. I thought we understood each other."

"You didn't say nothing about checking on a neighbor," Ralph said, that ugly sneer making an appearance. "You said not to propose to Catherine no more." He shrugged, but there was nothing nonchalant about the movement. "Ain't planning to do that again. *Nope.*"

But something behind his words sent a warning through her like the bolts of bright lightning that had accompanied the storm before.

He could still do her much harm without proposing marriage. He could force her physically. He could kill her.

Just how badly did he want her land?

Matty must have sensed the danger lurking behind Ralph's words, because his hand closed over Catherine's.

"I think you should head on home," Matty said firmly. "You aren't welcome on Catherine's land, and you'd best stay away from her, as well."

Ralph's lips twisted. "You can't stay here forever, *deputy.*" He drawled the title slowly. "When you got to go back home, back to your job, Catherine might take a little more kindly to the neighborly help I'm offering."

"I will *never* need or want your help," she said stiffly. "I've made that clear just about every way I know how."

His eyes slid up and down her, making her feel slimy as if he'd touched her physically. "A woman runnin' a place like this by yerself...you'll need me. Mark my words."

She stood stock-still, watching until he'd moved out of sight.

When Matty reached for her with a murmured, "Catherine..." she whirled away, stalking toward the soddy.

She couldn't accept his comfort, though she'd let him near in front of Ralph in a show of solidarity.

Because Ralph was right. Matty was going to leave. Sometime soon. And when he was gone, all the responsibility for the homestead would return to her shoulders.

And she would be left to worry about fending off Ralph on her own.

That night, they'd cleared the supper table, but a soft rain had begun falling and Matty seemed in no hurry to head outdoors. He'd stayed close all afternoon after the confrontation with Ralph. He sat on the stool but reached down and picked up a rusted can Catherine hadn't noticed before now, sitting near his boots.

"I finished my set of dominoes," he said. He upended the can and dumped several into his palm, then placed them on the table. "Will y'all play a game with me?"

"I've got mending to do." One of Catherine's pairs of socks was more holes than fabric. She didn't have time for games. And she was a little surprised that Matty wasn't out patrolling or something. Maybe he thought Ralph wouldn't return because of the rainy weather.

Or maybe he just wanted a break, didn't want to have to worry all the time. Too bad she couldn't escape it.

"Aw, Cath, you can spare time to play one game," Pop wheedled.

She considered her grandfather, who had been so against their social visit to the Elliotts just yesterday. His moods were as changeable as the weather, and tonight he was full of cheer and wanted to play.

And Pop so rarely asked for anything. "I suppose you're right."

Matty's face lit, like the lamp over his shoulder, and for a moment she found herself caught in the pleasure reflected there. All because she'd agreed to play a silly game?

Matty turned the dominoes facedown on the table and mixed them all around as he explained the rules and basic strategy. The dominoes clacked together, momentarily louder than the rain outside.

When Catherine and Pop had the gist of the game, they each drew several dominoes and began to play.

"I'll go easy on y'all, since it's your first time to play." Matty grinned.

"I played before, in the war," Pop said. "But I don't remember the rules, only that the kid that taught me was the most competitive person I'd ever met." He paused. "'Cept maybe for you," he continued with a nod to Matty.

"I just like to play," Matty argued.

Pop harrumphed, but his smile remained. Catherine loved seeing it—Pop didn't smile often.

"You've got a liking for games, too, gal," Pop said, and Catherine looked up from her dominoes in surprise.

"She used to pal around with this little neighbor girl," Pop said to Matty.

"I don't remember that," Catherine put in.

"Folks lived where the Chestertons are now. Moved on when you must'a been about six."

Catherine searched her memories but couldn't picture such a friend.

"The two of you were as thick as thieves, running the property, playing games and dollies."

Why couldn't she remember? And worse, why did her heart pang at the thought of having a friend?

Pop bowed out of the second game, but Catherine found herself agreeing to play again.

"You and Michaela seemed to get along," Matty said.

Was that what it had seemed like? Michaela had barely tolerated her presence. Had poked fun at her hair, though she wasn't meant to have heard.

"Did you ask Mr. Elliott to send word home as to your whereabouts?"

"No."

"Why not?"

He stared down at the dominoes as he pushed them around the table, mixing them up. His concentration on the simple act seemed out of proportion. Or perhaps she was imagining his discomfort in light of her own conflicted feelings about him returning home.

"I'm getting stronger, but I'd like to settle this issue with the...with the neighbors before I go." He glanced at Pop.

He cared.

She squelched that thought. Couldn't afford to depend on Matty.

"It's not your responsibility," she said stiffly.

"I told you I would be your friend, and I aim to keep my word."

She'd never had a friend, and later, after he'd excused

himself to the barn, she stared into the dark, unable to sleep.

A friend.

After the visit yesterday and Michaela's disdain…and in the face of Matty's constant support, Catherine realized she was starting to think of him that way.

She had a friend.

If only she knew what to do with him.

Chapter Fourteen

Matty woke from where he'd dozed off, rolled in a quilt just inside the barn's outer wall.

What was that?

The smell of cow was pungent, the soft coos of the chickens the only sound.

And then more noise came, a loud banging. From the cabin.

Matty took off at a dead run, ignoring the protesting pain across his chest. He'd spent the past two nights in the barn instead of closer to the house, not wanting anyone watching them to figure out where *he* was watching from.

Had someone gone into the soddy and attacked Catherine and Pop? He reached for the gun belted at his side even as he burst into the cabin.

Catherine was tangled in a quilt on the floor, caught between the cot and a table leg.

But the man who pinned her down wasn't a stranger. It was Pop. His hair was disheveled, but from the back Matty couldn't get a look at his face or see Catherine, other than her feet that kicked from beneath Pop. Then Pop raised his hand as if he would strike Catherine.

"Stop!" Matty cried. He couldn't pull his gun on the older man, not knowing what he did about Pop's mental state.

Pop looked over his shoulder. His eyes were wild.

"You don't wanna hit Catherine, Pop."

Matty eased in the door. Another step or two and he could get his arms around Pop and pull the man off Catherine.

"Don't know no Catherine," Pop spat. "This here yella-bellied Grayback snuck up on me, tried to smother me in my sleep. And you—"

Matty stepped forward in time to take Pop's wildly swung fist on his chin. His head knocked back, but he got his hand on Pop's shoulder.

"Catherine—"

Another fist to his midsection cut off Matty's words, but Catherine was already struggling out from beneath the blanket, pushing up against the cot. "Pop!"

Pop reached for Matty's gun, but Matty twisted to the side and got both his arms around Pop's shoulders.

"Stop struggling," Matty said in the older man's ear. "You're safe in your dugout. On the homestead where you've lived for thirty years."

Pop still fought.

"Calm down!"

"Geoffrey," Catherine said sharply.

She stood directly in front of him, and Pop went still in Matty's arms. Matty could see only the side of Pop's face, but it had gone pale and Pop went limp, leaving Matty to catch him.

His collarbone twinged as he took the unexpected weight. Burned from the unaccustomed movements while grabbing Pop that couldn't be helped.

"Cath?" His voice emerged weak.

"Is he—" Matty asked.

"Pop!" The alarm in Catherine's voice changed. She took the older man's arm.

Pop took a panting breath, and Matty helped wrangle him over to the cot, where he perched gingerly on the edge.

"You back with us?" Matty asked.

Catherine knelt before the older man. "Take it easy, Pop."

Matty went for the coffeepot, but it looked as if Catherine hadn't gotten the day started at all. Had Pop woken in a terror and surprised her?

He poured water from a pitcher into the coffeepot and put it on the stove to warm. Then thought again and knelt to open the stove door and stirred the coals, then added some wood chunks.

"I'm sorry, Catherine." Pop's voice was hoarse and low.

"I'm all right. Are you okay?"

From behind, Matty could see how Catherine's hands were shaking. She was putting off a calm demeanor, but she must be shaken up.

"Yep." But even as he answered, Pop looked frail and shaken himself.

Matty poured the now-steaming coffee into a tin mug and brought it to the older man.

"Thank ya."

"I think we'll all feel better when we've had some breakfast." Catherine couldn't stop shaking. She turned away so Pop wouldn't see the sheen of tears in her eyes, but the cowboy was right there and she completed a circle as she attempted to stay her composure.

She pressed a shaking hand beneath her chin and

drew in what was supposed to be a steadying breath. "Let me milk Elsie and gather some eggs and I'll whip up something. Pop, you should lie back down..."

She pushed out the door without waiting for permission, letting her voice trail off over her shoulder.

Outside, the sun glowed just over the horizon. How had things gone so wrong so early in the day?

"Catherine, wait—"

Matty's voice rang out behind her, but she sped her steps toward the barn. If she could just make it inside, she could huddle up next to Elsie and hide her tears and shaky hands.

It was not to be. His hand clasped her elbow and he halted her with a tug.

"I just need to—" A sob hiccuped out, interrupting what she would've said. *Be alone?*

How had that helped her this morning?

Without her permission, Matty hauled her in close.

And for once, she couldn't resist the comfort of his embrace. Her arms came around his neck. His hands rested lightly at her waist as she couldn't stem the tears. She cried against his chest, taking comfort from *not being alone*. From breathing in the faint scent of horses and stronger smell of man. From his steady breaths, his chest rising against her cheek.

"He w-was calling out in his s-sleep," she said, voice wobbling.

The cowboy's hands squeezed her waist gently. He was listening.

"And I th-thought to wake him before it got w-worse."

His chin rested on the crown of her head for a brief moment, and she allowed herself to feel safe and protected.

And then he ruined it all by saying, "It's all right."

She pushed away from him. His hold loosened, but he didn't let her go all the way.

"How is it going to be *all right*?"

His gaze didn't waver. She feared seeing pity there, but in his eyes there was only compassion. A brisk breeze whipped her hair into her eyes, and she pushed it away even as she glared at the cowboy.

"Then maybe it should be, *it's all right to lean on someone every once in a while.*"

His words hung in the space between them. A statement that seemed impossible, but almost an…invitation. To lean on him. To depend on him.

But how could she, when he was going to leave again? And when he didn't know the truth about her parentage?

She couldn't hold his gaze and let her eyes fall to the grass at their feet.

He nudged her chin higher with his knuckle, his eyes flickering to the bruise she knew must be forming on her jaw. It still throbbed.

"He hit you?" This time his gaze went dark.

Now she pulled completely away from the cowboy with his too-knowing gaze. Of its own volition, her hand came up to cover the tender place on her jaw. "He didn't mean it."

"He might not have meant to hit *you*, but he didn't know the difference, did he?"

His words were like hurled rocks, even though his voice was gentle.

"You can't keep staying in that soddy with him."

She shook her head against his words—maybe against the reality that loomed.

"I have to—" She jerked her thumb over her shoulder, toward the barn. She didn't wait for the cowboy's acknowledgment but stalked away.

On the milking stool next to Elsie, she let more tears fall with her face pressed against the cow's side.

Pop had been her only support after Mama had died. He'd worked hard to keep the homestead running. With his mind going and the paranoia getting worse, how could she ask him to move closer to town? Even if she ignored her own discomfort with the idea and worries that she would be ostracized, what if Pop attacked someone, thinking they were his enemy from a war that had been over for decades? He could be jailed, or even sent to a sanatorium.

And he didn't deserve that, not after everything he'd done for her.

And besides that, how could she ask him to leave behind the land he'd worked since before she was born? They'd cultivated this property. She had the blackberry bushes they shared with the mockingbird down near the creek. The maple that provided sap for syrup for the season. How could they leave behind those years of memories spent with her mama?

But…there was a small part of her that wanted what the cowboy offered. The chance not to have to be alone. Not to have to bear this burden by herself as Pop aged.

Maybe to have…a friend.

Doubts crushed the small seed of desire. If she hadn't been able to make friends as a schoolgirl, why should she think she would fit in now as an adult? Especially with the secret she carried?

The cowboy seemed friendly enough, but he was stuck here and needed her help. She couldn't ignore what had happened in the past.

She would have to figure out a way to prevent what had happened this morning from happening again. Some way to ensure Pop couldn't surprise her.

Chapter Fifteen

Two days after the scuffle with Pop, and Matty felt the distance Catherine had put between them keenly. Did she hate him seeing her vulnerable that much? He'd tried to draw her out with games of dominoes in the evenings, but she'd pled exhaustion.

She and that mule had spent long days finishing clearing the wheat field and he didn't doubt it.

The fist-sized bruise on the side of her face made his gut twist every time he saw it. How could he help her if she wouldn't open up?

And he was running out of time. His brothers would come for him in another two days. He wanted to see his family and he couldn't leave the sheriff without a deputy for any longer.

Pop had spent the past two days wandering the homestead looking frail and lost. Matty'd split his time between watching for an intruder and watching the old man, half afraid he was going to get lost in his memories again and hurt Catherine.

Why couldn't she see that it was dangerous to stay out here alone with him? Why was she so determined to make the homestead work when it was backbreaking labor with such little reward?

Tonight, she'd put the mule up for the evening and washed up with a bit of time before the sun went down. Clouds littered the horizon. Maybe a storm moving in.

She'd given him a brief wave where he'd been near the barn still working with the tools she'd asked him to repair. He wasn't any good at it, not as his brother Ricky was, and had spent most of the day frustrated.

Now he ran a hand over the whiskers itching across his jaw and neck and stood, stalking toward the soddy.

He pushed open the door and found Catherine and Pop in murmured conversation. They looked up when he entered.

"Can you give me another shave, Catherine? I'm starting to itch."

She said something in a low voice to Pop, who waved her on.

She followed him silently to the stump where she'd shaved him once before. Lightning flashed, far away on the horizon. Here, the stillness before the storm weighed heavily in the air.

"Thanks," he said as she knelt at the bank to work up a lather.

Her fingers were cold when she displaced the lather onto his cheeks.

She didn't meet his gaze. Up close, he could see the tired circles beneath her eyes.

"Storm rolling in tonight," he said when he really wanted to ask her if she'd thought more about what he'd said days before.

"Hmm."

"If I was up to no good, storm might be a good cover."

Now her eyes flicked to his face and he saw surprise

and trepidation in their depths. "You still think Ralph is watching the place?"

He would've shrugged, but she had the blade at his neck and he didn't want to get cut.

"I've been watching and listening and I couldn't guarantee it, but yes. He hasn't got what he wants yet."

Whether it was just the land or Catherine herself had yet to be seen.

"Don't suppose you want to tell me what you've got hidden in the barn?"

He felt the faint tremor of the blade against his cheek, though her expression betrayed nothing. "What do you mean?"

"Behind the false wall."

Her emotionless mien remained for the barest instant, and then her shoulders slumped. Thankfully, she'd moved the blade to wipe it on the towel over his shoulder.

"How did you discover it?"

"Spent a lot of time in there these past few days and nights."

She looked defeated and resigned, and stupidly, he still wanted to comfort her, even if she didn't want his comfort.

"I found it accidentally," he said. "I don't think the structure is real sound, at least not after the recent bad weather. I was walking around, tapping on things, and noticed that wall was hollow."

Her eyes remained shadowed.

"I didn't open it up," he said. "But I'd think by now I've earned enough of your trust to know what you're protecting."

"Grain."

So he'd guessed right.

"If I guessed it, the Chestertons might've, as well."

She wiped the rest of the soap free with the corner of the towel.

"We've built the stockpile over several years, and it'll save us from starving this winter," she said. "Once it's planted, there isn't much they can do."

Not in the manner of thieving, but if they had a mind to dispose of Pop and Catherine and take their crop, that was enough to frighten Matty. Catherine and Pop had no friends. No one to take up for them. Would anyone even notice if they'd suddenly disappeared? Not likely if they never showed their faces in town.

And they were too far away from town for Matty to be any help as a deputy. How would he hear about it if Ralph assaulted her?

"So you think someone will try to come after it tonight?" she asked, her back to him as she faced the stream.

"If they expect me to be in the soddy because of the weather, they'll get a surprise," Matty responded.

"You're going to sleep out in the elements?"

He quirked a smile. "Probably won't do much sleeping, but I'll stay out in the barn. I hope it'll come to naught, but…"

Maybe that wasn't entirely true. If he caught Ralph or his younger brother on the Pooles' property, he could likely get the sheriff to prosecute them. And that way, at least, Catherine would be out of danger from those men.

But the issues with Pop remained.

Catherine woke in the middle of the night. This time, instead of Pop stirring in his bed—as it had been the past several nights—it was a loud crack of thunder that startled her.

She tried to even out her breath, tried to sink back into the bliss of sleep.

But her mind had begun whirring like a whole field full of cicadas.

Was there a chance Pop might think the thunder was enemy cannons? Would he get lost in his memories? Attack her again?

"Pop, you awake?" she asked over the drumming rain. She hated how shaky her voice emerged.

But even more, she hated the fear that pushed her to disturb him. Shouldn't she be able to feel secure in her own home?

"Yes," he answered. His voice sounded lucid, but she couldn't be sure. She couldn't see much in the inky darkness—lightning lit up the sky outside the window at short intervals, but her eyes had trouble adjusting to the darkness in between.

"All right. I was just checking on you."

He didn't respond.

A question had been plaguing her since the conversation with the cowboy down at the creek. What would Mama have done if they'd been in this same situation with Pop? Mama had stayed on the homestead to avoid rumors and mistreatment, for Catherine's sake. She'd bartered with neighbors when necessary.

Catherine tossed and turned through the storms that abated just before dawn. She must've dozed off at some point, because Pop wasn't snoring beneath his blanket. His absence worried her, and she rushed outside.

Though the rain had stopped, the sky remained gray with clouds swirling overhead. The creek rolled and frothed, high but not yet threatening to overflow its banks. She prayed it didn't. Her eyes flicked to the barn, already damaged from before. Worrisome.

Her moccasins slipped and slid across the muddy yard. The rain still fell in sheets. She almost ran into the cowboy as he emerged from the structure, his hat slightly askew and his face softened from sleep.

"Everything quiet?" she asked, reaching out for the door frame to keep herself upright.

He stretched his arms over his head, giving her a glimpse of his sidearm and flat stomach as his shirt tightened against it. "Discounting the thunder that blasted my eardrums all night? Yes."

"Did Pop come out to milk Elsie?" She glanced over his shoulder, but in the low outdoor light and the shadowed interior, she couldn't see her grandfather.

"No. He's not inside with you?"

She shook her head. The niggle of worry she felt grew. "I…spoke to him, or woke him up maybe, in the night. He seemed fine then, but now he's gone." Was she attempting to reassure the cowboy, or herself?

"He likes to wander," Matty reminded her.

"Yes, but not in the rain. And it's barely light out. And what if the storms aren't over?"

And what about Ralph Chesterton?

Perhaps the lack of sleep these past few nights was to blame for loosening her tongue, but the cowboy only touched her elbow. He didn't laugh at her unease. His eyes met hers with that steady gaze that had become so familiar as he said, "If he's not back by lunchtime, *then* we'll start to worry."

She swallowed back her unease. He was right. Of course he was right. She was overreacting, jumping to conclusions.

But after the scuffle with Pop and his silence since, she couldn't shake the feeling that something was wrong.

Pop wasn't back by lunchtime, but the rain had continued.

Matty stood in the open dugout doorway. Rain pattered on the ground above his head and on his hat.

"We don't both need to get soaked. It's likely a fool's errand anyway."

Catherine threw a glare over her shoulder from where she was bent over a small rucksack, packing provisions.

Maybe he shouldn't have said it so bluntly, but it was the truth. Pop had pulled this same disappearing act several times in the nearly two weeks since he'd been with the Pooles.

"If it were someone you loved, would you be content to stay behind?"

For some reason, today, Catherine was spooked. He was willing to go out in the weather to track down the older man, but he didn't see why they both had to go.

Catherine shoved provisions wrapped in a towel into her rucksack and tied the drawstrings.

"How far do you think he could've gone?"

She shrugged. "I didn't think he would've gone out in this weather at all. Something could have happened to him."

Or he could have happened to someone. Catherine still hadn't told him about the Chestertons. If he'd come upon one of them out there, might he have attacked them?

Catherine straightened, slinging the rucksack over her shoulder. She mashed a floppy old hat over her curls.

He sighed as she moved toward him. There would be no changing her mind.

She snapped the door closed behind them, and he trailed her across the yard and into the woods. Water dripped from the trees in a different cadence than the rain on the grass.

"If the rain keeps up, it will obliterate any tracks he might've made." He didn't bother sugarcoating it for her. She needed to know that this was pointless. Pop would come back when he was ready, just like always.

His brothers would probably laugh at him if they saw him trailing the diminutive woman like a lovesick pup.

How had he gotten here? He'd changed his view of Catherine since the beginning, that was for sure. He'd come to realize that it took a smart, independent woman to run a homestead and care for her ailing grandfather.

He ducked under a low branch and received a stream of water down the back of his neck for his trouble.

"Careful," he said when her footing slipped and she lost her balance. Grabbing a nearby sapling for support, she straightened.

What could he say to make her see that she couldn't continue on like this? Ignoring his growing affections, just trying to think of her as a friend, he couldn't see her isolation on the homestead ending well. He'd told her he was sorry for what had happened between them in their school days, but he hadn't opened up to her about those dark days after his parents had died.

Maybe if he did, she would understand how she could lean on others, depend on her neighbors—and *him*—to help as this difficult time only got worse.

But that meant opening up about the one thing he hated talking about. Jonas knew the most, but he'd shared the bare minimum with the rest of his siblings. He just couldn't talk about losing the two people who meant the most to him—and those few days when he thought he would die alone, too.

Being so reliant on the Pooles those first days after his injury had brought all that old grief back. It felt too close to share.

But if he didn't, would Catherine continue her stubborn thinking that everything was fine just the way it was right now?

Chapter Sixteen

Hours later, soaked to the bone, Catherine admitted to herself the cowboy was right.

There had been no sign of Pop. They'd started their searching in the woods near home and made increasingly larger circles with the soddy and barn in the center.

The cowboy had gone silent, though he had stayed with her. Every now and then, his hand came beneath her elbow as she traversed a treacherous patch or she slipped on the damp, leaf-strewn ground.

As the crow flies, they weren't far from home, but she hated to turn back. Her feeling that something was wrong with Pop had only intensified as they'd continued on without seeing a trace of him.

The birds that usually chirped and made plenty of racket were silent. The only sounds were of their movement as they hiked through the difficult terrain, and even that was muted.

She couldn't shake the feeling that she'd done wrong when she'd asked him if he was awake in the night. They hadn't spoken openly about his worsening nightmares or whatever condition it was that made him faint and short of breath.

And she had thought to spare him additional stress by not telling him of the Chestertons' threats. Had that been the wrong decision?

"It'll be coming on dark soon," the cowboy said, startling her out of her increasingly morose thoughts. "And your Pop might've turned back and be snug and warm in the soddy, wondering where we are."

She picked her way carefully on the rocky, leaf-covered ground. Trees and woods were at their back and right side, but to their left, the ground sloped away in a hill that had become steep. "Or he might be lying injured, cold and wet."

The cowboy started to say something else, but she couldn't listen. She turned on him. "If you're tired of hiking in wet socks, why don't *you* go back to the dugout? You're the injured one, after all, and I don't need your help."

Her inattention to her footing had been a mistake. Her boot slipped on a slick rock face, and she lost her balance. She struggled to right herself, reaching out for anything to grab on to, but there was nothing.

She tumbled down the hill, end over end. Views of green then gray sky swirled through her head. Water splattered her face.

"Catherine!"

She heard the cowboy's cry from a distance, but couldn't speak when a hard landing on her back knocked the breath from her lungs. She kept rolling, knocking her shoulder against a rock.

She scrabbled for a handhold, but the wet grasses provided nothing to hold on to.

And then finally she came to rest on a flat bed of grass. She gasped once, twice, trying to draw in a breath.

Lying on her back, her head was turned toward the hill she'd just tumbled down, and without moving she saw the cowboy scrambling down the hill, sliding on his hind end at times, his face a study in concentration.

He was upset. At her words?

I don't need your help.

It was ironic that she lay prostrate, unable to even stir herself to get up, when she'd spoken such nonsense just moments ago.

Her body's natural instinct took over, and she was able to draw a deep breath at the same time that he skidded to a stop and knelt at her side. She'd lost her hat somewhere along the way and soft raindrops washed her face.

"Catherine," he breathed. What was that expression crossing his face? His brows were drawn and his eyes intense as he reached for her. He didn't help her sit. Instead, his hands came to cup both sides of her jaw.

He was trembling.

"Are you— Can you feel your extremities?" Even his voice shook.

She inhaled and exhaled once more. "You mean the bruises I'll have come tomorrow?"

He didn't smile. His hands moved from her face to her shoulders. "Does anything in particular pain you?"

The breathless concern in his voice pinched her stomach, and she pushed up with her hands on the wet grass, sitting upright. "Just my pride."

His hands fell away, but he didn't move back as she expected. He was close enough that if she turned just so, their shoulders would bump. Close enough that water dripped off his hat and onto her muddy hand, lying in her lap.

His closeness discomfited her. "I'm fine," she said through stiff lips. Except now she needed a bath, and she was still shaken from the fall.

"I've been trying to show you that you don't always have to be." His voice was hoarse, and his hand returned to cup her cheek.

What was he—

He leaned forward, and his lips brushed hers. The kiss lasted only seconds, and she was so stunned that she sat frozen as he pulled back several inches. Still close enough that she could see the fine stubble that had grown back where she'd shaved him last night.

His hand remained cupping her jaw while his lips spread in a slow smile.

Heat boiled in her belly and flamed in her face, but for once she had no idea what to do. She didn't want to pull away.

He'd *kissed* her.

She was shaking now for a different reason, her heart in her throat. She couldn't keep her thoughts from the mad whirl they'd gone on.

What did it mean? Where did they go from here now?

She had to focus. Pop was still missing. He could be hurt.

"We…we need to go. Pop—"

Matty's eyes remained steady on her face, but he seemed to understand that she needed time to think as he helped her up with a hand beneath her elbow.

Matty had seen the flare of panic cross Catherine's face as he'd pulled back from the kiss.

Even now, as he helped her stand up and watched her stretch both legs out, checking for injuries, a knot of worry lodged behind his breastbone. His heartbeat still hadn't slowed after seeing her tumble down the hill. She could've broken a bone or even hit her head on a rock and been killed.

And as he'd slipped and slid his way down the hill after her, the realization had shocked him to his core. He cared about her. He was falling for her.

He hadn't been able to stop the kiss. He was just glad she hadn't pushed away from him or slugged him. He still half expected it, but the sidelong glance she gave him was more filled with confusion than anything else.

"You sure you don't want to go back to the dugout and dry off a little, get some rest?"

Her expression clouded, her brows drawing together. "I can't shake a feeling that something isn't right. I want to keep looking for him."

The day had worn on. Darkness would fall soon, and what then? If she insisted on continuing her search, he'd follow her. She hadn't brought a weapon, and he wore one at his waist.

More rain seeped between his hat brim and collar. There were no parts of him that remained dry.

And even with his socks squelching in his boots, he wouldn't leave her out here alone.

"I'm wishing I had my horse," he said. Riding horseback would hasten their search, allow them to cover more ground more quickly.

"Do you think you could ride now without pain?" Her question was laced with curiosity.

"I...don't know." His collarbone still tweaked occasionally, but the overall ache had dulled these past few days. He could probably manage riding without pain, as long as his mount was calm and he didn't try any daring movements.

Which meant that when his brothers came for him, he'd have no excuse not to go with them.

Even though a part of his heart would remain here with Catherine.

* * *

Twilight had fallen, everything growing darker in hues of blue and gray. The rain hadn't stopped, and Catherine slogged forward even though her moccasins felt as if they each weighed several pounds.

"We should stop," Matty said again. She knew he believed it was ridiculous to continue searching for Pop in this weather, but her dread had continued to mount as the day wore on.

Tears clogged her throat, though she cleared it so she could speak. "I don't want to stop."

But she drew to a pause in the shelter of a tall birch. Beneath the canopy of its branches, the relentless rain was more of an occasional drip.

"We won't be able to see anything in the dark," he said. "We could walk right by Pop and miss him."

"What about a lantern?" She ran a damp hand down her face. Exhaustion weighed her down, but the feeling that something was terribly wrong with Pop persisted.

She hadn't brought a lantern in the rucksack she'd packed. "Or a torch," she added belatedly.

"Doubt you'd find any stick of wood dry enough to light," he said.

Her stomach rumbled. They'd consumed the biscuits and handful of jerky she'd packed earlier in the afternoon.

But she couldn't just give up, not when Pop could be injured.

Matty's hand closed over her elbow. "What if we go back and get a few hours' sleep?"

It was a good idea.

After a slight hesitation, he went on, "And I was thinking I might ride to Elliott's place and ask if he could spare his hands. If they're willing to help us search, we could cover more ground."

Her head jerked up. She searched his face, but beneath the shadow of the tree and the rapidly darkening sky, she couldn't make out his expression.

As if he sensed her uncertainty, he reached out and clasped her hand.

"How can you be sure… Can we trust them?"

He squeezed her hand. "If it was any of my pa's neighbors, I would say an unconditional yes. But if something has really happened to Pop, we may have to chance it."

He believed her that Pop wouldn't have just run off, not in this weather. He believed her that something was wrong.

Silly tears burned her eyes and one overflowed, rolling down her cheeks. She used her wrist to brush it away, breaking the connection between them.

She didn't know what to think since this afternoon. Since that kiss. Did he really see her that way…? Could he possibly be sweet on her?

Her? Homemade happy Cathy?

"I thought…you wouldn't want to go searching with me again. That you'd think I was foolish."

She started away from the tree, back out into the relentless rain. Though she remained upset and uneasy about not finding Pop, it would be a relief to be inside and out of the elements.

Matty followed, as faithful as ever. They were maybe three-fourths of a mile from home. A hike that would normally take less than an hour.

He didn't speak until they'd climbed the top of the hill she'd fallen down earlier. "When I was nine, when the sickness came over my family…it was the winter after you'd come to school… I don't like to talk about my parents' deaths, but maybe there's a lesson to be learned here."

He who was usually so jovial, never lacking for words, seemed unable to find them now.

"I'd succumbed to the fever first. When I finally came out of it, came back to an awareness of myself, it was so *quiet*."

She skirted a cedar, brushing against a lower branch, the motion sending a shower of raindrops falling to the ground.

"There was no fire burning in the stove. No sound of my ma's knitting needles clicking. My pa wasn't a quiet man. He was always talking. Always."

Perhaps Matty had inherited that trait from his father, then.

"And I realized I didn't hear his voice or his laugh. I was lying in my bed, quilt soaked with sweat, and I was scared."

She stopped. His voice... The emotion underlying his tone told her how serious he was, telling her this, that maybe he still felt scared thinking back to that time.

"I was weak as a newborn foal, but I made myself get outta bed. I found their bodies, and I knew. No one was coming for me."

She didn't think, she just reached out for him. Where his hand had closed over hers earlier, offering her comfort, she now repeated the action, taking his larger hand in hers.

He didn't pull her closer, didn't pull away. Just accepted the comfort she offered.

When he spoke again, his voice was coarse with emotion. "I think your Pop is real blessed to have you to come after him."

She had to swallow the lump in her throat before she could form any answer for him. "I'm real glad someone did come along and find you."

He squeezed her hand, the same way he had earlier.

And it was nice to have someone to hold on to. To know that she wasn't alone. She didn't know if it could last past the next few days, but for this very moment, she couldn't let go.

Complete darkness had fallen now. It was going to be difficult to find their way back, even though she could recognize the familiar landscape.

She didn't let go of Matty's hand as she carefully picked her way through the woods, knowing they would have to be careful crossing the creek when they came upon it. It would be swollen from today's rains, and in the dark...

An unnatural noise startled her.

Chapter Seventeen

"What was that?" Catherine's voice held a fine tremor. She'd gone still beside him.

He hadn't heard a thing, but let go of her hand and rested his own hand at his hip, just above the butt of his revolver.

"Did you hear it?" she asked, her voice barely a breath.

"No."

The rain had finally stopped as it had gone dark and now only occasional sounds of water dripping from the trees around them came. In the distance, a bullfrog croaked. Farther even than that, some kind of night bird chirped.

Beside him, Catherine barely breathed. Probably straining her ears to hear. Was she hoping so hard that they'd stumble on Pop that she'd imagined it?

Or could it be someone else out there? Ralph, spying again? Or Floyd?

He didn't want to think about them stumbling onto someone with nefarious intentions in the dark—especially if that other someone was armed. Not for the first time today, he wished for his brothers and his pa. They would've been able to cover much more ground today—and they were handy in situations like this, where he didn't know if he'd need a couple more guns to protect Catherine.

A low sound came. A hum? A moan? It was several yards away. In the dark, here in the woods, he couldn't make out the landscape, and he couldn't remember well enough from when they'd circled through here earlier. Had there been a large fallen log over that way?

Catherine started to move in that direction, but he stopped her with an outreached hand. It landed at her waist, and she froze. He nudged her closer.

"Wait." He whispered the word, not wanting to alert whoever was out there to their presence.

He could feel her panting breaths at his collar, warm against his rain-chilled skin, sending gooseflesh spreading down his chest, beneath his shirt.

"It might be someone else," he whispered, his mouth close to her ear, or as near as he could estimate in the darkness.

"Who's that? I'm armed, ya corncrackers."

The growl was definitely Pop's voice, and Matty felt a rush of relief. They'd found him.

Catherine's palm rested against his chest for a brief moment before she began moving through the darkness. "Pop? It's us. Catherine and Matty."

"Catherine?"

Matty wanted to hold her back, knowing that if Pop was lost in one of his memories, he could hurt her, as he had the other day.

But he just followed a pace behind, hoping to stay close enough to intervene if he had to.

"It's me, Pop," Catherine said. "We were worried about you when you were gone in the rain all day."

She rounded a darker, large shadow—the fallen tree

that Matty remembered—moving more slowly now. His boots crunched over broken tree limbs.

"Where are you?"

"Here, girl."

Pop sounded lucid, which was a blessing in itself.

Catherine knelt, her movement so sudden that Matty almost tripped over her.

"Are you hurt? Where'd you go today?"

"Ssh. They're out there."

The hair on the nape of Matty's neck stood up. He reached for Catherine, intending to put his hand on her shoulder and stop her, but in the darkness he missed completely, his hand flailing ineffectively as if to keep her from Pop.

"Who, Pop?"

"I went out to attend to my personal business and I saw someone hidin' in the woods down by the creek— right where it bends, you know the good fishin' spot."

Matty tensed. He'd guessed that Ralph might make an attempt at coming onto Catherine's property during the storms. To what purpose? Had Pop scared him off? Or was he still out there?

He bent low, coming shoulder to shoulder with Catherine. "Did you get a look at the man?"

He held his breath as he waited to see if Pop would describe a Confederate soldier.

"It looked like the younger Chesterton boy. I didn't get close enough to see him—he ran off, and I was trying to catch up with him when I fell."

Catherine must have turned toward him, because he felt her warm breath on his jaw when she spoke. "He's hurt. Favoring his left leg."

"I don't think it's broken," Pop said, but now his voice was rough—with pain? Catherine must be prodding his injury. "I couldn't walk on it, and I kept thinking I heard voices during the day. This place gave me the most cover."

Had those voices been his and Catherine's as they'd searched for Pop? How had they not noticed him? They'd crossed within twenty feet of the fallen tree, but then, if Pop had thought they were someone else, he would have tried to make himself *less* noticeable, not more.

"I've been hiding all day. Figured the leg'd be a bit better tomorrow and I could make my way back home then."

Matty's mind spun. If the Chestertons had been out in the woods today, might they have tried something at the homestead? Had they watched Matty and Catherine searching for Pop? Used the advantage to try to steal the wheat Catherine was worried about?

"Thought I saw a lantern a little bit ago. Wondered how you were keeping it lit."

Matty went still.

Catherine must've had the same thought, because she said in a low voice, "Pop, we didn't have a lantern."

The three of them went silent as realization washed over them.

Matty's hand went to his gun for a second time. His heart beat in his throat.

Had they been too noisy getting to Pop? Was someone watching them even now?

Catherine touched his sleeve.

He leaned toward her. "I'm going to scout back toward the house."

"What if—" Pop was right and someone was out there?

"I'm armed," he reminded her. "And I wish I could carry Pop back home, but with my collarbone…" He couldn't. "I'll get the mule and make my way back once I'm sure everything is clear."

Catherine wasn't given a chance to argue as Matty bussed her cheek with a kiss and disappeared into the night.

She might've said she knew the property better than he did, but he wore the badge and she didn't know if she could point a gun at someone, much less shoot if the situation called for it.

"Is it your ankle?" she asked Pop, kneeling on the ground next to him. "Not the leg?"

"It don't feel broken," said Pop, his voice barely audible. "Just too sore to put my weight on it."

"What were you thinking, going after someone?" She wrapped both hands around his left knee and squeezed, slowly moving her hands down his leg and repeating the pressure.

Pop grunted as her hands hit just above his boot. His leg was swollen and hot against her skin, even through the layer of his soaked pants. "I was thinking about protecting my family. Protecting you."

"Were you really? Or were you caught in your memories again, thinking it was an enemy soldier?" The words were out before she'd really thought about them.

Pop went still for a minute. She couldn't tell if he was even breathing. "I believed I was lucid, but…" He let out a harsh breath. "I don't know. Maybe I only imagined I saw someone."

Her heart performed a slow flip in her chest. They never spoke of his episodes after he'd calmed. "Or maybe you didn't."

She hadn't planned to tell him about the tracks Matty had found, but after a day spent worrying for his health, the spill she'd taken and her wildly rolling emotions over Matty…the words had slipped out. She told him all of it. Their visits to the Chestertons and Elliotts, the repeated visits and proposals. The threats.

He breathed a sharp, shaky breath. "So maybe some of what I was imagining was real?"

She hadn't thought about it before, but, "What if you've been sensing the Chestertons sneaking around? What if it's made your delusions worse?"

He was silent as they both contemplated it. Now that he knew about the Chestertons, was there a chance that Pop's mental faculties could improve?

"What about your breathing troubles…? When you feel faint…"

He hesitated, but she waited, let the silence draw him out.

"That might've happened today, as well."

Her breath caught in her throat. "Oh, Pop." Tears burned her eyes.

He cuffed her shoulder. "What're you going to do about that cowboy?"

She sniffed, not following where he'd gone with the conversation. "What do you mean?"

"I've seen the way you watch him."

Heat slipped into her face, even though it was dark and he couldn't possibly see her blush.

"It's just because he's a novelty. I'm not used to having another person around. It's been years since Mama passed."

Pop was quiet for a moment. "It's been…different, having another man around the place. Makes me feel better that you haven't had to take all the burden of running the place. He's… I guess you can count on him."

Catherine couldn't help but think of Matty's steady

presence. He'd been beside her all day, even though she got the feeling he hadn't believed they would find Pop.

She...liked it. Liked knowing that he was out there protecting her, even now.

Liked him.

But the niggling remembrance that he would be leaving soon remained. What if she allowed herself to depend on him, got used to it...and then he left?

He didn't know that she'd been born to an unwed mother. She clearly remembered the whispers when she and Mama had gone to town.

She could easily imagine being snubbed by Luella McKeever again, and possibly all of the friends in her quilting circle, if she had one. Because of Catherine's parentage. Something she couldn't help and couldn't change.

Worse would be if the way Matty looked at her—sometimes exasperated, sometimes with that warmth that took residence in her midsection and spread outward—changed. Would his eyes turn cool when he knew the truth?

She couldn't allow herself to depend on him. Pop couldn't survive in town, and she needed to remain self-sufficient if she were going to survive the next several years here on the homestead.

Chapter Eighteen

More than an hour after he'd left Catherine and Pop, everything was quiet as Matty made his way into the clearing just behind the barn. He'd taken the long way around, keeping his eyes and ears focused for any hint of the lantern that Pop thought he'd seen, any shadows moving where they shouldn't be or any out-of-the-ordinary noises.

There was nothing. Had Pop dreamed it all in a fevered hallucination?

But the tracks that Matty had seen before were no dream. And neither were Ralph Chesterton's threats.

He visited the house first, bundling two of the quilts together and taking time to stoke the fire so that when they got Pop back they wouldn't have to build it from scratch. Nothing inside had been disturbed.

The barn was the same. The cow and mule stood placidly in their stalls, dry as could be. Unlike him. The chickens cooed softly from their perches.

The mule didn't protest as he found the harness Catherine had used with the plow and connected the buckles. It was harder in the dark, but Matty didn't want to draw attention with a light if someone was watching the house.

He retraced his steps back to Pop and Catherine slowly, leading the mule by its halter and stopping every so often to listen for sounds that didn't belong.

The night was dark, the moon and stars still obscured by clouds, though it had stopped raining at last. He felt as if he was steaming in his wet clothes after all the maneuvering and walking.

For a moment, he got turned around and didn't recognize his surroundings, but then got his bearings with the curve of the creek. He splashed through the shallows, noting how they seemed deeper than usual. Normally the water level wouldn't be above his boots, but tonight it was nearly to his knees.

He heard Catherine's melodic tones before he could even make out the outline of the large fallen tree.

"Hullo the tree," he called out. "It's me."

There was a beat of silence, and then Pop growled, "About time."

He reined in the mule as he neared, making sure it wouldn't step on Pop. He tied it off on a low-hanging branch.

"You run into any trouble?" Pop asked.

"No. Didn't see or hear any sign of anyone else. The house and barn were untouched."

Matty reached for the blankets he'd tied onto the back of the mule and untangled them. With one hand, he patted the top of the horizontal tree and found it only slightly damp, so he set the blankets down on top.

"Let me help you stand," Catherine said.

There was motion where her voice had come from, and Pop groaned. Matty stepped in that direction to assist, coming on the opposite side from Catherine. When he threaded his arm behind Pop's back, his hand bumped

Catherine's. Together, they helped Pop hop the few steps to the mule.

Matty guided Pop's hands to the harness, so he'd have something to grip. He bent over and threaded his fingers together, bracing himself to take the man's weight.

Catherine's palm rested on his back. "Your collarbone."

"It'll be all right. It's just for a second. You help him so he doesn't lose his balance."

Pop's booted foot rested in Matty's cupped hands for a moment, and then the weight was gone as Pop swung his leg over the mule's back.

Catherine steadied him, her shoulder brushing Matty's chest as he straightened. His collarbone had protested the movement, but the pain hadn't been nearly what it was before. For a moment, his heart beat in his throat. He had no excuse to stay when his brothers came back for him.

None except the way he felt about Catherine.

She said something soft to Pop while Matty turned back to the fallen tree. He grabbed one of the quilts and brought it to Pop.

"Here. Let's wrap you up a little, keep you warm for the way home." He tossed the blanket around Pop's shoulders, and Catherine helped the older man tuck it under his armpits so it would stay on.

When she turned back to him, Matty let his hands rest on her shoulders. "I brought a quilt for you, too. Figured you might want to switch it out for your slicker."

He sensed more than saw her looking up at him from the close proximity. He knew the kiss he'd bestowed on her earlier had confused her—he'd seen the panic in her face.

They were slightly behind Pop on the mule. He wouldn't be able to see them unless he turned completely around. And in the dark, he would only be able to see their shadowy silhouettes anyway.

"Want me to help you off with your slicker?"

"All right," she whispered, turning her back beneath his hands on her shoulders.

She was soaked, like him, and he held the slicker as she pulled her arms free. The wet material clung to her as if it never wanted to let go.

He could empathize.

Finally, she knocked free of the slicker. He tossed it on the back of the mule behind Pop and retrieved the quilt. He swung it around her shoulders, bringing the two corners to meet just beneath her chin.

She reached up and he dared to twine their fingers together even as he hung on to the quilt.

Catherine's heart was pounding as she stood so near Matty. She couldn't see his features in the darkness, but she could imagine those dancing eyes and the smile that had become dear to her.

"Thank you," she whispered, allowing his clasp of her hands.

The simple words seemed so ineffective for everything he'd done for her today and through the night. Searching for Pop, scouting for danger and retrieving the mule, and then his thoughtfulness on top of everything.

He'd brought her a quilt. It was a simple act of kindness, but one she hadn't expected. Since her mother's death, she and Pop had become equals in caring for each other, sharing chores. And these past years, as Pop's health and mind had begun to decline, she'd been forced to take on more and more.

When had she stopped expecting simple kindnesses altogether?

His breath brushed her forehead. They were so close that if he ducked his head, he could kiss her again.

Her mind had worried over that first kiss all day, but now she realized that she would welcome it if he kissed her again. Was that foolish, knowing he was leaving soon?

They were still connected through their hands. Maybe she tugged him closer, or maybe he leaned of his own accord, but suddenly, his breath was hot against her mouth, and then his lips touched hers.

This time, she didn't freeze. She returned the sweet pressure of his lips, tilted her chin up. He exhaled sharply through his nose. As if her response pleased him.

The moment suspended between them.

"We gonna move anytime soon?"

Pop's gruff voice was an intrusion. She was breathless from Matty's kiss and the emotion swirling through her. Matty squeezed her hands once more, his forehead pressing against hers for a brief moment.

"Patience, old man," Matty said. "Remember, you'd be stuck out here all night if we hadn't come for you."

But Pop *was* hurt. This wasn't the time for kissing—no matter how much she might wish differently—so she clasped the quilt to keep it wrapped about her shoulders and moved toward the mule's head.

"I'll scout out ahead," Matty murmured, brushing her elbow with his hand as he strode past.

Emotion swelled in her chest as they started off. Matty walked several yards ahead as she guided the mule over the dark ground. It was slow going with no moon out and what stars might've been visible covered with clouds.

But she wasn't alone.

She'd never expected to come of something with Matty. Not knowing how he'd acted as a child, and not with her circumstances on the homestead and caring for Pop.

But something had changed between them, and she couldn't bring herself to regret it.

There were still obstacles. She must find a way to tell him about her parentage. But surely if he cared enough to kiss her... She had hope that he would be understanding.

Also, she knew his place was with his family and back in Bear Creek. She couldn't picture herself there. Or Pop.

Not to mention the troubles she was having around the homestead.

But why would God have brought him into her life if there wasn't the possibility of more for them?

She wasn't good at depending on others. On the homestead, nothing got done unless she took the initiative. Pop and Mama had taught her to rely on herself, to take care of herself.

But these past days, leaning on Matty...

What if they could be more than friends? Maybe in a few months or years, if things changed with Pop, Matty could come courting. She could find a place in his family...

Despite the obstacles, hope filtered in her heart like sunlight through trees in the woods. What if...?

She'd kissed him back.

Though he kept his ears and eyes attuned for anything out of place, Matty hardly registered the landscape passing.

Catherine had kissed him back in those stolen moments in the dark. And given him hope that his growing feelings weren't one-sided.

He was going to force Ralph to stop accosting Catherine, and he was going to figure out a way to come calling.

Dawn was lighting the sky as they trekked through the offshoot of the creek. Catherine gasped, and he looked back to her. Thanks to the lightening sky he could see she was knee-deep in the stream. She pulled the mule out the opposite side and stopped. Pop looked as if he was dozing, even sitting bareback on the mule.

Matty moved back toward her. "What's wrong?"

She handed over the mule's halter lead to Matty and bent to swipe at her pant legs. "My feet had just started to dry," she complained.

He gave her a sympathetic smile, unable to keep his eyes off the way her curls had gone wiry, probably thanks to the dampness. "We'll get you home and dried out."

And since they'd found Pop on their way home, they wouldn't have to go back out after him. Matty was looking forward to doing what chores couldn't be put off—like milking the cow—and rolling up in a quilt himself for a few hours' sleep.

He kept the mule's lead when Catherine would have taken it from him, instead taking her hand. It was light enough now they should be able to see danger.

She walked beside him, tilted her head up once to look at him, and he squeezed her hand. *This.* This was what he'd been looking for with Luella—or maybe what she'd realized he couldn't give her.

Wanting to protect Catherine. Hoping to give her comfort just by being at her side. Getting through difficulties together.

He was paying more attention to the woman beside him and not enough to their surroundings, because he was caught off guard when she stiffened beside him and then froze.

His head came up, his opposite hand dropping the mule's lead and automatically reaching for his weapon.

But it wasn't a thief that her eyes were locked on.

"No!" she cried out.

The barn had collapsed. Or part of it had. On the side closest to the stream, the outside wall had fallen. The roof had separated from the supporting outside wall, which leaned precariously inward.

Catherine pulled free of his hand and started running toward the structure.

"Cath— Wait!"

But she didn't. Matty vacillated between chasing her and helping Pop. Finally, he turned to the older man.

"Catherine, don't go inside!" he called over his shoulder. He didn't hold out much hope of her listening, but reached up to help Pop off the mule.

"It could come down on her head," he muttered to himself.

Pop kicked his good leg over the mule's side and slid to the ground, Matty steadying him once he was on his feet. "Go after her," the older man ordered.

He'd seen the danger, too.

Matty rushed across the yard just as Catherine was squeezing inside, her back brushing against the post holding up the far side of the barn.

"Cath—"

He spared a glance around, noting that hens had nested in the branches of the nearest tree overhanging the stream. Had they all managed to get out? Likewise, the milk cow had squeezed out somehow. She grazed off in the distance, at an angle where he hadn't been able to see her until he'd come even with the barn.

There was debris up against the corner where the collapse had happened. The stream was only inches from the barn. It must've risen from the lengthy driving rains they'd battled yesterday and then begun to lower again.

He could hear Catherine muttering to herself and ducked inside, clamping a hand on his hat when it brushed against the low roof and threatened to fall off. Dust sent him into a coughing spasm.

It took a long moment for his eyes to adjust to the dimness inside.

Light streamed through a hole where the back wall had come free and the roof had fallen inward. The stall walls had collapsed and hay was scattered over every surface. He couldn't see the mismatched items or even the barn floor for the soil and wood pieces strewn about.

There was nothing here to salvage. But Catherine had her back to him, fumbling with a panel on the back wall, just beneath where sunlight streamed in.

He picked his way carefully toward her. They should get out of here. Wood creaked, as if the one wall that remained protested having to stand up alone.

"Catherine—"

She ignored him. "It can't be gone," she muttered.

"It's not safe in here." He reached for her, but when his hand closed over her shoulder she shrugged him off. Something was wrong.

"It looks like the cow and chickens got out all right. We can clear some of the beams and dig out your junk—"

She didn't respond to his quip and his shoulders sank lower.

"It's *got* to be here." He heard the desperation in her voice even if she wouldn't look at him.

"Cath. *Catherine.*"

The tenor of his voice must've finally gotten to her, because she went still, both palms pressing against the wood.

"What do you need me to do?"

She shot him a tight-lipped smile over her shoulder.

"I have to see—I have to get into the wall. Can you lift that beam?"

She pointed to where a heavy crossbeam leaned against the top of the board she was attempting to remove. He shoved a shoulder beneath it, praying that what remained of the ceiling wouldn't come down on his head.

He pushed up, biting back a grunt when his collarbone twinged. He managed to lift it enough for her to wiggle a board free from where she'd created the false wall. Then another.

She gasped.

"I can't hold it—" he bit out.

She shook her head, backing away a half step.

He released the beam and it settled back into place, sending a rain of dust on top of his head.

"It's gone."

He barely heard her words, she'd spoken so softly.

He moved to where she'd stood and looked into the space that had been revealed when she'd removed the planks.

He had a clear view out to the risen stream. The spot where she'd hidden her grain stockpile must've been swept away by the floodwaters.

The structure creaked ominously again. Another rain of dust fell on his head and sent him coughing into his elbow again.

"We've got to go." He turned back to Catherine, who stood stock-still. One hand covered her mouth. She'd gone pale and he didn't like the bleak expression in her eyes.

"C'mon."

She let him take her arm and guide her back outside. Her compliance worried him even more.

He took both her elbows in his hands. Unlike during

the dark part of morning, she didn't lean toward him. She only clutched her midsection tighter, as if she was barely holding herself together.

"Catherine, talk to me."

Chapter Nineteen

The seed wheat was gone.

Catherine felt numb from the inside out.

She couldn't believe it. How could this have happened?

After the flooding had destroyed their crop, the seed wheat had been her only hope for them to make it through the winter months. Without the grain and hay the wheat would produce, she and Pop wouldn't have flour. And there would be no hay for the animals to subsist on during the long winter months when they couldn't graze from the fields.

They had no cash. Nothing to trade.

How would they make it through?

Matty was speaking, but she couldn't focus on his words. She felt the weight of his hands at her elbows. More, she felt the weight of expectation.

So much that she couldn't bear it.

She stepped away and watched his arms fall back to his sides.

He sighed. "I know you're upset, but—"

Upset. The word didn't begin to reach through her numbness to the bitter devastation she felt.

"That wheat was going to get us through the winter," she whispered.

"I'll help you figure something out. I'll fix this—"

She let her eyes slide away from the cowboy. Pop stood next to the mule where they'd left him, but she could see the pinched lines of his face. Her stomach constricted.

How could she depend on Matty when he was going to leave? She'd been foolish to believe that there could be anything between them. They were too different.

Even now, when she knew what this devastating loss meant, he wanted to look on the bright side.

"This isn't your problem to fix," she said. "I have Pop to think of, and you'll soon be returning home."

"Cath—" The cowboy's face darkened.

She couldn't bear his presence, not in the face of this loss.

"I need to care for Pop," she said. She turned and walked away, leaving the cowboy near the barn.

Two days later, Matty still couldn't get Catherine to open up to him.

She'd avoided him yesterday. He'd spent the day attempting to dig out the barn, salvaging what wood he could and unearthing Catherine's junk piece by piece.

It was backbreaking work, and he was sore today. But he wouldn't take it back.

Maybe she thought he was going to walk away because she'd had this setback. He didn't know what she was thinking because she'd shut him out. And that was starting to frustrate him.

He finished washing up the breakfast dishes—earlier she'd stuffed her mouth full of bacon and rushed out the door with two biscuits in hand—and dumped the dishwater outside.

Pop had stayed in bed with his leg propped up and was grumbling to himself when Matty brought the tub back indoors.

"I thought I'd go out and check on Catherine."

"Yes," Pop agreed.

"Any advice?"

Pop looked at him long enough to make Matty uncomfortable.

"I only want to help her," Matty said. He didn't know how much Pop had figured out about their kiss during the early morning, or if Pop could tell how much he'd grown to care for Catherine over these past weeks.

"Catherine's mama was an independent spirit. She had to be."

The cryptic words brought to mind something Catherine had said days ago. That it had been the three of them.

"It ain't easy for Catherine to lean on somebody. She ain't had much practice."

He nodded. He knew that. He just needed her to trust him long enough so he could prove he was strong enough to carry her. That leaning on someone didn't mean she was weak.

He straightened his shoulders and pushed out of the dugout. Where would Catherine hide today?

Catherine loitered at the edge of the plowed wheat field. The loss of the seed wheat had finally sunk in.

This would be a hard winter. They'd find a way to get through, whether it was trading the mule or possibly her finding work. She'd already thought of asking Harold Elliott if he'd take her on as a hand.

It was the death of the germ of a dream that had just begun that she grieved more. With Matty at her side as they'd found and rescued Pop, she'd begun to think things she never should have thought.

What it might be like to have someone to depend on. Friends.

Maybe even learn to read.

Not to have to work through Pop's declining health on her own.

But those were all the silly dreams of a child. The only thing she had to look forward to was a long year— years—of work.

There would be no time for social calls.

And what man would want to be with a woman who had no time for socializing?

Especially a woman with her background.

Even if Matty wanted to be with her now—which she still couldn't fully believe—it wouldn't last.

It was better to harden her heart and send him on his way now.

A sharp whistle and the sound of hoofbeats brought her head up.

Two riders and a third riderless horse approached. The men were dressed similar to how Matty dressed— trousers and woolen shirts, boots and Stetsons—but she didn't recognize either of them.

Should she scream? Run for the dugout?

Pop would be so disappointed that she hadn't seen or heard them coming. She'd been so distracted by her thoughts that they were almost upon her and she hadn't reacted one bit.

"Halloo!" called one of the men as she remained frozen in indecision.

An answering whistle came from behind her, and she whirled to see Matty striding confidently toward her.

"My brothers," he called to her.

Maybe he'd seen her panic in her stance, or maybe he just knew her well enough to know she was thinking of bolting.

"Two of them, at least," he said as he drew abreast of her.

He was calm as the men drew up a few yards away and dismounted. Was he unsurprised to see them? Or just hiding it? He'd told her in the beginning that they would come for him.

How had they found him?

A man with blond hair peeking from beneath his Stetson, a well-trimmed beard and twinkling blue eyes was the first to approach, cuffing Matty on the shoulder. "Good to see you, little brother."

Behind them, a younger man of eighteen or so took off his hat. His brown hair was matted to his head. Brown eyes peered at her and his mouth formed a wide smile.

"Is this her? Catherine?" The younger brother moved forward with his hand outstretched.

His question crystallized Catherine's suspicion. How did he know her name?

She shot a look at Matty, who wore a chagrined expression. "This is Edgar," he motioned to the brother closest to him. "And that knucklehead is Seb. Yes, this is Catherine."

She accepted the young man's outstretched hand.

"You've been here before?" she guessed.

Now Seb had the grace to look abashed, even though he hadn't lost his smile that hinted at orneriness.

"You didn't tell her?" the brother named Edgar asked. He shoved Matty's shoulder, making Matty wince slightly.

He huffed. "It's complicated."

She propped her hands on her hips, her mouth twisting. If Matty's brothers had been here before, it meant he could have gone home with them before.

He must've read some of her thoughts as they crossed her face because his hand flexed at his side. "I couldn't have ridden back with them. And I wanted a few more days to try to make sure Chesterton wouldn't bother you."

His words battered her. He could've gone days ago. The omission changed everything.

"Our ma was pretty riled when we didn't bring him home with us," Seb offered. She was aware of the way his gaze bounced between her and Matty, watching them closely.

"You convince the guy to leave her alone?" Edgar asked.

Matty shook his head. He knocked his hat back and rubbed the bridge of his nose. "I need a minute with Catherine. You mind?"

Edgar and Seb exchanged a glance that said much without words, but they didn't comment as Matty touched her elbow and propelled her several yards away.

"I can't believe you didn't mention that your brothers had found you," she snapped.

"I wanted to stay. Our friendship…had begun to mean something to me, and I didn't want to leave without discovering what I could about the threat to you."

He looked so sincere that she had to swallow hard and remember all the reasons it wouldn't work between them.

"I'm still concerned about Chesterton—"

She waved off his words, interrupting him. "The seed wheat is gone."

"But what about the land—"

She cleared her throat. Stuffed all those hopes and dreams far, far inside where she couldn't feel them anymore.

"We both knew this day was coming. You should go."

Matty wanted to reach out for Catherine, but didn't dare, not after she'd pushed him away for the past two days, and not with his brothers looking on.

He could feel the almost palpable touch of Edgar's and Seb's intense curiosity. And he was sure that they would report anything he said or did to his ma and the rest of the brothers at home.

But he didn't care all that much. If he had an inkling that Catherine would open up to him if he fell on his knees, he'd do it.

He hated thinking about leaving her vulnerable to the Chestertons.

"Chesterton made some pretty direct threats against you. I doubt he only wanted the wheat." His voice was rough with the emotion he was holding back. Not only his concern for her, but the feelings he thought she shared.

Her chin came up. "Pop and I will take care of ourselves."

She'd been taking care of herself for years.

His throat started to burn. "I wanted— Can I come back and visit?"

Her eyes darted away, her gaze skittering over his shoulder. "I don't think that's a good idea."

Edgar and Seb conversed in low tones behind them

and she glanced over her shoulder, as if the reminder of their presence bothered her.

"Things will be busy around here," she said. "And you'll be back at your job."

"That doesn't mean I won't have time to ride out for a visit."

She took a deep breath and he braced himself for her next argument.

She looked right at him. "I'm illegitimate."

For a moment, her words didn't register. She must've seen his confusion in his drawn brows, because she went on.

"My mother was never married." She spoke the words in a stilted tone. "I never knew my father."

He shook his head, denying that what she said mattered in any way that would push her away from him.

Suddenly, her fierce independence and desire to stay away from town made more sense. His mind rushed back to their school days. He'd never heard a word about her parentage, but he remembered vividly her tears on that last day he'd seen her. Had one of the other children found out? Had they teased her about it? Hurt her? Or something else?

He started to reach for her. "That doesn't matter to me—"

She knocked his hand away. "It matters a great deal to me." Her gaze didn't waver. "I won't go into town. I won't attend socials. And I have Pop to think about. I think you should go."

"Catherine, wait." He reached for her elbow when she would've turned away, and he caught sight of the slight tremble in her lower lip. "I don't want to just leave like this."

She jerked her arm from his grasp. "Goodbye."
She strode away toward the dugout.
And left him to turn back to his brothers. Alone.

Chapter Twenty

"Get on!" Matty used his hat to slap a slow-moving calf, urging it out of the corral. Behind him, the branding fire burned hot, and he was wielding the iron today in deference for his injury.

He wiped his forehead with his sleeve before replacing his hat where it belonged.

"This the last batch?" he called out to Oscar, who was closing the gate after sending ten more animals into the corral. They worked in one of the corrals on the far edge of his pa's property.

Oscar acknowledged him with a grunt.

They'd started before sunup with only a short break at noon, and now it was almost sunset. His eyes were gritty with smoke and dust. He'd sweated through his shirt by lunchtime. He was exhausted.

Maybe he'd be able to sleep tonight.

Or maybe not. Thoughts of Catherine plagued him day and night. It hadn't even been a week, but he couldn't keep his thoughts from returning to the homestead, especially those moments in the dark with Pop nearby. When she'd let him hold her close.

"You ready to talk about it yet?" Jonas asked from near his elbow where his knee held the calf in place.

"What?" Matty grunted.

"Whatever's got you moping around these past few days."

"It's that gal," Seb called out from where he'd roped the next calf inside the corral. "Catherine."

Matty gritted his teeth. Their final goodbye had left him too raw. He didn't want to talk about her.

"Little brother fell in love, huh?" asked Oscar as he helped Seb bring the calf to the ground.

Matty ground his teeth harder. During his weeks at the Pooles', all the times he'd wanted to be back home among his noisy, rambunctious family, now all he felt was frustrated. As if he was a square peg that didn't fit the round hole of his family anymore.

He hadn't been to see Luella since he'd returned home. Those last days at the Pooles' he hadn't even spared her a thought. And the more he thought about it now, the way she'd left things had been final. Hadn't it?

"I've been holding off your ma," Jonas said, as calm and implacable as usual. "But her patience is gonna run out. Just warning ya."

Maxwell had left Hattie in charge of the clinic and had been working alongside his brothers all day. He looked up at Matty from across the calf's shoulder as Matty pushed the red-hot brand into its hide. Maxwell didn't have to say anything. His small smile said enough.

And Matty vividly remembered years ago ganging up on Maxwell with the rest of his brothers and giving him a dunking when he'd been out of his mind over Hattie.

He could only hope Jonas's presence would prevent something like that from happening today.

"I'm still mad I didn't get to meet her," Breanna added

from her perch on the corral rail. She was in her element, in trousers and on horseback all day. "I wanted to go…"

"Edgar and Seb know the way," Davy put in from his perch astride his horse, just outside the corral. "We could make a social call."

"Oh!" Breanna exclaimed.

"No!" Matty barked.

He hadn't meant for it to come out quite so harshly, but everyone went silent.

He felt as if he'd hit his face with the branding iron, as if steam was rising from his skin. So much for hiding his feelings for Catherine.

Slowly, he raised his head.

They were all staring at him. Jonas and Maxwell with expressions of compassion, Davy, Oscar, Edgar, Seb and Breanna with ornery grins.

"When're we going to meet her?" Oscar asked.

Matty shook his head. "You can't. Her grandpop— She doesn't want to see me."

"Aw, c'mon—"

His brothers protested even as Jonas shushed them and refocused them on finishing the grueling task.

The final few calves branded, Matty hung back. He was seriously contemplating taking a dunk in the creek instead of following the rest to clean up in the bunkhouse before the family would gather for supper.

It was difficult to be around his family when all he wanted was to be back on Catherine's homestead.

Was she getting any rest? Working herself to death trying to figure out a way to get a wheat crop to last them through the winter?

Was she still being threatened?

The steers turned loose out into the field, his brothers

had ridden ahead, leaving Jonas and Matty to walk home together.

They walked in companionable silence for a bit. He appreciated that his father was a good listener. And that he didn't try to fill the silence with advice or teasing.

Matty sighed. He took off his hat and used the other hand to run his fingers through his sweat-matted hair. "I can't stop thinking about her," he finally admitted.

"You care about this girl?"

He let his eyes slide to the far horizon. "Yes." The answer was easier than he'd expected. "But it's complicated. Her grandpop is aging and...sometimes imagines things that aren't there. Doesn't like to be around people."

Jonas hummed in his throat. Still listening.

"And...Catherine has a reason to be distrustful of some folks in Bear Creek. I don't know if she'd ever want to be a part of the community, not like our family is."

Jonas seemed to consider his words as they climbed the last hill toward the house and barn.

"Do you think there could be a time she'd come around? Maybe if she spent some time with folks in a smaller setting—" like their family? "—she'd start to like it."

Matty shrugged. He didn't know if Pop would ever come around, not with his history. And he risked alienating Catherine if it backfired.

Hat hanging by his side, he rubbed the back of his neck with his opposite hand. "There's more. She's in a bad way—or her homestead is. She needs a wheat crop to make it through the winter and her barn needs to be rebuilt."

Jonas didn't speak for a long moment, and Matty turned his head toward his father.

One side of Jonas's mouth quirked in a half smile. "Seems your brothers are right. You've never been this discombobulated by a gal before."

"What do you mean?"

"You're so twisted around you can't see straight."

That about summed it up.

Jonas clapped him on the shoulder. Matty's collarbone barely twinged.

"What if there was a way to ease her back into society—and solve her most pressing problems. Might help her a little with trustin' others."

Matty let the idea take root. Hope soared. What if his pa was right? What if there was a way he could be with Catherine?

"What did you have in mind?" he asked.

Catherine washed up at the creek, the cool water soothing against her heated skin.

Dust and dirt turned to a thin film of mud and then dissolved in the brook, streams of brown disappearing in the clear, burbling water.

It had been a week since the flood. The water had receded to its normal levels, and the dirt had cleared, leaving behind evidence of what had been—moss, limbs, branches strewn along the banks where none had been before.

A week since Matty had gone.

And she felt a gnawing emptiness inside. She missed his steady presence. His conversation. Playing games with him.

His kisses.

She'd spent the past days digging out the barn. With the creek changing direction, she vacillated on whether to rebuild there or find another location. If she couldn't rebuild here, digging out a brand-new building large enough for two animals and the chickens would be back-breaking work.

She hadn't brought up with Pop yet the possibility of her hiring on at Elliott's for the remainder of the summer. She didn't know if Harold Elliott would hire a woman, or whether Pop would be able to handle being alone for long workdays.

But she was running out of time. The field she'd spent days clearing after the first flood lay dormant, with no wheat to plant.

She pushed up from her squat, pushed her damp hair out of her eyes and headed for the dugout.

Inside, Pop had made a hearty-smelling stew. She dried off her hands and face with a small square of a towel and sat down at the table.

"You doing okay today? No spells where you're short of breath?"

He grunted, and she took that to mean *no*. He would tell her if he had one, right?

Later that night, he moaned in his sleep and she awoke. Darkness enclosed the room.

Her breaths came fast, as blood pounded in her temples, in her ears. Should she wake him? Was he having a nightmare about the war?

She couldn't forget what had happened the last time. Being pinned to the ground, stuck beneath the table and bed, unable to roll away.

Afraid that he wouldn't wake up.

And tonight there was no cowboy staying in the barn to intervene.

She sat up in the bed, wrapping her arms around her knees.

It was too much to bear alone.

The homestead, their livelihoods. Pop.

She buried her face in her knees, trying to stem the tears that threatened, but it was no use. They fell anyway.

Why did Mama have to die? Why did Pop have to fade into his memories the way he was?

She was afraid. And there was no one to turn to.

Chapter Twenty-One

The sun was still an orange ball on the horizon as Catherine leaned back against the soddy door. She hadn't been able to go back to sleep after she'd woken in the night.

Pop had stayed asleep. Restless, but asleep.

She desperately needed to find the peace she'd felt the early Sunday morning she'd shared a few quiet moments with Matty. Had it only been two weeks ago?

He had arrived in her life like a tornado, upending everything.

Hoofbeats startled her, brought her gaze up. Pop would advise her to duck inside, where they'd both have a modicum of protection.

But she hesitated.

And her heart leaped as she saw a familiar cowboy ride into sight.

Matty.

He balanced easily on the horse, keeping his saddle naturally. He caught sight of her and lifted his hat in a wave.

Her eyes followed his movements and then were drawn past him. Several riders followed him. Farther behind that, two wagons rumbled toward her.

What was going on?

Heart beating with both hope and trepidation, she walked out to meet him.

He dismounted, holding the reins of a fine chestnut gelding in his hand.

"What are you doing here?"

He smiled, but his eyes remained uncertain. "Mentioned your troubles to some folks—my family, mostly. We decided to give you a barn raising."

Her heart thrummed in her chest, her mind going immediately to Pop.

Matty jerked his thumb over his shoulder. "We've got the manpower and enough lumber to get you a nice, snug barn that'll last decades. We can finish it today."

"I can't believe you did all this." She shook her head, her throat clogged with emotion. She crossed her arms. "We can't accept it. What if Pop—"

He reached out and touched her upper arm. "And what if he's fine? Can I at least talk to him?"

Over his shoulder, the two wagons creaked to a stop. They were piled high with lumber that she hadn't noticed before.

Two men sat astride fine horses, pointing to the flat swath of land behind the soddy, away from the creek bank. If she blinked, she could easily imagine a wood-sided barn there.

"Fine," she whispered. "You can talk to him. He's inside."

Matty squeezed her arm gently. He moved past her and disappeared into the soddy.

She stood where she was, half afraid to believe this was even happening. Matty had come back. Even knowing about her parentage.

She didn't know whether to pray that Pop would send him home or that he would allow it. Thinking of having a new barn—a freestanding structure!—was wonderful.

She had to force herself to slow down. Take a breath. Matty might've come back, but that didn't mean he wanted to be with her. Even if he did, how could they be together with his job in town and her working the homestead?

Perhaps he simply felt sorry for her. Wanted to pay her back for helping him when he'd been injured.

She couldn't hope for more than that.

A young man rode forward at a gallop, finally reining in just behind Matty's horse. His animal tossed its head and the rider laughed—a trilling, melodic laugh.

Catherine gasped as the young *woman* dismounted, removing her hat to reveal a long blond braid down her back. She was slender, blue-eyed and dressed like a man. Just like Catherine.

"You must be Catherine. I've been *dying* to meet you. I'm Breanna." She came forward with a wide smile and hand outstretched.

Catherine couldn't seem to find her voice. "Hullo," she said finally.

Breanna pumped her hand in an exuberant handshake. "Matty has told us hardly anything about you, other than you live alone out here."

More riders arrived, men dismounting behind Breanna's horse. From a distance, another wagon moved slowly toward them. This one appeared to be full of... *women*.

"Did my brother drive you crazy when he was here?" Breanna barely took a breath between words.

Catherine couldn't seem to tear her eyes away from the approaching women. She'd begun to tremble.

"Breanna, quit bothering Matty's girl," one of the men called out.

She opened her mouth to retort that she wasn't *Matty's girl*, but Breanna linked arms with her.

"I'm only trying to warn her about *you*," Breanna called back to the men. To Catherine, she murmured, "Our family might be big, and noisy, but we're all behind you."

Why?

"Let me introduce you to everyone."

Breanna kept her close with that arm threaded through the crook of her elbow, though Catherine could have pulled away at any time. She met brothers and then wives and Jonas and Penny, Matty's *parents*.

They all greeted her warmly. There were no sidelong glances, no whispers after she and Breanna turned away. Only a simple curiosity.

Matty must've told them about her isolation on the homestead, about her lack of education, but they seemed to…*like her*.

She couldn't understand it. Matty obviously hadn't told them about her parentage—she couldn't see them accepting her so easily if he had.

But regardless…they didn't turn their noses up at her because of the way she was dressed or her simple home.

"Breanna!" A young boy ran up and threw himself at Breanna, forcing her to let go of Catherine in order to catch him.

"Watch out, you hooligan!" Breanna laughed. To Catherine, she said, "My brother Andrew." And to the boy, "We're trying not to scare off Catherine, remember?"

They were?

"Who's that?" Breanna asked.

Catherine looked up. A wagon approached from the north—the opposite direction all the Whites had come from.

"It looks like…" Catherine's voice trailed off as realization hit. Mr. Elliott, and his family.

Inside the soddy, Matty sat on Catherine's cot with Pop across from him, his leg still propped on the bed.

The old man looked more frail than Matty remembered, but he was just as stubborn and moody. Matty hadn't had enough time with Catherine outside, time to check for bruises or the haunted look in her eyes that she'd had in the days after Pop had attacked her.

"I've brought some help for Catherine," Matty said. "Just for today."

Pop's brows scrunched together like two white, fuzzy caterpillars. "Who?" he barked.

"My family. My pa and ma, my brothers and sisters and their wives—the ones who are married. Sent an invite to your neighbor Elliott. And a couple of friends from town."

"We don't need no charity." Pop's jaw was set, his eyes squinty and unreadable.

And Matty started to get riled up. "If you'd like, think of it as repayment for all the food you fed me while I was here. And the lodging." Such as it was.

Pop snarled.

"You know how hard she works to provide for you," he infused the words with all the fervor he felt, especially that Pop would make things difficult for Catherine when it didn't have to be that way. "You don't have to come outside if it's going to stir up bad memories."

Pop considered for a long time, staring at the wall. Finally, he nodded.

"I brought someone to see you, as well. If you feel up to it, my brother Maxwell—the doctor—could examine you. See if he can't figure out why you're getting short of breath."

Pop's eyes narrowed. "That's awful presumptuous of you. I don't wanna see no doctor."

"It's not presumption. I care about Catherine, and Catherine loves you."

He shrugged. "I ain't interested in someone poking and prodding me, just to tell me what I already know. When it's my time, the good Lord will take me home."

"But—"

"I ain't talking about it no more!"

Frustrated, Matty rose and thrust his hand through his hair before mashing his hat back on his head. With the old man in this state of mind, there was no way he was changing his decision. Matty could come back in later and try again. He hadn't gotten Maxwell all the way out here just to walk away when Pop might benefit from an examination.

Chapter Twenty-Two

Catherine had been stuck in place, afraid to disrupt the tentative friendship Breanna offered. It would've been rude to just walk away. Thus, she hadn't been able to escape as the Elliotts' wagon had rumbled up to the homestead.

Did you see her hair?

She was incredibly aware of the dirty state of her clothing—she'd missed a wash day in her scramble to salvage what she could from the flattened barn and keep the homestead afloat. And her clothing had been worn to start with.

And the soddy behind her was so simple compared to the Elliotts' fine home.

But she would look like a scared rabbit if she ran away, abandoning Breanna.

Michaela descended from the wagon, helped by her father, just as one final wagon approached in the far distance. Just how many people had Matty invited out here?

As if summoned by her thoughts, the man exited the soddy. His expression was serious, maybe upset. Had Pop refused the assistance, after Matty had gathered all the help out here? But he nodded at Catherine, his eyes crinkling slightly.

Pop had approved.

Matty joined the two men she'd seen earlier who seemed to be discussing the placement of the barn and maybe its dimensions. They didn't ask for her okay, but she didn't mind all that much. Having a sturdy free-standing structure would be a huge blessing, and Matty would make a good decision for the placement. He'd proven himself knowledgeable enough while he'd been here before.

Which left her to greet folks.

Not a position that was comfortable for her.

"Thank you for coming," she said awkwardly as Michaela approached, her arms bundled with a large wicker basket.

The conversation immediately lagged as Michaela's eyes flickered over Catherine's attire and then to the young woman at her side.

"I'm Breanna White," Matty's sister offered.

Michaela's eyes snapped with recognition, and she smiled.

Could anyone else see how sickly sweet—and false—it seemed?

"This is one of our neighbors, Michaela Elliott." Catherine didn't know if it was a proper introduction or not, but at least she'd made the effort.

"Mama wanted to come but was feeling a little under the weather."

"It was kind of your father to bring his cowhands. I know Matty will appreciate the extra hands." Catherine's teeth ached as she clamped down on her real feelings even as she forced the words out. Why had the Elliotts come? Although they'd offered conversation, they hadn't been particularly neighborly when she and Matty had visited before.

The last wagon rolled to a stop, and Breanna inhaled sharply.

Catherine's eyes flicked to follow Breanna's gaze to the wagon, but she didn't understand what had caused the other young woman to tense. There were several people inside, a couple of young women and two men who appeared to be around Matty's age.

"Hey, Ma? Where are we setting up the food spread?" Breanna belted out the words, causing both Michaela and Catherine to jump, though Catherine caught herself and—hopefully—hid her reaction quickly.

Penny took charge of Michaela and her basket of foodstuffs, just as the newcomers unloaded from their wagon.

And Catherine got a good look at the nearest young woman. Instant recognition flared.

Luella McKeever.

All the noise, voices and horses stamping and even the creek burbling nearby faded away as Catherine registered the other woman's presence.

Had Matty invited her? Why, when he knew their history?

"I—" Catherine turned to Breanna, her earlier plans not to abandon this new friend obliterated. She couldn't breathe to find words to explain, to escape.

Too late.

"Morning, Breanna." Luella's voice rang out sweet and fresh.

Catherine closed her eyes briefly, then allowed them to fly back open. Better to face whatever she would find in the other woman—friend or foe.

She turned back to greet Luella. There would be no

hiding for her. She wasn't the same girl she'd been at eight.

Catherine caught the surprised widening of Luella's eyes. The matching recognition as Luella realized who she was.

"Hullo. Is it…?"

"Catherine." She tried to keep her voice steady, but couldn't stop the tremble. *Homemade happy Cathy.* The words from the past reverberated through her mind— including ones that Luella hadn't said. *Illegitimate. Shameful.*

Luella didn't seem to know what to say, and Catherine wasn't ashamed of the prick of gratefulness that her flapping mouth engendered. Finally, the other woman nodded to Breanna. "Eileen and I overheard Seb inviting Jim and the boys and we begged to come along."

Her eyes flicked to where the men were gathered, now laying out boards in a rough square on the grass.

And suddenly Catherine remembered Matty's statement on one of their very first days together. She'd asked him if he was sweet on someone and he'd answered with, *It's complicated.*

Because he'd been seeing *Luella*?

"It'll take a lot to feed this group of men. I'm sure Ma will be happy for the extra help," Breanna was saying, even as Catherine's thoughts whirled in circles.

She nodded when Luella moved off to speak to Penny, who seemed to be coordinating the women's efforts. It took everything in her to keep her lip from trembling as it wanted to.

She knew Matty had a life back in Bear Creek. Hadn't she just told herself this morning when he'd arrived that he had likely come out here today as repayment for taking him in?

And then he'd leave again. He'd go back to his life, his friends. Maybe even Luella.

She squinted against the sun shining directly into her eyes, making them water. When she couldn't help it, she brushed a hand against the moisture and excused herself, slipping into the woods when no one was looking.

Catherine stood in the shade of a large poplar, half hidden behind the wagons and ground-tied horses. A bucket hung from one hand, but she'd finished watering the animals minutes ago, about the same time Penny had called the men away from their work for lunch.

The lot of them had gone down to the creek to wash up.

And she remained hidden, here, out of the way.

The morning was gone, but the men had already constructed the frame of the building, beams that stretched to the sky. The women had spread picnic blankets across the grass in the sunshine and laid a bounty of food across them. The noise and movement of so many was unfamiliar and she was uncomfortable with the attention, though she'd forced herself to spend time with each of Matty's sisters-in-law and his mother and to express her thanks for their part in today's event.

She'd studiously avoided both Michaela and Luella.

Catherine felt bad that she had nothing to contribute. But she'd had no notice of this event and knowledge that it was coming.

And the ladies didn't seem to mind in the least.

Earlier, Matty had been up on the crossbeams with several of his brothers preparing the roofline. He looked as if he'd never been injured, carrying boards, swinging a hammer, doing everything as if his collarbone had healed completely.

She watched the easy camaraderie he shared with his family and found that she was the slightest bit jealous of the other men. They called out to each other in teasing tones, and he answered right back. There was a part of her that desperately wanted to be out there with them. But she didn't know if she fit in. And that indecision had held her immobile.

Now as the men traipsed eagerly toward the food-stuffs that had been prepared, Catherine saw the women, those who were wives, go out and greet their men. Sarah, who had a baby clinging to her hip, accepted a buss on the cheek from Oscar. Davy greeted his wife with an arm around her shoulders. And then Catherine saw something that made her gut tighten up. Both Luella and Michaela had joined the group and now stood talking to Matty and Seb. Both women wore stylish dresses that fluttered like flags in the stiff breeze. Both had their *long* hair pulled into what must be fashionable styles behind their heads, pinned artfully into place.

Seeing Luella smile up into Matty's welcoming face twisted Catherine's insides. Her hands fisted at her sides. She felt sick.

But her feet remained rooted in place. What would she do, go out there in front of everyone and attempt to bill and coo up at him, just like the other girls?

And when he laughed outright at her?

The memories of the past wouldn't let go of her, and she'd almost decided to slip back into the woods—and perhaps not return until everyone was gone—when Breanna accosted her, giving her a shove toward the picnic blankets.

"C'mon, I'm starving."

No doubt she was. Breanna had been among the men,

hammering boards into place, although Catherine had seen her brothers shoo her away at times.

Now that Breanna had pushed her out into the open—out of her hiding place—several pairs of eyes turned on her, including the two doctors, Maxwell and Hattie. It would make more of a scene if Catherine ran away, so she left the bucket behind and swallowed hard and moved toward Matty's mother on one of the picnic blankets.

"Is there anything left that I can help with?"

Penny looked up and smiled. "I'm sure Matty would appreciate it if you made him a plate."

"Oh, but—" Wouldn't that look as if she was courting his attention? *She couldn't.*

If he snubbed her for Luella, Catherine would look foolish.

But Penny didn't seem to sense her turmoil as she pressed a tin plate into Catherine's shaky hands.

Blindly, Catherine filled the plate with a mix of foods.

Why hadn't she been paying better attention? She should've snuck off before Breanna had found her hiding place. But she'd been frozen, all because she'd seen Luella talking to Matty and…she'd been jealous. There. She admitted to the ugly emotion.

The solution came to her as she scooped some kind of salad onto the now-overflowing plate.

She could take the plate for herself and escape somewhere quiet. Pretend that she'd meant to do that the whole time.

And then it was too late as a shadow fell over her.

"That for me?"

Catherine opened her mouth to tell him that it was *her* plate, but his mama beat her to it.

"That's right."

He took the plate before she could protest, switching hands and clasping her now-empty hand in his. He gave her a warm smile, his eyes crinkling at the corners.

"I'll wait while you make a plate for yourself."

He would?

She should make sure the other men were all taken care of—they'd been working all day to help her, after all.

A quick glance around showed that everyone seemed to be either chatting or eating.

"Go ahead, dear," Penny encouraged.

Her cheeks burned as she added a piece of fried chicken and a biscuit to her plate. Her stomach churned so she wasn't sure she could eat at all.

When she straightened, Matty was quick to put his hand beneath her elbow.

"Let's try to find somewhere quiet," he murmured.

And she didn't shake his hand away. Didn't run off into the woods.

An empty picnic blanket at the edge of the gathering seemed like a safe place, but as soon as she and Matty settled on the blanket, Breanna and one of her nieces—Cecilia?—plopped down with them.

"Go away, sis," Matty growled playfully. But Catherine thought she heard a note of seriousness beneath his teasing tone.

"You had Catherine all to yourself for two weeks," Breanna returned. "We want to get to know her."

He muttered something under his breath.

Breanna smirked at him. "Was my brother a huge annoyance while he was in your care?"

Catherine glanced up from her plate to see the cowboy's cheeks had gone pink in the shadow of his hat.

"In some ways," she said.

Now his eyes cut to her, narrowed slightly.

"He was helpful cooking meals…but his penchant for games was…interesting."

Matty's irritation with his sister was minor in comparison to the joy of sitting next to Catherine.

She picked at her food, kept glancing all around. Her gaze seemed to keep hanging on Luella, who'd sat down with friends from town and Michaela. The men he'd invited. They were good workers. But the two gals had turned it into more of a social.

He'd seen Luella unload from the wagon with her friend Eileen and immediately sent a prayer winging heavenward that she wouldn't do anything to humiliate Catherine. When she'd first arrived and gone to greet Breanna and Catherine, he'd been in the middle of discussing the final layout of the barn with his brothers and afraid that it would've made things worse if he'd rushed away from that discussion to bust into a female conversation.

But that didn't mean he wasn't worried about Catherine's feelings getting stomped on all over again. He'd stopped noticing her trousers after those first days spent lying on the cot at her place, but he knew womenfolk could be persnickety about clothing and didn't want a repeat of their school days.

He'd been glad when Luella had kept her distance and thankful that the women in his family seemed to make Catherine feel welcome. He trusted his ma and his sisters-in-law to keep any kind of gossip from spreading.

But now, seeing Catherine still nervous about the other fillies had his own nerves strung tight.

So of course he made a joke, guiding the conversation

back to his games. "Don't be fooled by her shy nature. Catherine whupped me at dominoes. Twice."

Breanna and Cecilia laughed.

"I hope he wasn't a sore loser," Breanna said through a mouthful of his ma's fried chicken.

"Do you remember the time he got so mad at Ricky—" Cecilia began speaking but broke off in a fit of giggles.

"Accused him of cheating," Breanna agreed with a nod and a fit of giggles herself.

"Don't believe anything they say about me," he told Catherine.

As she watched the two younger women, a smile played at the corners of her mouth. "I don't know. Your family might have other interesting stories about you I'd like to hear."

For a moment, he got caught in her eyes. His chest seized up and he just let himself look, not caring that his sister and Cecilia were looking on.

"Oh!" Breanna exclaimed. "What about the time he put a snake in the teacher's desk drawer—"

"Not *that* one," he told his sister, aware of Catherine's curious gaze. He didn't want her to have any reminders of the ornery boy he'd been during his school days.

"Mmm—" Cecilia swallowed. "What about when your brothers put his saddle on backward?" She leaned toward Catherine as if they shared a confidence. "He was out courting—was it Luella?" She turned toward Breanna as if to confirm her statement.

Catherine's eyes flicked to him. He met her gaze head-on. There was nothing between him and Luella now. He knew she'd been right to end it. If he'd felt an inkling of what he felt for Catherine for the other woman, they would've been married already.

But he hadn't.

God must've known he was waiting to meet Catherine.

"So his brothers snuck onto her family's farm and resaddled his horse, only backward. When he went to mount up, the horse was so confused it went one way and Matty the other."

Catherine looked to him for confirmation. His face was hot, but he nodded. "Tumbled off head over feet. My backside was bruised for days."

His sister and niece had dissolved into giggles again. Catherine looked as if she didn't know whether to join them or to interrogate him more.

He'd finished his food and now set his plate on the blanket in front of them. "Don't worry." He leaned back on his hand, letting his fingers slide over hers where she reclined on the blanket, as well. "I'll protect you from my siblings." And he'd protect her from any trouble, whether it was gossip or a threatening neighbor.

"Oh, yes!" Breanna sat forward again, her eyes dancing.

He narrowed his eyes at her, warning her not to tell another story on him.

And Breanna being Breanna, she promptly ignored him.

"It was maybe a year after he came to live with us. What were you, ten? Eleven?"

Matty remained silent with his eyebrows raised. He wasn't going to help his sister tell this story.

"Matty had gotten ahold of this storybook. Something about knights and Camelot. He made this sword out of a tree branch and rode around on his horse protecting his *kingdom*."

"A prince, hmm?" Catherine's head tilted toward him. Her eyes had gone soft.

"Knight," he corrected softly.

Her mouth turned up in a smile.

If his sister telling stories about him made Catherine look at him like this, he'd sit through a thousand of them. Ten thousand.

A stifled giggle interrupted his perusal of Catherine's lips. Breanna and Cecilia had gone suspiciously silent.

He looked over to find them hiding smiles behind their hands. Catherine cleared her throat. Her cheeks had turned pink.

"I have another surprise for you," he said. He got to his feet and held his hand out to her.

She glanced back at where his ma sat. "I should help with cleaning up…"

"It'll keep." He held her gaze. "Please."

She took his hand and allowed him to help her up. He tucked her close to his side and they walked on a path that would take them past the barn. And leave his family behind.

"Are you completely overwhelmed?" he asked.

"Not…completely. A little."

It was a start.

"I'm wondering…did you tell them about my parentage?"

"As far as I'm concerned, it's your business and no one else's. I don't know who used it to shame you before, but…if you choose to tell people, my family will support you."

There was a beat of silence as they passed the unfinished corner of the new barn. Part of the wood sides were up, but it was still a skeleton. Give them the rest of the afternoon and it would be complete.

"I don't know how to thank you for this," she murmured.

Then they were past the structure and crested a small

hill, and finally they were upon his next-to-last surprise for her.

She went still at his side.

"What are they—"

Her feet moved, as if she was going to rush forward, then went still at his side. She looked back at him. Her eyes were suspiciously bright.

"Are they…?"

He didn't care if Oscar and Edgar saw from where they sowed wheat seed—that he'd bought from the mercantile in town—he put his arm around Catherine's shoulders.

"As long as the weather holds and there's no plague of locusts, you'll have your crop at the end of summer."

Her eyes had a sheen of moisture as she looked up at him. He let his hand move to cup her cheek.

"Eye spy something blue," he whispered.

She rolled her eyes, shook her head slightly. "The sky," she murmured. The intimacy of being in close proximity kept their voices low.

He shook his head, not looking away from her face.

"The jay in the tree."

"Wrong again."

Her gaze flicked briefly over his shoulder and then back to his face. "I can't think of anything else."

Neither could he.

"Your eyes," he whispered. He cupped her cheek and did what he'd wanted to do since he'd ridden in this morning. He kissed her, his lips moving softly against hers. Completely heedless of his brothers in seeing distance.

Her hand came up to rest against the nape of his neck.

When he finally drew away, they were both breathless. He hugged her close before releasing her, but he couldn't seem to let go of her hand.

He thought about stealing a second kiss, but shouts and movement from the dugout had them both whirling in that direction.

Pop rushed from the soddy doorway, wielding what might've been a hoe. He ran straight at the picnic blankets. Oscar and Sarah were nearest the soddy with their children and Oscar jumped up, throwing himself toward Pop.

Matty started toward the melee at a run, barely registering Catherine behind him. Seb, Davy and Jonas had joined Oscar, all of their voices blending into a cacophony of noise. Someone—a woman—shrieked. Matty's breath burned his chest as he got close. "Stop!"

And Catherine's cry above it all. "Pop!"

Chapter Twenty-Three

Pop's eyes were wild, his hair sticking out in all directions, as Catherine elbowed her way past two of Matty's brothers and tried to get close to him.

Pop swung out with the garden hoe again and the man nearest—she thought it was Maxwell—grabbed hold of it, wrenching it from Pop's grasp.

"Don't hurt him!"

"Cath—" Matty's exclamation was a warning, but he didn't understand. He couldn't know how scared Pop was going to be when he woke up from his memories.

And then there were still two bodies between them, but she was close enough to see sweat bead across Pop's forehead and upper lip. His face went white as death and his eyes rolled back in his head as he collapsed.

"Pop!" Her shoulder bumped someone's side, throwing her off balance.

"Everybody get back," Matty ordered as she banged her knees hard in her bungled attempt to kneel beside her grandfather.

"Maxwell." The quiet woman's voice was followed by a shadow falling across Pop's face.

Catherine smoothed back his hair from his sticky

forehead, looking up to see Hattie's compassionate expression as she extended a black doctor's bag to her husband.

"Let's take him inside," Matty suggested.

He gently took her elbow and helped her stand, and that's when she noticed the silence.

With so many people around, it hadn't been quiet the entire morning. But now…she could hear a far-off bird chirp. The splash of the creek over the rocky streambed.

She began to shake.

Matty and one of his brothers carefully bent to lift Pop, ready to carry him back into the soddy. And she knew she shouldn't, but she couldn't keep her eyes from darting to the faces surrounding her.

Concern. Pity. Fear. Uncertainty.

And there, hidden deep in Luella's eyes, something more. She would never forget this. She might even go home to Bear Creek and tell all her friends.

But Catherine refused to duck her head in shame. This might be her lot in life, but she was proud of it. Proud of the man who'd cared for her until he couldn't anymore.

Even if her eyes burned with tears as she followed the men into the soddy.

"What does that mean? *Cardiac hypertrophy?*" Catherine asked.

She stood just outside the front door of the soddy, Matty at her side. Not touching. She'd kept a careful distance between them since Pop's spell earlier this afternoon.

The hammering had started up again first, after they'd brought Pop inside. Matty had hovered until Maxwell had told him to go back to work.

She'd been allowed to stay.

When Matty had opened the door, just long enough to slip outside, she'd heard the soft buzz of conversations. And been glad for the reprieve.

The doctor had been patient as Pop had recovered from his faint. And thorough, listening to Pop's chest with a funny-looking hollow tube, asking Pop question after question—quietly, so that Pop didn't get agitated again.

He'd given Pop a sedative to help him sleep and then asked to talk to her outside.

She'd been surprised to find the sun setting and most everyone gone. Only a few hammer strikes sounded from the barn that was now complete, down to the doors and a window high on one side. Matty must have been watching, waiting, because he joined her as she repeated the question to Maxwell.

"What does that mean?"

Maxwell's expression was serious, compassionate. Not pitying, as some of the others had been. "It means that his heart is slowly giving out. One of these times, he'll have a spell so bad that he won't recover."

"Like Walt?" Matty asked.

Maxwell nodded, and Matty explained. "Penny's granddad lived next door to Jonas—that's how they met, but that's not here or there. He was around your Pop's age when he started having symptoms similar to Pop's. Weakness in his limbs. Shortness of breath."

"He died a few months after the first episode," Maxwell said quietly.

Matty's arm came up. Reaching for her. She turned slightly so that it dropped away from the back of her shoulder. His action was presumptive. Though she guessed it was no more presumptive than showing up with several wagons full of wood and wheat for her field.

She…wanted his support. She brushed an errant tear that threatened to track down her cheek.

But after what had happened with Pop earlier, any seed of hope she'd had was crushed, just like the wheat stalks in the hailstorm.

"There's no telling how long he might live," Maxwell said gently. "Some cases I've read, the person suffering weakness and shortness of breath lived on for years."

"But not every case," she whispered.

He shook his head.

She could tell he was a good doctor. He'd delivered the news honestly, gently.

But his gentle manner didn't soften the blow. Pop might have only months to live.

"And the delusions? The mood swings?" Matty asked. Of course he would ask the difficult question when she was so very shaken.

"The dementia is a separate issue."

Dementia. How could one word hurt so badly?

"It probably exacerbates the heart problem when he runs or flies into a rage. His heart can't do the extra work," he explained gently.

She couldn't stop shaking, but she held on to both of her elbows. She could hold on for a little longer. They were going to leave. Not long now.

Maxwell said something else to Matty, but his words flowed over her like water over a streambed. He took his leave, mounting up on one of the few remaining horses and riding out.

Leaving her alone with Matty.

The couple of men finishing out the barn were no-where in sight. Her memories played tricks on her as she heard again his whisper from weeks ago, *It's all right to lean on someone.*

But he wasn't going to be here anymore.

He would be going soon, as well. His job, his life were in Bear Creek.

And hers was here with Pop. After today, she knew there was no way he could interact with others safely.

And if he had mere months left on this earth, she wouldn't force him into a situation that would make his final days dangerous for him and for others. They would stay on the homestead, where he'd been happy for so many years of his life.

And she wouldn't ask Matty to stay, either.

Before the dustup, she'd loved seeing him interact with his family. Even when he'd acted annoyed with Breanna at lunch, there had been an affectionate undertone to their conversation. He'd spent the morning working on the roof and ribbing his brothers.

She knew he'd chafed under the isolation of the homestead. How many times had he mentioned going home in those first days?

She cared about him enough to want his happiness, and she doubted it could be here, so far from the people and the job he loved.

Her heart was torn from wanting the cowboy she couldn't have, and battered from the dire news of the seriousness of Pop's condition.

Twilight fell around them as Matty looked down on Catherine. She appeared to be barely holding herself together, clutching her elbows as if she might fly apart unless she held tightly enough.

The joy he'd felt earlier, the closeness when they'd

kissed…it was all gone. Stolen by an old man's health problems.

He didn't want to leave like this.

He wanted to reassure her but knew that words weren't always a comfort in situations like this. Only time and God's presence would comfort her as Pop slipped away.

"You should go. You'll be riding in the dark." She didn't look at him as she said it.

It skewered him when she raised one hand to wipe away residual tears from her cheeks.

His voice emerged hoarse when he said, "There's one more thing."

"What more?" she asked, and where earlier her words would have hidden a laugh, now there was only a tense uncertainty. "How can there be more when you've done so much? More than we can repay."

"I— They didn't do this so you'd feel a sense of obligation. Any more than you rescued me and put me up for weeks."

She kept her head down but allowed him to draw her along to where he'd tied off his horse. He took a brown wrapped package out of the saddlebag.

Her hands dropped with the weight of it. She looked down on the package, leaving him with only a view of the top of her head.

She tapped the coarse brown paper, then fiddled with the bow in the twine that held it all together.

He swallowed when he wanted to urge her to open it. It was her gift. If she wanted to savor it, she should.

Slowly, she untied the bow. The twine fell away. She unfolded the paper methodically. Finally, *finally* his gift was revealed. Three primers of different levels, all bought new from the store.

She didn't look up from where her fingers traced a pattern on the first book's cover. "How did you know?"

Her subdued reaction was not what he'd hoped for. He'd hoped that in this moment, she would open up to him. *Let me in.*

"I found your old schoolbook tucked in the wall. I'm sorry I'm nosy."

She exhaled what sounded like a laugh. A sad laugh. "No, you're not."

"I suppose not."

"Thank you," she whispered, looking up at him again. A tear spilled over and he reached for her, raised his hand to brush it away.

He hadn't meant to make her cry.

But she flinched, and he let his hand fall to his side. "Last time I left you told me not to come back," he said.

She still wouldn't meet his gaze. He felt the distance between them yawning like that dangerous, overflowing creek.

"I'd like to have permission to come back this time."

Slowly, she shook her head. Swiped at another errant tear. "It's not a good idea."

"Cath—"

"I appreciate what you wanted to do today, but this was a bad idea. And so is you coming back."

His head knocked back as if she'd physically struck him. Maybe he even took a step back, and then she was looking up at him, her eyes sorrowful.

"It's not that I'm not grateful. I *am*. Without your help—and your family—we might've starved this winter. But you saw what Pop did—"

Was he wrong to want to try to grow this relationship between them? Jonas had encouraged today's visit, had thought they could kill two birds with one stone:

introduce Catherine into the family, and help her with the homestead. But everything had gone hopelessly wrong after Pop's outburst.

She blinked. She'd shown him more emotion today than almost the entire time he'd been with her before.

"What did you think would happen after today? That we'd grow closer?" she asked.

He'd hoped.

"Maybe you thought if you were able to come visit—" she swallowed audibly "—come courting, then eventually we'd get married?"

He hadn't thought that far ahead. But it wasn't a *bad* idea. He wanted a family, as his brothers had. And Catherine could use the help.

"I wasn't going to push you into it, not like—" *Ralph.*

She waved away that stray thought. "Do you really think you could be content to live isolated out here?"

No. He hated the thought of being so alone, so vulnerable. He'd thought it over and over again, how vulnerable Catherine was to Ralph's threats because they were so far out of town with hardly any neighbors, no one to rely on.

"But Pop—"

"I think after today it's pretty obvious that Pop can't be around people."

He wasn't imagining the wobble of her lip as she said the words. She *did* care. But she was also right. The obstacles stacked between them seemed insurmountable.

Which left him with nothing left to do but say goodbye.

He couldn't just *leave.* He wrapped her shoulders in his arm. A friendly hug, in contrast to how he'd embraced her earlier when they'd kissed.

He kissed the crown of her hair. Tried to think of any argument that would hold water.

But in the end, he simply mounted up and set off for home.

Chapter Twenty-Four

Three days after the barn raising, Catherine still woke to conflicting emotions. Partly, a state of disbelief at how the homestead had changed. The worries that she'd had about housing the animals and feeding them through the winter had disappeared, thanks to Matty's help and the help of his family.

The other part was grief. She had harbored some small hope that Pop wasn't as bad off as she'd thought him to be, but the doctor's examination had only confirmed her worst fears.

She attempted to bury her grief in work. With the help planting the wheat field, she'd recovered all the time lost to the first wave of storms that had come through. And the barn was amazing. Snug, watertight, strong enough to survive the sometimes-blistering Wyoming winds.

Which meant her sense of urgency had waned. Today she would perform more normal tasks like making bread and washing clothes.

But first, her investigation. Last night, just before sundown, she'd noticed a wisp of smoke dissolving into the sky. Too close to be one of the Chestertons. Unless one of them was trespassing on her property.

Now it was just after dawn, and she'd snuck through the brush and woods, thinking she must be right upon the trespasser.

And then she literally stumbled over him as she stepped over an old rotted log, twisting and landing on her rump with an "Oof!"

"What—"

She scrambled backward, unable to get a look at the man wrapped in his bedroll, now struggling to get free of the blanket.

She sought a branch or something to use to protect herself among the fallen leaves—she'd only wanted to get a look at the trespasser. She hadn't brought a weapon.

But then his head poked out of the blanket. That tousled brown hair, those brown eyes—it was Matty's brother.

"Seb! What're you doing here?"

He finally kicked free of the blanket and sat up, rubbing his face with both hands. He wore trousers and a woolen shirt so like Matty's that Catherine's heart thumped once, hard.

"I, uh…" He reached for his boots, turning each one upside down before stuffing them on his feet.

Now that she was looking, she saw his horse tethered several yards away, and the ashes from a small campfire. That must've been the smoke she'd seen last night.

He seemed to be alone, but… "Is Matty with you?"

"Naw."

The momentary hope she'd harbored dissipated.

He crossed his arms over his knees.

She mirrored his pose several feet away. "Then what are you doing here?"

He exhaled loudly. Ran one hand through his hair and then seemed to realize he wasn't wearing his hat.

He reached for it where it sat on top of the fallen log that had blocked her view of him—that's why she'd tripped on him in the first place.

And that's when she saw the rifle leaning in the fork of two branches.

Realization rushed over her in a wave. "Matty sent you. To watch out for me."

"Yep." His expression was slightly chagrined, but he didn't sound apologetic.

She shook her head but couldn't help the small smile that wanted to play about her lips. She'd told Matty not to return, but once again, he'd ignored her.

Unlike Chesterton's threats, Matty made her feel cared for. Somehow he saw beneath the walls she showed to everyone else and knew that she was afraid of her neighbor.

"I think he woulda rather been here himself, but the sheriff's got him hunting down some missing cattle. Rustlers been hitting up some of the smaller ranches closer to town."

"So you're…camping? For how long?"

He shrugged. "I dunno. Couple days. Oscar's going to swap with me."

What? She shook her head, standing up. "It's a lot of trouble over nothing."

"It ain't that much trouble when you consider how upset Matty would be if something happened to you."

She rolled her eyes, but deep inside she did feel… protected. But it was probably over nothing.

"My seed wheat was swept away in the flood. With the field replanted and the new barn…the only things of value I have that could be taken are my livestock."

"Or yourself. I think Matty's worried *you* were the target all along."

She laughed at the ludicrous statement. "But *why*? I think you're wasting your time."

"Matty don't. And a man's gotta trust his gut."

She realized she wasn't going to change the young cowboy's mind, so she stood, brushing off her pant legs where leaves and dirt clung. "I suppose if you're staying, the least I can offer you is a cup of coffee."

Two days later, Catherine finished filleting the two perch she'd caught with Pop. They'd taken advantage of the sunny morning and spent hours next to the gurgling stream. After days of slipping in and out of his memories, he'd been remarkably lucid, and she was thankful for the time spent in quiet activity.

Now the midday sun beat against her uncovered head. She'd sent Pop ahead to stir the fire and peel some potatoes while she finished with the fish.

Her mind had wandered to Matty—was he eating the noon meal with his boisterous family right about now?—and she didn't register the presence of another until it was too late.

Strong hands grabbed her from behind, immobilizing her arms.

She shrieked and flailed, kicking out her feet. She connected with what might be a shin, but whoever had grabbed her only grunted.

"Let—me—go!" she cried out.

"Who's gonna make me?" came a growled voice she recognized. "Your cowboy ain't here to save you."

Ralph Chesterton, just as Matty had thought.

A frisson of fear traveled through her. She hadn't seen Seb since that first morning she'd come upon him. He'd said another of the brothers would be coming to relieve him, but what if something had happened? What if Matty had agreed that he'd been worried about nothing and told the brothers to return home?

"Get your hands off me!" she cried again, struggling and twisting, to no avail.

He only laughed, an ugly, desperate sound.

"Ralph!"

Ralph whirled at the second voice, taking her with him, her back to his chest. She experienced a dizzying rush. Floyd stood yards away, his hand raised with a finger in front of his lips.

"Quiet!" Floyd growled. "I think someone's coming."

The band of Ralph's arms around her made breathing difficult. Catherine tried to breathe shallowly.

"Probably that feeble granddad of hers. Just get a sturdy branch and hit him over the head."

No! Catherine couldn't let them hurt Pop.

Floyd scrabbled around in the underbrush.

"What do you want?" She croaked the words, her voice raspy because he still held her so tightly. "Grain's. Gone."

"You." Ralph shook her, rattling her down to her bones. "You been teasing me the last six, seven months. Traipsing around in those men's clothing—it's indecent."

"Told you. No marriage."

Floyd had found a large, lopsided branch and now wielded it like a mallet. If Pop was anywhere within hearing distance, she prayed he would stay away.

"Figure if you're so opposed to marriage, there are other ways to break you." He ran his nose along the line of her cheek and she shuddered in revulsion. She jerked her head to the side and that's when she saw a shadow moving through the underbrush. Seb!

"I aim to have what I want from you." He shook her again and she coughed.

"Ralph—" Floyd started, but a cold voice had both brothers freezing in place.

"That's enough."

It had come from the opposite direction Catherine had seen movement. Who?

"Get your hands off her." The voice sounded familiar, but Matty had so many brothers...

"You gonna shoot both of us?"

The metallic click of a gun being cocked rang loud in the stillness.

Another voice, this from the opposite direction. "You get away from her." That was Seb for sure.

Catherine was released, but as her feet hit the ground her legs refused to support her and she collapsed, catching herself on her hands and knees. She coughed and spluttered as breath rushed to fill her lungs.

Floyd and Ralph were talking over each other with interjections from her second rescuer. Their voices seemed very far away.

And then Seb knelt next to her, his hand coming to rest on her back. "You need a doctor?"

She shook her head, finally drawing an unencumbered breath. She was able to sit back on her haunches, and then he helped her stand.

"I'm glad you were here." Was that her voice? She sounded hoarse and scratchy.

He grimaced. "Shoulda been here a little quicker. You sure you're all right?"

She nodded. But she was still shaking.

And to her horror, her eyes filled with tears.

Through the blur in her eyes, she saw his expression shift from uncertainty to panic.

"Oscar—"

Oscar. Her second rescuer was the oldest brother. She remembered he had a wife and...five children?

"Hug her, why don't you?"

A hysterical laugh bubbled out of her throat as Seb closed her in a brotherly hug, patting her back awkwardly.

Shock continued to spiral through her—both that the Chestertons would do something like this, and that Matty's family had come to her rescue.

She'd never had anyone to lean on before...and this even after she'd pushed Matty away.

In another time, before Matty had been dropped into her life, she would have resented him sending help to her. But she now found that she didn't know what she'd do without them.

If only things could be worked out with Matty... If only he *could* come courting. If only Pop could stand to be around people.

But as far as she was concerned, they remained at an impasse.

Chapter Twenty-Five

Matty was heading out of the sheriff's office for the evening, ready to head home and more than ready to find his bunk.

His boots had just hit the boardwalk when a sharp whistle drew his head up. Oscar and Seb approached on foot, leading their horses. His pulse sped when he saw the one man hog-tied and slung over Oscar's saddle. Another rode Seb's horse, hands tied in front of him.

"Catherine?" he called, rushing toward them.

"She's all right," Oscar responded quickly, immediately knowing what Matty meant.

"What happened?" He met his brothers at the corner of the boardwalk.

They tied off their mounts to the hitching post.

"They ain't got no call to truss us up like this," Floyd Chesterton fussed.

Matty grabbed the man's shoulder as Oscar pushed him off the saddle, preventing him from falling face-first in the dusty street.

"How about assaulting a lady?" Oscar wasn't gentle as he pushed Floyd toward the boardwalk steps.

Matty's head started pounding. "He touched her?"

"Barely," Seb grunted. He'd helped Ralph off the horse and onto his feet and now followed him up the steps. "I was on 'em as quick as I could get close enough."

They went inside the one-room sheriff's office—that doubled as the jail with three cells along one wall.

"It was a mistake," Ralph said. He wasn't struggling like his brother. His head and shoulders were hunched. He was docile.

Floyd pulled his arm away from Oscar's hold, but met gazes with the sheriff, Al Dunlop. Maybe it was Al's six-shooter at his belt that kept Floyd from struggling more.

"These two can't arrest us—they ain't deputies."

Al shared a look with Matty. Matty had explained the situation to him in great detail after he'd returned to town.

"Seems like I remember deputizin' these two men just this morning," Al said.

It was a fib. Oscar and Seb had already been out at Catherine's place this morning. But he appreciated Al's support.

Al steepled his hands in front of him. "You boys wanna tell me why you're terrorizin' a neighbor? A *female* neighbor with an aging grandfather?"

Floyd's chin jutted up almost to the ceiling, while Ralph stared at the floor.

"It didn't start out that way," Ralph said, voice low.

Floyd grunted, but Oscar poked him in the side and he hushed right up.

"Explain," the sheriff ordered.

"Between the ice last winter and the storms last month, we lost everything. I know it wasn't right, but we thought if we could find out if she had a stockpile of grain, we could convince her to share it with us. Or give it to us." This from Floyd.

"Convince, or threaten?" Matty demanded.

Ralph glared. "Wouldn't have been no threatening if she woulda agreed to marry me."

Matty met his glare evenly, though his heart drummed in his chest. "A lady's got a right to say 'no.'"

"She ain't no lady. Not dressed like that," Ralph growled, his lips curling in that ugly, familiar sneer.

Anger boiling over, Matty started to move toward the other man, but Oscar halted him with a hand to his arm.

"Let the law handle him, handle them both," his older brother said.

The sheriff took over questioning the two men, leaving Oscar, Seb and Matty to exit out onto the boardwalk.

Matty rubbed at the ache behind his neck.

"Was Catherine— You said she was all right," he parroted Oscar's statement from earlier when they'd first ridden up.

"She's fine," Oscar said. "Ralph grabbed her, shook her up a little, but he didn't actually hurt her."

"I shoulda been out there," Matty grumbled beneath his breath. He'd been on duty in town while the sheriff had been tracking a couple of rustlers. Broken up a couple of fights down at the saloon and found Mary Jo Robert's missing cat.

But he would rather have been with Catherine. She'd needed him.

Matty left in the dark of night to ride out to Catherine's place the next morning. He had to see her. Had to know for himself that she was all right, even though his brothers had assured him—repeatedly—that she was fine.

It was early still when he arrived. The homestead

was quiet. Likely Pop was still laid up, barely walking thanks to the foot he'd sprained.

And Pop wasn't the one Matty wanted to talk to anyway.

He found Catherine in the barn, her face pressed up against the milk cow's belly, shooting streams of frothy white milk into her pail.

She rose when his shadow crossed into the open doorway and fell across her boots. Nearly kicked over the half-full pail.

"What are you—"

He took her in his arms before she could finish the question. His mouth found hers and she responded to his kiss with the clutch of her hands on his shoulders, the sweetness of her lips moving against his.

He reassured himself that she *was* safe—she was perfectly safe—until they both panted for breath.

Then he clutched her to his chest, his hands at her shoulders. His breath sawed in and out of his chest.

"You really all right?" he asked finally. The words stirred the fine hairs at her temple and they tickled his lips.

She nodded, but he felt her trembling against him. Whether from the kiss or residual fright from yesterday, he didn't know.

"You didn't have to come all the way out here." Her voice emerged slightly muffled by his shirtfront. "Didn't your brothers tell you I was all right?"

"They did, but you're wrong. I *did* have to come out here and see for myself."

He set her back slightly, far enough that he could look into her face.

"I care about you. A lot. I mean, a man doesn't go

around constructing *barns* for a woman he cares nothing about."

Her eyes filled with tears at his words.

"Cath—"

She moved away from him and his arms felt incredibly empty. "We— I shouldn't have kissed you like that." Her eyes downcast, she went back to her milking stool. "Nothing's really changed between us."

His emotion swung widely, like a pendulum. He knew she only pretended calm as she methodically forced stream after stream of milk into the pail at her feet.

He hadn't expected her to fall at his feet and declare that he'd been right, that she didn't want to be alone anymore.

But he also didn't expect indifference.

When his brothers had told him of Ralph's vile verbal threats—and physical threats—to Catherine, he'd been unable to control his reaction.

He didn't just *care for her.*

He was in love with her.

But she wouldn't even look at him.

Two days after the dustup with the Chestertons, Catherine spent her morning scrubbing laundry.

The effort of scrubbing the fabric on the washboard used her entire body, and she was soon sweating, her hair clinging to her temples.

But she was still shaking as badly as she had been two nights ago.

She couldn't stop thinking about what might've happened if Matty had never been injured, had never stopped at their homestead. Couldn't stop thinking about his kisses. About what it might be like to really lean on him. For real.

If she hadn't been able to rely on him and his family, what would the Chestertons have done to her?

For years, she'd prided herself on her independence, on not needing help from others around them.

And then Matty had crashed into her life with the force of a thunderstorm. She'd tried to keep him at a distance, but being near him had crushed the walls she'd constructed to keep her heart safe.

And now he was gone.

She'd turned him away. The obstacles with Pop were too big.

But she still wished he'd come back.

Pop wandered out of the soddy, leaning heavily on his walking stick. She'd told him what had happened. She'd had no choice but to divulge everything when Seb escorted her back. She couldn't blame him; she'd been completely shaken up.

She'd worried that Pop would get lost in his memories, but he hadn't. He'd first been angry, then quiet as he took in everything that Seb had told him.

After what had happened keeping secrets about the Chestertons' threats, she knew that telling him was the right thing, but it didn't keep her from worrying that he would disappear in his memories and not come back to her.

"You're gonna scrub those pants to shreds, girl," he said, hobbling her direction.

She looked down at her hands. The trousers she'd wadded up had become damp instead of wet as she'd scrubbed them against the board. She dipped her finger in the water—it had gone cool, she'd been woolgathering so long.

She sighed and shook out the trousers. They had gone partly dry and were a wrinkled mess.

She dunked them in the tepid, sudsy water.

"I suppose my mind was wandering," she said.

Pop grunted. "Straight to that cowboy, I 'magine."

Heat flushed her cheeks. Yes, Matty was part of her muddled thoughts.

"You've always been content on the homestead—until recently."

Because she'd let the fears born from that terrifying and humiliating week in the schoolhouse strand her out here.

She wrung out the trousers, twisting them between her hands. Water trickled down into the tub.

She wanted something different now. She hoped that she could have a family. Friends.

But with Pop's health in decline, those things would have to wait.

"I've been thinkin'…"

"Dangerous words," she said over her shoulder as she clipped the trousers to the clothesline.

"I ain't gonna be around forever."

Her heart leaped. But she spoke carefully. "Don't talk like that."

She pushed her sleeve up and fished around the bottom of the washtub, searching for any remaining clothing articles. There were none, and she stood with water dripping off her hand.

"It's true," he said gruffly. "And it's time—past time—you started thinking about yourself. What're you going to do when I'm gone?"

She flicked the water off her hands violently. "I don't want to think about that now. There's no use in it."

"Do you think I don't know how hard it's been on you when I'm…not myself?"

Dementia. The word, the diagnosis the cowboy doctor had given rang through her head.

"What if I lash out at you again? What if I hurt you again? I don't like you being here alone anymore. Not the way things are going."

Hot tears burned her throat, but what could she say to that? "There are no easy solutions here, Pop," she whispered.

"Not if you're scared."

She held up her damp hands helplessly.

"Ever since you were a little thing, you hated taking risks. But a man like that ain't gonna wait around forever."

Now she whirled to face Pop head-on. "What?" Her words were laced with a laugh, but it was mostly hysterical.

"Your cowboy. Matty White. If he ain't in love with you now, he's well on his way. And unless I'm imagining things again, you feel the same for him."

Heat rushed into her cheeks, but she couldn't deny it.

"So what're you gonna do about it?"

She shrugged, keeping her eyes low so maybe he wouldn't see the pain caused by his words. "What can I do? He's firmly ensconced in town. In his family. And you and I belong here."

He scrutinized her with narrowed eyes. "Who says you can't belong in town?"

Luella. Michaela. Those women years ago who'd belittled, insulted her mother.

"I had my reasons for hiding out on the homestead when I came back from the war, but your mama… well, maybe she could've made people forget what they wanted to talk about, if she would've tried a little harder.

What she thought was a big deal, don't have to be a big deal for you."

She swallowed hard, hope beating painfully in her chest. "What are you saying?"

"I'm saying, I think you should make plans to attend worship services in town tomorrow."

Chapter Twenty-Six

Catherine slipped into the Bear Creek church after worship had already started. The voices of the congregation rose in mostly harmonious singing as the people stood in praise.

An empty pew at the back beckoned and she slipped in there.

She'd donned her mother's dress again, and being out of her usual outfit had her feeling uncomfortable in her skin. But if she planned to be in society more, shouldn't she get used to dressing this way?

Did she really plan to be seen in town more? The truth was, she didn't have a real plan. Not yet. But if Matty hadn't given up on her…

She couldn't do anything about her shorn hair. It was the most noticeable thing that made her stand out from the other women.

Through the sea of people—enough to make her stomach constrict with nervousness—she spotted Matty's blond head near the front of the sanctuary. Upon closer observation, she saw his family in the pew next to him. And behind him.

They were such a large part of the community.

Nervousness made her hands shake as she gripped the pew back in front of her. There was no use pretending to use the hymnal when she couldn't read the words inside. The tune was something she'd heard her mother sing as a child, but she was too afraid to mess it up to sing loudly.

A young woman in the pew directly in front of Catherine turned to glance over her shoulder as the preacher gave the direction to sit down. Her eyes widened even as Catherine smiled tentatively at her. She whirled back to face the front. But moments later, she leaned to whisper to the older woman—her mother?—sitting next to her.

Surely the timing of that whisper was coincidental. It would be vanity to think the young woman was talking about her.

The preacher shared several pieces of community news.

Two rows up, a pair of heads twisted, maybe drawn by the movement behind them. Catherine recognized one of the two women. Luella McKeever.

Their eyes met for a fraction of a second before Luella whipped back to face the front.

Catherine *must* be imagining the whispers that seemed to be traveling through the entire sanctuary. Why would anyone care that she attended church?

But that didn't stop her hands from trembling or the hot flush that no doubt turned her face tomato red.

She tried to regulate her breathing and focus on the preacher leading the congregation in a prayer.

But after his rousing amen she was sure that she heard whispers perk right back up.

Those long-ago doubts and insecurities rose like a tide. She fisted her hands in her lap and bowed her head, squeezing her eyes closed. She was imagining things. Giving things a meaning when they had none.

And she wasn't eight years old anymore.

She was strong enough to maintain an entire homestead.

And Matty believed in her.

She raised her head and worked at releasing her fisted fingers, relaxing her hands. She had a right to be here, a right to hear the message just like anyone else.

She stopped looking at the other worshippers and focused on the man in the pulpit, delivering a reading from the Bible.

But with her eyes focused forward, she couldn't help but see when Matty twisted in his seat. His eyes traveled over the gathered people until he met her gaze squarely.

The wide smile that spread over his lips loosened some of the tension coiling so tightly inside her.

Then, to her utter shock, he stood and edged his way toward the center aisle.

"'Scuse me."

Though his voice was pitched low, in the quietness of the sanctuary, Matty's words were plainly audible.

He moved past his mama, Seb and Breanna and then out into the aisle. Seb and Breanna craned their necks back until Penny must've hissed something at them, and then they grudgingly turned to face forward.

And then Catherine couldn't see anything other than the handsome cowboy who filled the aisle and her view. He scooted into the pew next to her.

Her face still burned at the commotion they'd jointly caused—more people had turned to look at them—but joy filled her. Her cowboy had come for her.

He closed his hand around hers. Their shoulders brushed.

"Hi," he whispered softly.

The preacher called them to stand for another hymn. Matty's strong baritone rang out from beside her, giving her courage to follow him in song.

When the preacher directed them to sit again and began his sermon, the crowd's attention remained with him. Whether it was because they'd gotten a look at the newcomer and their curiosity was satisfied, or because of Matty's presence beside her, she didn't know.

But the courage she'd gained before he'd stood up and come to sit with her was enough.

Matty kept Catherine at his side after worship was over.

He didn't know why she'd come, but joy filled him at her mere presence beside him.

They stood with the midday sunlight beating down on their bare heads. For a while they were surrounded by his family. His sisters-in-law all took turns hugging her, while his brothers welcomed her. The nieces and nephews and Jonas and Penny's younger kids swarmed around, running through the adults and then off to play with friends.

Penny stood to one side as the rest of them filtered away, talking with friends or loading up.

"We'd love for you to come out and join us for the noon meal." Penny's face was shining. She placed a hand on Catherine's arm.

Before Catherine could respond, Luella approached.

"Matty, can I talk to you for a minute?"

Catherine stiffened at his side.

"Morning, Catherine," Luella greeted belatedly.

"Morning," Catherine murmured.

He didn't want to leave Catherine, not when she'd

taken such a big step in coming—alone—to worship this morning. And he couldn't imagine what it would look like if he abandoned her for Luella.

"Please. It's important," Luella said.

"I'll keep Catherine company for a few moments," his ma said. Curiosity shone in the depths of her eyes, but they'd had a few talks about what Catherine meant to him and he knew Penny wouldn't let her come to harm, even from the town gossips.

He followed Luella toward her family's wagon, though they stopped well out of earshot of both her family and his.

She clutched her hands together in front of her midsection. A sure sign of nervousness.

"Well?" he asked.

She frowned at him, but then must've thought better of it because she suddenly smiled. "I think...I made a mistake. When I told you not to come courting anymore."

Her words caught him completely by surprise. "What?" He took off his hat, rubbed a finger up the bridge of his nose.

"I... We'd been courting for a while and you didn't seem to be interested in moving any faster. I didn't want to wait forever to get married. So I thought..." She swallowed nervously. "I thought if I ended things, it might spur you on to making a decision once you saw what you were missing."

"So you broke things off...to get me to be more serious about our relationship?" It didn't make sense to him. At all.

Tears filled her eyes, and she shrugged. A few weeks ago, he would've been taken in by her visible emotions. He would've done whatever she wanted, got down on one knee and proposed right then and there.

But now he looked over his shoulder, wanting to make sure Catherine was being taken care of.

When he turned back to her, Luella leaned to one side, her eyes following the path his gaze had taken only seconds ago. Her expression hardened slightly. "I never expected you to get hurt, or to…"

"To fall for someone else?" he finished gently. Because it was the truth. He'd fallen hard for Catherine and there was no going back. "Luella, I'm glad we were friends during school and I'm glad we're still friends, but…what I feel for you doesn't go anything past that. Not anymore." And it probably never had.

"I'm sorry."

Her eyes flashed. "What do you see in her anyway? She's…"

"She's a woman I care very deeply for," he said firmly. "And if I hear anyone spreading gossip about her, malicious or otherwise, I'd have a problem with it. We didn't treat her right when we were children, but we can choose to do differently now."

He paused.

"And that's what I expect from you, my friend."

Catherine knelt near one of the Whites' two wagons—because their family was so large they couldn't travel in a single conveyance—listening to Oscar and Sarah's toddler girl explain something about the Bible class the young children had been dismissed to.

She couldn't decipher all the words and was relieved when Matty came around the side of the wagon.

"Unca Matty!"

He swung the girl up in his arms, and she laid her head on his shoulder.

Kind of like Catherine longed to do.

One small thumb popped into the little bow mouth.

Curling up against the cowboy probably wouldn't be appropriate, not here in the churchyard. What a little girl could get away with…well, didn't mean Catherine could get away with it. And she desperately didn't want to embarrass him.

But he surprised her even as he took her hand, laced their fingers together.

Her eyes cut to where she'd last seen him standing with Luella. She'd experienced such a powerful pull of jealousy she'd had to fist her hands at her sides. But she'd somehow maintained a facade of calm in front of Matty's mother and then been distracted by the young girl.

"I can't come for lunch," she said softly. "Not this time. Will your mother be offended?"

He squeezed her hand. "No. Not if there's a next time."

She lifted her chin. After all he'd done for her, saying the words was the least she could do for him. "I'd…I'd like it if you would come calling."

He held her gaze for a long moment, then very deliberately set the little girl down and told her to go find her ma. When he straightened, he took both of her hands in his, edged her slightly closer than she had been before.

"I thought you were dead set against me. Too many things in the way. What changed your mind?"

"Pop." She swallowed back the grief. This wasn't the time for that emotion, not yet. "He's been slowly sinking into the…*dementia*—" she barely stumbled over the word "—for years. This season has been especially bad. And *he* told me in a lucid moment that he didn't want me to be alone. That I shouldn't let fear stop me from being with you. Because I…"

Her eyes had flitted around during her confession, not settling on any one place on him. But now Matty squeezed her hands firmly, and she forced her eyes to meet his gaze.

"Because you…"

"…care about you, too," she whispered.

"I wish we weren't in such a public place," he said. "I'd really like to kiss you right now."

Frantically, she glanced around. Until he jiggled her hands slightly. "I might've been a tease back in our school days, but I'll do my best to keep from embarrassing you now."

She believed him, believed the sincerity of his intense gaze.

"I can't make any guarantees for my brothers, though."

She laughed a little. "I like your brothers."

"Good." His eyes crinkled around the edges. "I was real pleased to see you this morning. It wasn't so bad, coming to town, was it?"

It had been terrifying, not that she would admit it to him.

"I— It— I did it," she concluded.

Again came that soft smile, the one that he seemed to give only to her. "You don't have to face things alone anymore," he reminded her.

That would take some getting used to.

Chapter Twenty-Seven

Almost a month to the day after Catherine's appearance at Sunday worship, Matty patrolled the boardwalk on a Saturday afternoon. One of the other deputies would be coming on duty at sunset, and Matty had promised to ride out in the morning and collect Catherine for worship. It meant he would only get a few hours rest tonight, but she'd finally agreed to come for lunch, and he was thrilled for her to have the chance to interact more with his family.

He hadn't gotten to see her as much as he would've liked in the weeks since she'd shyly asked him to come calling. Between his responsibilities at home and work as a deputy, he'd had only two free days. And he'd spent both with Catherine on the homestead. She'd come to town for Sunday services, so he'd seen her then, too, but had to be conscious of all the eyes on them, the expectation of those who believed he had to have a spotless reputation just because he worked for the town.

Pop's health was a worry. He was more and more out of breath at even the slightest exertion, and Matty feared the old man didn't have long left on the earth.

Matty was ready to get married, but he'd hesitated

bringing it up, knowing that Pop's health was so precarious.

And there was still the issue of where they would live.

At least the Chestertons were no longer a worry. They'd been locked up and were awaiting sentencing for their assault against Catherine.

He still didn't like the idea of living so far away from community and from his family. But he couldn't imagine asking her to leave the homestead behind, either, not with it being the place she associated with her mama and with Pop.

Tonight, he had to take one more patrol down the boardwalk and report back to the sheriff's office.

But as he was passing the bank, he saw suspicious movement inside. Maybe it was just old Mrs. Belvedere, in one of her visiting moods, but it was awful close to quitting time. He ducked in the door, just as a man in a mask leveled a shotgun at him.

"This is a stickup."

Blood pounded through his head, for moments overpowering the shrieks of two women and the fast talking of the bank teller behind the bars at the counter.

"All right, everybody take it easy." Matty held his hands up, making no move to draw his weapon.

The man with the gun had shaky hands. And shaky hands meant danger. Matty watched for any opening he could use to get closer, get that gun or draw his gun.

The bandit didn't seem to register the tin star at Matty's chest, nor did he ask Matty to shed his weapon. He just kept that shotgun leveled at Matty.

The bank teller was still fast-talking, but all of a sudden, everything around Matty went to white noise.

He might be in town, but what was going to stop this thief from shooting him and everyone else in the bank? How *exactly* did being in a populated area keep him from dying?

All along, he'd told himself that he wouldn't like living on Catherine's homestead because of the isolation, because it reminded him too much of what had happened during his childhood.

But what if it was all in his head?

What if there was just as much danger of falling off a horse at his pa's ranch and getting killed? Or being held up in a bank robbery? Or surviving a train crash, as Edgar's wife, Fran, had?

He was an idiot.

He'd been thinking about it all wrong.

It wasn't the *place* that was important. It was *whom you were with*.

And if he got out of this alive, he didn't want to spend one more day without Catherine. She needed him. Pop needed him.

And Matty needed her.

He loved her.

Afternoon sunlight turned Matty's hair golden as Catherine glanced over her shoulder to where he pushed her gently in the wooden swing. The swing was secured to a large tree not far from the ranch house. Behind the home and across the yard was the barn and combined bunkhouse, along with a corral that held several beautiful horses.

Catherine had walked around in a state of awe for most of the afternoon. She'd now heard the story of how Jonas had started the homestead with just one plot and grown it by purchasing land when each of his sons had come of age.

She'd seen the fine horses Oscar raised and admired

the large herd of cattle the family cultivated. They were almost a town of their own.

Daniel, a family friend and brother to Edgar's wife, Fran, had started a small school from his home at the edge of the ranch property.

Catherine had spent the good part of an hour talking with Hattie, one of the two family doctors. She'd been surprised to discover that Maxwell hadn't learned to read until he was in his teens—and he'd gone on to pursue his passion in medicine.

It gave her hope that one day she could learn to read, could gain the education she'd always wanted.

And the best part of all was the man now pushing her swing, although he'd shared with her and the family about the frightening bank holdup he'd been involved in yesterday. It still made her shiver to think about it.

"You're quiet," Matty said, his voice floating over her shoulder as his hand met her lower back.

"I'm adjusting to the lack of noise."

He laughed. "They were extra rowdy today, trying to impress you."

"Impress *me*?"

"And humiliate me."

She leaned back, letting her arms take her weight on the ropes, so she could see him. "I liked hearing all the stories about you."

His neck had gone red, but he grinned at her. "Good."

"But we didn't get to play any games…"

He grabbed the ropes and stopped the swing, then came around to the front.

His hands clasped hers on the ropes. "We can save the games for the next time." His eyes sparkled down at her. "I might be a lawman, but I'll steal some alone time with my girl if I have to."

His words sent a thrill through her, but she struggled to keep a straight face.

"Next time? Your girl?"

He used their linked hands to draw her up out of the swing.

"Haven't you guessed by now how I feel about you?"

She let her hands rest on his chest as his went to her waist. His hat shaded his eyes, but he didn't hide the vulnerability there.

"I'm not good at attributing motives to others' actions. Remember?"

His mouth twitched. "Then I'll have to speak plain. I'm in love with you."

Warmth infused every inch from her toes to the top of her head. She couldn't believe he'd said the words.

Breath caught in her throat and she had to give a slight cough to expel it. "You are?"

He lowered his head until their foreheads touched. "Why shouldn't I be? You saved me. Taught me to slow down and appreciate the beauty that was right in front of me—and that includes you."

His words made her eyes prick with moisture. Her mouth trembled.

He was offering her his heart. How could she refuse to share hers, especially when it belonged to him already?

"I love you, too," she whispered.

His expression, eyes slightly crinkled in his nervousness, opened up. Joy shone from every pore and he drew her in for a tight embrace, his chin resting on top of her head.

His exuberant hug changed as he loosened his hold on her and then raised a hand to tip her face up for his kiss.

She met him eagerly, showing him through her touch the depth of her feelings. He deepened the kiss and she clung to his shoulders, her entire body thrilling to his touch.

Finally, he broke their kiss, holding her close again as they both worked to catch their breath.

"Will you marry me?"

His softly murmured words startled her out of the daydream she'd fallen into. She moved back, far enough to see into his face. "What?"

That vulnerability had come back to his expression. "I asked if you'd marry me."

The reality of what he was asking, what that would mean, burned through her, erasing the sense of contentment she'd just experienced. "Matty…"

"Look, I know you value your independence," he said quickly. "And I don't intend to undermine that."

She lowered her eyes. "I have Pop to think about. I can't… I can't ask him to move into town. And your job—"

His hands rested on her shoulders and he squeezed slightly. "I wouldn't ask you to. I was thinking we could either have a long engagement…or if you want Pop to be a part of the wedding ceremony, I'll ask the sheriff for some leave and move out to the homestead with the two of you."

More tears burned her throat. She'd seen the way he loved being a part of his family. "You'd move into the soddy with us?"

His mouth tipped up. "I might do my best to persuade my brothers to give us a house raising—build a little two-room cabin…"

Now she couldn't keep her tears from spilling over. Matty brushed her tears away with his thumbs.

"I didn't mean to make you cry. If you want to think about it, I'll wait—"

She shook her head. "I don't need to think about it. Yes, I'll marry you."

He whooped, picking her up and swinging her in a wide circle.

She laughed and swatted his shoulder. "Put me down!"

But he didn't, even when his brothers spilled out of the house to see what all the commotion was about.

"She said *yes*," he called out to them. "We're getting married!"

The rowdy bunch gathered around them, talking and teasing and arguing as she'd learned was their usual routine.

She stood hand in hand with Matty, basking in the glow of being a part of a family again. God had brought her here—she could trust Him with the future.

Epilogue

Christmas Eve, 1902

This would be the first Christmas Catherine could remember without Pop.

The grief of his passing earlier in the fall still caught her unaware at times. After battling the demons of his mind and his heart, he'd slipped away quietly in his sleep. Just never woken up.

The grief had finally lessened somewhat, knowing that he was in a place where his mind and heart had been healed completely.

And the love of her husband and the boisterous family that had folded her into its bosom had gone a long way toward healing her heart.

Yesterday morning, before dawn, she'd gone out and visited the still-raised plot of land where they'd buried him, near his favorite fishing spot. The days of tears were gone but that didn't mean that she didn't miss him and she'd stood there praying and missing him for a long time. Long enough for Matty to come looking for her.

Later, they'd bundled close together beneath a swath of blankets in the sleigh and Matty had made Catherine laugh with his stories of Christmases past as they'd traveled to Jonas and Penny's home. Harold Elliott had agreed to send a hand to see to the animals for a couple of days.

She'd never expected to have a big family like this, though she'd longed for a father almost all of her childhood. Jonas's and Penny's abiding love went a long way toward filling those empty places in her heart.

She and Matty had stayed overnight, tucked into the back bedroom. It had been different, noisier somehow, sleeping in a house that wasn't the soddy. But she supposed it was something she could get used to. Especially if the gift she planned to give Matty for Christmas panned out.

"Good morning."

She startled from her thoughts at the whispered greeting.

When she'd woken early and with no chores to do, she'd settled in one corner of the big parlor sofa, not wanting to wake anyone else. Today and tomorrow would be busy with making meals and celebrating and children running amok and no doubt everyone needed their rest.

Now Ricky and his wife, Daisy—whom she'd met for the first time last night—emerged from the hall. Matty was on their heels, running a hand through his rumpled hair.

He leaned over the back of the sofa and bussed her cheek with a kiss, and then the two brothers moved into the kitchen, jostling each other along the way. She heard a pot banging and knew they were probably making coffee. They spoke in low voices.

She found herself smiling absently after them, thankful for this time Matty would spend with his family.

Because of the distance, Ricky and Daisy rarely made it home.

"I'm sorry if Katie-bug's crying kept you up last night," Daisy said. "She wasn't used to the unfamiliar crib. Or her daddy snoring in the same room." Their baby was right at a year and had spent last night crawling around the house, examining everyone's boots.

Catherine shrugged. "It wasn't so bad. Is she still sleeping?"

"Yes, the little ornery thing."

Catherine had liked the other woman on sight, even if she had been shocked to discover that Daisy had been in an accident that had required her right arm be amputated close to the shoulder. Maybe it was because they'd both come late to the family, or because they were both slightly different.

At her insistence and with Matty's support, she'd told the family about her parentage. And been happily shocked when it hadn't mattered one whit to them.

It had taken time for the townspeople to come to accept her in Bear Creek. Though Luella and her friends made a noticeable effort to be amicable with Catherine, sometimes she still walked past the post office or passed someone in church and would swear she heard a whisper. And it still made her uncomfortable.

But she'd learned that it didn't hurt so much anymore because she had the support of her husband and his wonderful family.

"Is it Christmas yet?" Noah, Oscar and Sarah's young son, bounded into the room. Someone shushed him from the direction he'd appeared.

A cool draft and stamping feet from the kitchen must mean that Oscar's brood had arrived, though it was early yet.

"Auntie Cathy, is it Christmas yet?" The tyke made a beeline toward Catherine and settled his elbows on her knees, looking up at her adoringly.

From the day of their small church wedding in late summer, she'd been given a new nickname, one that erased all those old memories and hurts from the past. *Auntie Cathy.*

"Not until tomorrow," Matty said, ruffling the boy's hair as he settled next to his wife on the sofa. He curled an arm around her shoulders and she couldn't help pressing in against the warmth of his side.

He handed her a steaming mug of coffee, which she accepted with both hands. "Thank you."

With the hand that wasn't wrapped around her shoulder, Matty traced the curve of her cheek with his forefinger. "You all right? You got up awful early."

She blew on the steaming beverage. "I'm fine. Just… reminiscing."

"Rem-in-what-ing?" Noah's nose wrinkled as he botched the word.

"It means remembering," she said gently.

"'S good to remember," he said, his expression serious as if he imparted all his four-year-old wisdom to them. "I gots to remember to be good today or Santy won't bring me nuthin' in my sock."

Catherine hid her smile by sipping her coffee.

"I'm afraid your uncle Ricky will be getting coal in his sock," Daisy said gravely from the opposite sofa, and Noah turned his attention to her.

"Has Uncle Ricky been naughty this year?"

"He always is," Seb chimed from the doorway. Behind him, Breanna tumbled in the door, shaking snow from her hat and coat. She hadn't cut her hair, but threatened to shear it off like Catherine's, though for now it rested in a long braid down her back.

"If you need to take a break from all the noise later, you just give me the signal," Matty whispered.

She sipped her coffee again, contentment seeping through her. "What's the signal?"

"A wink will do."

Matty had received his wink after the noon meal and whisked Catherine out for a horseback ride. The air was brisk, but the wind had died down overnight and they wouldn't be out long.

She was a fast learner and improving her riding skills rapidly, but had elected to ride double with him today. He didn't mind. It was warmer.

Her hands clutched his sides, but then she pointed to a copse across the meadow, sounding entranced by the play of snow on the pines.

"Can we walk for a bit?" she asked before they'd made it across the meadow.

"Whatever you like, sweetheart." He took her gloved hand in his and led the horse. They trudged through the snow, sometimes laughing when their boots found an unexpected hole.

"Have you thought about returning to the sheriff's office?" she asked.

He shrugged. He'd asked for time away from being a deputy when she'd accepted his proposal earlier in the summer. She and Pop were more important to him than the job, but there were days he missed it.

"I'm enjoying getting to spend quality time with my wife," he said with a waggle of his eyebrows that never failed to make her laugh.

She elbowed him in the side where their hands were

connected. "Maybe I'd like a little *less* quality time with my ornery husband."

He tilted his head to one side as if contemplating her words, then shook his head, keeping his expression very serious. "Nah. That can't be it."

She laughed, as he'd meant her to, and an easy smile spread across his lips.

He wasn't in a rush to go back to the job. Sometimes Catherine's melancholy worried him, but it seemed it was just her way of dealing with her grief. And he liked spending his days with her, working the land.

He'd been careful not to push her to make plans for their future. She'd faced a lot of changes this year. They weren't in any rush to make more.

She tugged his elbow and he followed her willingly, bemused when she did it again moments later, and then again, leading them in a circle. Or, when he looked back at the pattern their footprints had made in the snow, a rectangle.

With the copse behind her and the sky as blue as her eyes… "You are a picture," he told her. He leaned in for a kiss and she obliged him, her arms coming easily around his neck, his settling about her waist.

But she broke away too soon, a mischievous smile playing about her lips. "I didn't bring you out here *only* to steal kisses," she said.

"No?" He grinned lazily.

"And I didn't need to escape your family *that* desperately."

He quirked an eyebrow at her.

"I suppose they've grown on me. Especially the children."

He'd noticed how the little ones seemed to gravitate toward her.

Catherine gestured to the path they'd broken in the pristine snow. "I also brought you out here to see this."

She seemed almost as excited as his young nieces and nephews would be tomorrow morning, bouncing on her toes.

Of course he would humor her. "And what am I seeing?"

"Well, if you picture a front door here, a kitchen here, bedroom…" She paced and pointed across the rectangle she'd made and his chest got tight all of a sudden.

"It's a house?" he asked, voice gone hoarse.

She looked up at him almost shyly. "It could be. You said your brothers would help us build…"

"I thought you'd want to build on the homestead."

He let the horse's reins go. The animal was placid and not real interested in going anywhere at the moment and he needed both hands to catch Catherine's waist.

She looked up at him, her eyes clear. "I think I'd like to be closer to…our family."

It warmed him from the inside out that she'd begun to think of his family as her own.

"And Daniel promised to teach me to read if we lived closer."

He buried his nose in the crown of her head. "Oh, he did, did he?"

She nodded, the movement brushing his chin against her hair.

"And…"

Now she trailed off. He felt a tremor in her hands as they rested on his shoulders. She pushed slightly back and he watched her face, concerned.

"And…I don't know much about babies. So it might be nice to be close to Penny. And Sarah. And…and Rose."

"Babies?"

He knew he must appear stunned. He felt stunned, his hands frozen spanning her waist.

Something in her eyes shifted, a shadow, and he didn't want her to think for one second that he wasn't happy.

He whooped, the sound echoing off the layers of snow. The horse neighed his displeasure with the unexpected noise, but Matty had already swooped Catherine into his arm and twirled her.

They kicked up snow as his fervor slowed and he set her feet back on the ground.

"So you're…happy?" she asked tentatively.

"Incredibly so." He took her lips again in a brief expression of joy, then hugged her to him as they looked out over the snowy landscape.

Who could've guessed that God would use a storm and an injury to open his eyes to Catherine's need? And her love.

He'd been searching for contentment with his job, thinking he'd never find it isolated on a small homestead, but he couldn't be any happier than he was now.

God had blessed him immeasurably. A hundredfold, until his cup spilled over.

"Merry Christmas," she whispered, her words warm against the skin of his cheek that had grown cool in the elements.

"Merry Christmas," he returned. "Our first one together, and you couldn't have given me a more precious present."

"Hmm." She looked up at him coyly. "Then I suppose you don't want the gift I snuck into the sleigh for you while you weren't looking…"

His eyebrows rose of their own accord. "Are you kidding? Let's get back to Ma and Pa's place right now. We've got celebrating to do."

She laughed as he hoisted her onto the horse behind him, the sound pure joy.

God had definitely sent a rainbow after the storm.

* * * * *

Dear Reader,

I hope you enjoyed this visit to Bear Creek and the White family. My family has always enjoyed playing games together, from Candy Land and Monopoly to card games and dominoes. We've also found Settlers of Catan for when we have a grown-up game night! Now that I have kids of my own, they also enjoy the simple fun of a game of Eye Spy, which is where I got the idea to have Matty play that game with Catherine. I found historical references to Eye Spy that fit the timeline of my story—and that makes it kind of fun to think that someone was playing the same game I play with my children over one hundred years ago.

I would love to know what you thought of this book. You can reach me at lacyjwilliams@gmail.com or by sending a note to Lacy Williams, 340 S Lemon Ave. #1639, Walnut, CA 91789. If you'd like to keep up with the Wyoming Legacy series and find out about all my latest releases in an occasional email blast, sign up at http://bit.ly/lacyw_news.

Thanks for reading!

Lacy Williams

REQUEST YOUR FREE BOOKS.

2 FREE INSPIRATIONAL NOVELS
PLUS 2 *FREE* MYSTERY GIFTS

Love Inspired HISTORICAL

LIHI

SPECIAL EXCERPT FROM

Love Inspired HISTORICAL

A marriage of convenience to rancher Shane McCoy is the only solution to Tessa Spencer's predicament. He needs a mother for his twins, and she needs a fresh start.

Can two pint-size matchmakers help them open their guarded hearts in time for Christmas?

Read on for a sneak preview of
THE RANCHER'S CHRISTMAS PROPOSAL
by Sherri Shackelford,
available in November 2015 from Love Inspired Historical!

"We could make a list." Tessa's voice quivered. "Of all the reasons for and against the marriage."

She had the look of a wide-eyed doe, softly innocent, ready to flee at the least disturbance. She'd been strong and brave since the moment he'd met her, and he'd never considered how much energy that courage cost her. For a woman on her own, harassment from men like Dead Eye Dan Fulton must be all too familiar. He felt her desperation as though her plea had taken on a physical presence. If he refused, if he turned her away, where would she turn to next?

A fierce need to shelter her from harm welled up inside him, and he stalled for time. "It's not a bad idea. Unexpected, sure. But not crazy."

These past days without the children had been a nightmare. Being together again was right and good, the way things were supposed to be. He hadn't felt this at peace since he'd held Alyce and Owen in his arms that first time nearly two years ago.

LIHEXP1015

"We don't need a list." Her hesitant uncertainty spurred him into action. "After thinking things through, getting married is the best solution."

"Are you certain?" Tessa asked softly, a heartbreaking note of doubt in her voice.

"I'd ask you the same. It's a hard life. Be sure you know the bargain you're making. I don't want you making a mistake you can't take back."

"You're not a mistake, Mr. McCoy."

"Shane," he said, his throat working. "Call me Shane."

The last time he'd plunged into a marriage, he'd been confident that friendship would turn into love. Never again. He'd go about things differently this time. With this marriage, he'd keep his distance, treat the relationship as a partnership in the business. He'd give her space instead of stifling her.

She was more than he deserved. Her affection for the children had obviously instigated her precipitous suggestion. Though he lauded her compassion, someday Owen and Alyce would be grown and gone, and there'd be only the two of them. What then? Would they have enough in common after the years to survive the loss of what had brought them together in the first place?

"You're certain?" he asked.

Her chin came up a notch. "There's one thing you should know about me. Once I make up my mind, I don't change it. I'll feel the same in a day, a week, a month and a year. There's no reason to wait."

Don't miss
THE RANCHER'S CHRISTMAS PROPOSAL
by Sherri Shackelford,
available November 2015 wherever
Love Inspired® Historical books and ebooks are sold.

SPECIAL EXCERPT FROM

Love Inspired®

When an Amish bachelor suddenly must care for a baby,
will his beautiful next-door neighbor rush to his aid?

Read on for a sneak preview of
THE AMISH MIDWIFE,
the final book in the brand-new trilogy
LANCASTER COURTSHIPS

"I know I can't raise a baby. I can't! You know what to do.
You take her! You raise her." Joseph thrust Leah toward
Anne. The baby started crying.

"Don't say that. She is your niece, your blood. You
will find the strength you need to care for her."

"She needs more than my strength. She needs a
mother's love. I can't give her that."

Joseph had no idea what a precious gift he was trying
to give away. He didn't understand the grief he would feel
when his panic subsided. She had to make him see that.

Anne stared into his eyes. "I can help you, Joseph,
but I can't raise Leah for you. Your sister Fannie has
wounded you deeply, but she must have enormous faith
in you. Think about it. She could have given her child
away. She didn't. She wanted Leah to be raised by you,
in our Amish ways. Don't you see that?"

He rubbed a hand over his face. "I don't know what
to think."

"You haven't had much sleep in the past four days.
If you truly feel you can't raise Leah, you must go to
Bishop Andy. He will know what to do."

"He will tell me it is my duty to raise her. Did you mean it when you said you would help me?" His voice held a desperate edge.

"Of course. Before you make any rash decisions, let's see if we can get this fussy child to eat something. Nothing wears on the nerves faster than a crying *bubbel* that can't be consoled."

She took the baby from him.

He raked his hands through his thick blond hair again. "I must milk my goats and get them fed."

"That's fine, Joseph. Go and do what you must. Leah can stay with me until you're done."

"*Danki*, Anne Stoltzfus. You have proven you are a good neighbor. Something I have not been to you." He went out the door with hunched shoulders, as if he carried the weight of the world upon them.

Anne looked down at little Leah with a smile. "He'd better come back for you. I know where he lives."

Don't miss
THE AMISH MIDWIFE
by USA TODAY *bestselling author Patricia Davids.*
Available November 2015 wherever
Love Inspired® books and ebooks are sold.

LIEXP101:

Find out more about Forever Romance!

Visit us at
www.hachettebookgroup.com/publishing_forever.aspx

Find us on Facebook
http://www.facebook.com/ForeverRomance

Follow us on Twitter
http://twitter.com/ForeverRomance

NEW AND UPCOMING TITLES

Each month we feature our new titles
and reader favorites.

CONTESTS AND GIVEAWAYS

We give away galleys, autographed copies,
and all kinds of exclusive items.

AUTHOR INFO

You'll find bios, articles, and links to personal websites
for all your favorite authors—and so much more.

GET SOCIAL

Connect with your favorite authors, editors, and
other Forever fans, and share what's important to you.

THE BUZZ

Sign up for our monthly romance newsletter,
and be the first to read all about it.